SMILE FOR THE CAMERAS

SMILE FOR THE CAMERAS

A Novel

MIRANDA SMITH

B

BANTAM
NEW YORK

Bantam Books
An imprint of Random House
A division of Penguin Random House LLC
1745 Broadway, New York, NY 10019
randomhousebooks.com
penguinrandomhouse.com

Copyright © 2025 by Miranda Smith

Penguin Random House values and supports copyright. Copyright fuels creativity, encourages diverse voices, promotes free speech, and creates a vibrant culture. Thank you for buying an authorized edition of this book and for complying with copyright laws by not reproducing, scanning, or distributing any part of it in any form without permission. You are supporting writers and allowing Penguin Random House to continue to publish books for every reader. Please note that no part of this book may be used or reproduced in any manner for the purpose of training artificial intelligence technologies or systems.

BANTAM & B colophon is a registered trademark of
Penguin Random House LLC.

Hardback ISBN 978-0-593-98316-4
Ebook ISBN 978-0-593-98317-1

Printed in the United States of America on acid-free paper

2 4 6 8 9 7 5 3 1

First Edition

BOOK TEAM: Production editor: Cara DuBois • Managing editor: Saige Francis • Production manager: Richard Elman • Copy editor: Annette Szlachta-McGinn • Proofreaders: Ethan Campbell, Catherine Mallette, Tess Rossi

Book design by Caroline Cunningham

Title page blood splatter pattern: Charlie's/Adobe Stock
Chapter opener film cell: happyvector071/Adobe Stock

The authorized representative in the EU for product safety and compliance is Penguin Random House Ireland, Morrison Chambers, 32 Nassau Street, Dublin D02 YH68, Ireland. https://eu-contact.penguin.ie

To all the women who were once little girls watching scary movies through splayed fingers

SMILE FOR THE CAMERAS

FADE IN.

EXT. BLACKSTONE COTTAGE—NIGHT

Tall trees loom over us. Moonlight filters through clustered foliage, the only light source. Insects whistle, leaves rustle.

Another sound slices through the night. The sharp THWACK of a blade hitting wood.

ELLA runs toward us, still shrouded in darkness. She stumbles across uneven terrain, dodging fallen branches and hanging vines. We hear her labored breathing, her thumping heartbeat. Each time her feet collide with the earth, she winces in pain (an injury from earlier in the night), but she can't stop now.

Someone is chasing her.

We don't know who or why. We only know our heroine is in peril.

As she ducks under a moss-covered branch, we get a glimpse of the maniac behind her. A terrifying image: long dark gown sweeping the forest floor, a lion mask streaked in blood. Gripped between two hands is an axe, mottled with soil and splinters and more blood.

Ribbons of blood streak Ella's clothes, too. Her arms and hands are painted with mud, now dry and cracking as though she dug herself out of her own grave.

In many ways, she has. Her mistakes brought her to this point. Her cowardice and naivety. And yet, with each staggered stride, she is shedding those former skins. She must keep going.

If she emerges from the forest, this maze of madness and mayhem, she'll be a survivor.

If she doesn't, she'll end up dead like all the others.

FADE OUT.

1

Now

The August heat sticks to my skin. I've been back in New York City for only two weeks and I'm already wishing I'd waited until fall, when the breeze is more forgiving and pedestrians aren't as buzzy.

I'm here because my agent, Fiona Thatcher, told me it's where I need to be if I'm serious about reviving my acting career. And she's right. Of course she's right. I'm not big enough to make a name for myself living somewhere else, like Nicole Kidman in Nashville or Sandra Bullock in Austin. That's why I've dragged myself out of the small corner of my hometown upstate.

After years away from the spotlight, being here—or any place with more than three stoplights—results in a sensory overload. Upstate, I could go weeks without seeing people if I wanted. Even if I didn't want. Here, I can't go anywhere without bumping shoulders with strangers, hearing catcalls and the endless rumbling of cars as they pass.

Here, I'm one of the thousands trying to turn their dreams into reality. Except my dreams already came true once. I'm just trying to get them back.

I arrive at Pendulum's ten minutes earlier than expected, but

Fiona's already beat me here. This establishment is another realm that presents the best of what the city has to offer. The hostess leads me toward the back of the restaurant, passing linen-clad tables and a strikingly beautiful waitstaff.

"You're early," Fiona says when she stands, greeting me with air-kisses on both cheeks. She looks almost identical to the way she did three months ago, when I last saw her. Black blazer and slacks, short dark hair tucked behind her ears. A mauve color on her lips, which part to reveal perfect teeth. "Happy to be back?"

"I suppose," I say, taking my seat. I've never been very good at small talk, and I've found since returning to the city, I'm out of practice. For so long, it was only Mom and me. Now I'm surrounded by people again, trying to earn my way back into their good graces. "Are you here long?"

"No, I fly back this afternoon. I wanted to talk to you in person first."

Fiona, like most agents, is based in Los Angeles. For someone only a few years older than me, she's already been quite successful. Her most famous client just signed on to join a superhero franchise. Another client stars in a network hospital drama. She reps a slew of up-and-coming teen actors.

And then there's me.

"You look good," she says, her eyes appraising each detail of my ensemble. I'm not sure she means it. I wasn't sure what to wear, so I ended up throwing on a vintage sundress that was popular several seasons ago.

I'm about to ask her if she approves of my look, if she thinks it'll help me stand out in auditions, when our waitress arrives at the table. She's tall and slim, with flowing hair and expertly done makeup. I'm sure she, like most of the staff, is an aspiring actress or singer.

If she knows who I am, she doesn't let on, a sign she's on the right track. No one makes it in this industry by fangirling. The goal is to act like you're one of the elites, not an admirer.

We order our drinks—gin for Fiona, water for me. The waitress wanders off, stopping at another table. That's when I spot her. A famous actress from the nineties who hasn't been in anything for a while. She's wearing sunglasses and a summer cardigan, and her posture suggests she doesn't want recognition.

"Did you see her?" Fiona asks.

"Is that—"

"Mm-hmm." She smiles and nods. "Word on the street is, she's going to be in the new Scorsese film."

"Really?"

"It's a smart move for her. Revitalizing her career at the perfect moment."

I watch the actress as she takes delicate sips of her drink. Even though she's far more famous than I ever was, if she can take off a few years and come back successful, maybe I can, too.

"Are you going to drag this out?" I ask Fiona. Again, I'm not great with the small talk, and since she insisted on meeting in person, I assume she has news about my last audition.

"Straight to business. I can roll with that." She smiles conspiratorially and wiggles in her seat, like an exec about to give a pitch. "It's down to you and another actress, but the producers loved your intensity."

I inhale, and it's like the air around me is cleaner, fresher. Full of hope. Then worry returns.

"What's the catch?"

"It's a big role. We're talking press tours, premieres. Possible award show buzz. This is everything you need to get your career back on track."

"Which is why I want the part." I so fucking want the part, and I'm afraid my eagerness is peeking through. I repeat, "What's the catch?"

"Shooting won't start until the spring, which gives you plenty of time. Meanwhile, the production company is going full steam ahead on another project, and they want you to join."

Two jobs at once? My heart flutters with excitement.

"What is it?"

Fiona's lips tighten. "It's the *Grad Night* reunion."

Just as quickly, that same enthusiasm plummets. The possibility of a reunion has been mentioned a few times before, but I've always refused to get involved. "No, Fiona. I told you—"

"I know. You don't want to do it. You've never wanted to do it. But you're now the only holdout."

"They have Leo?"

"He signed last week."

Leo is the biggest star to come out of the *Grad Night* franchise. He's more than an actor. More than a celebrity. And he also happens to be my ex-boyfriend, although we've since lost touch.

"Why would he agree to a reunion? His career is on fire."

"For the same reason you should agree to do it. One *yes* now leads to more down the road. Leo knows how to play the game, and his career is proof."

"I don't want to participate in a reunion. I'm trying to branch out. Distance myself from the franchise."

"Right now, it's more important to remind people who you are. Reunions are all the rage. Every big cast is getting together for either an interview or a reboot, and this is the perfect opportunity to get your face back out there."

Reclaiming my career is the first step in finding myself again. I want my face out there. I do, more than anything. But not for the *Grad Night* films. I've spent the past twenty years trying to forget about that shoot, even though it's the gig that kick-started my career.

The waitress returns with our drinks, giving me a few seconds to compose myself. The role I want could relaunch my career and make people forget I was ever part of a horror film all at once. Emotional drama. Big director. But I can't land that project without committing to the reunion, and I promised myself I'd never participate.

"This was a mistake. I should have known better than to think I could waltz back to New York and pick up with my career where I left off."

"Don't be like that. I told you they want you for the film, they just want you to play along for the reunion, too."

I sip some water, trying to settle my rising anxieties. "Tell me the details."

"It's a two-day shoot. They have the original cast back together. Including Leo. And Cole will be there, too."

Cole Parks. The director behind the *Grad Night* films. His father, Daniel Parks, is one of Hollywood's most popular directors. If Leo has been the biggest success on-screen, Cole has been the biggest one behind the camera. I'm shocked he'd take the time to participate, too. But then again, maybe it's not that surprising. *Grad Night* has always been Cole's passion project, and it ended up being far more popular than any of us could have predicted.

"Where and when?"

"Shooting starts this weekend."

I let out a sound that's half-laugh, half-gasp. "Are you serious? I just got back to the city."

Her eyes dart to the left. "I may or may not have given the impression you were considering getting involved."

"Fiona—"

"Hey, I'm doing this for you. I know you're trying to take things in a different direction, and I support that." She pauses. "But you need this."

I stifle my outrage, staring at my water glass, drops of condensation dampening the tablecloth. Fiona is smart. Probably too smart to take on a has-been actress, but she did anyway because she believes in me. And she's far more supportive than Gus, the last agent I had. She wants me to succeed, and she wouldn't push for this if she didn't believe it could open the door to bigger opportunities.

"Where?" I repeat.

"Blackstone Cottage."

My palms slap against the table. "Are you kidding me?"

"They want to shoot on the original location. Have a big nostalgia vibe, getting the whole gang back together in the same place."

But that place is precisely what I want to avoid. There are too many secrets there. Too many ghosts. And the same people participating know all of them. I can't be the only one bothered by the idea of returning.

"I don't know if I can do this. It's all too soon."

I'm referring to the two decades that have blinked by since I was last at Blackstone Cottage, but she thinks I mean something else.

Fiona slides her hand over mine. "Grief is hard."

Instantly, a ball of tension feels stuck in my throat. I clench my eyes to hold back tears. Mom has been gone six months, and I'm still not used to the fact that I'll never hear her voice again. What I'd give to be back in my sleepy hometown with her, instead of here, pretending to be a person I'm not.

"My parents died when I was young," Fiona continues. "I struggled for years, but once you process those emotions, it clears a path for you to do what you're meant to do with your life. She would want this for you."

Fiona is right. The person who was always most supportive of my acting career was Mom, and she'd want me to pursue it again.

I exhale. "Making *Grad Night* wasn't an easy time in my life." It's not the whole truth but as close as I can get. "I was young, and the shoot was stressful. There was a lot of drama with the people on set."

"Are you talking about Leo?"

Like the rest of the world, she thinks it's because of him. As though the only thing keeping me from accepting the job is a few days with my ex-boyfriend.

"That's part of it," I say, my voice strained. "It's all too overwhelming. I can't handle it on my own."

"It's a closed set, but each cast member is allowed to bring a companion," she says. "You can bring anyone you want."

Problem is, I don't have anyone. When I walked away from my career, I cut off my professional and personal ties, too. Mom was the only person I needed in my life, but she's not here anymore.

"Could you come?"

"Me?" Fiona's posture stiffens, her hand pulling back slightly. "I hadn't planned on it. I have some commitments the rest of this week, but I might be able to fly out this weekend."

"Don't worry about it." I slump forward, defeated. "Even if you tagged along, I'm not sure I could make it through an entire weekend."

"Look, you're conflicted about whatever happened back then. And your feelings are valid," she says, leaning forward again. "But people don't want to hear about how much you hate the franchise. They want to see the gang back together. It'll remind them of how much they loved the movie when it came out. And how much they loved you."

"But none of that is real."

"You're an actress, Ella," Fiona says. "Fake it."

"I don't know if I'm that good."

"There's a fine line between what's real and what's fake. You have to learn to tell the difference." She pauses. "Give the audience and the cameras and, most important, the producers what they want. Your career will thank you."

I'm about to respond when there's a clattering sound across the room. I look. The beautiful waitress with the luscious hair has dropped a platter of food right in front of the other actress's table.

"This is ridiculous!" the actress yells, no longer caring if there's attention on her.

"I'm so sorry—"

"Are you moronic or something? Where's Teddy?" The actress turns her head from left to right, searching. "If he expects me to frequent his establishment, he needs to hire someone with an actual brain."

An awkward silence blankets the room. You can hear the clanking of broken porcelain as the waitress cleans up the mess. After a few seconds, Fiona speaks, her voice lowered.

"If you remember, she was *People*'s Most Beautiful years ago," she says, her eyes on the actress. "Nothing in this business is what it seems."

Before our food arrives, I excuse myself for the restroom. Truthfully, I need a few minutes away from Fiona to think. I know that she wants me to participate in the reunion, but I'm not sure I'm up for it. I don't know if I can return to the set of *Grad Night* and all its secrets, even if my career depends on it.

I stare at myself in the mirror. Same face, new highlights, familiar dread. There's so much to unpack by going back to Blackstone Cottage. Frightening stuff happened that never made it on-screen. The world wouldn't believe me if they knew the truth, and a lot of people would be punished, including me.

A commode flushes, and a stall door opens. The waitress who broke the dishes exits the stall and stands beside me at the sink. I can tell by her splotchy cheeks she's been crying. Our eyes catch in the mirror.

I smile. "Hi."

"Hi." Her tone is kind but false.

"Don't worry about her. It could have happened to anyone, and she didn't have to handle it that way."

"You know, I always admired her." She smiles weakly. "Never meet your heroes, huh?"

"Not everyone is like that, even if a place like this makes it seem that way."

"I appreciate it," she says, making her way to the door. Before leaving, she stops and turns. "By the way, I wasn't going to say anything, but I'm a huge fan of the *Grad Night* movies. It's one of the films that made me want to be an actress."

"Thank you," I whisper, looking back at the mirror, ashamed of my own reflection.

2

Now

I barely ate at lunch. I suffered through the last half hour listening as Fiona told me about other future prospects. None of them is as important as the film for which I already auditioned, and I sense all of them are contingent on whether I complete that job first, which I can't do without committing to the *Grad Night* reunion.

It's the way this business works. One *yes* leads to another leads to another. One *no* can end your career. I never would have embarked on this journey again if I'd known it would all come down to the first project I did, twenty years ago.

Technically, it wasn't my first project. I'd been in two films before, although they were minor roles. Pizza Girl in a stoner comedy called *Green Bloods* and Friend Number Two in a romance called *Lovebird*. I earned both of those roles after I graduated from the Performers Academy, a creative arts school in New York City.

Even though I lived here for a few years—from age fourteen until eighteen—it still never felt like home. Bedford was home, ninety minutes north of the city. It's where my mother was born and raised. She, too, had a small showbiz stint. Mom was a gifted dancer and had dreams of making it on Broadway. Her plans were cut short when she found out she was pregnant and moved back home to give birth to me. Sometimes, I can't remember whose idea it was for me to study acting, if I was starting my own dream or finishing hers.

Since childhood, I jumped at any and every opportunity to be in front of an audience. School plays. Community theater. I even booked a few commercials advertising toothpaste and sunscreen. Instead of enrolling at my local high school, I sent my résumé and demo reel to the admissions team at the Performers Academy. They invited me to audition for their program and eventually offered a scholarship reserved for low-income families.

When I received the acceptance letter, Mom and I were sitting on the secondhand sofa in our Bedford apartment. She'd recently returned home from her closing shift as a cashier at the local pharmacy, and boxed macaroni and cheese was cooking on the stove for supper. "This is a make-or-break moment," she told me. "Most aspiring actors would kill for an opportunity like this."

"We'd have to move to the city," I said, overwhelmed by the enormity of what was to come. "There's no guarantee I'd ever be a real actress. I don't want to uproot both our lives just to fail."

"If you don't accept this, you'll regret it for the rest of your life," she said. "I believe in you. It's time you start believing in yourself."

I was fourteen. Eating the same dinner I'd had the night before. Wearing clothes the local church had donated the week before. A month before that, I'd had my first period. Yet there I was, making a decision about my future. For both our futures, it seemed.

My years at the Performers Academy marked the beginning of a new adventure, one that brought us even closer together. Mom held down two or three jobs to pay our way, all while I bounced between different classes and workshops. Whenever I had a performance, she sat in the front row cheering me on; her support helped me see past my insecurities, allowed me to achieve more than I ever would have on my own.

When I was eighteen, I landed the role in *Grad Night*. We didn't yet know it would turn into the cultural phenomenon it became. At the time, we were simply happy I was offered a role with more than three lines. I was the lead, and I knew from reading the script I was the Final Girl, the one to survive the vindictive serial killer at the movie's center.

It was the beginning of a dream and nightmare all at once, the latter of which no one else knows about. Rather, very few people know about it. And if I agree to participate in the reunion, I'll be coming face-to-face with those individuals in a matter of days.

I climb the concrete steps leading to the brownstone Fiona's agency has rented for me while I'm in the city. The lease is active for another two weeks, and then I'm homeless. After Mom died, I sold the farmhouse in Bedford. All that's left there is dust and painful memories, and I couldn't maintain the property while simultaneously reviving my acting career. The money from the sale will help me lease an apartment and provide a nice cushion, but truth is, I don't know what the future holds for me after I leave New York. It's very much a fly-or-fall moment in my life, much like when I received that acceptance letter all those years ago.

The brownstone is in a nice neighborhood and updated, but it's still small because, well, New York. The kitchen and living room bleed into each other, separated by a refurbished barn door leading into the single bedroom. I immediately take off the outfit I'm wearing, switching into some joggers and a tank top instead. When I'm in the closet, I catch a glimpse of my movie box. That's what I call it anyway: the box containing all the posters and memorabilia I've taken from different films over the years.

It seems vain to carry this stuff to a temporary residence, but with the Bedford house gone, it's not like I have another place to store my belongings. I hardly ever look inside the box anymore, but the conversation about my career with Fiona has left me feeling nostalgic. I carry it over to my bed and sit, crisscross applesauce, sorting through the contents. Each item tells a story. Silk flowers and old tubes of lipstick. An unlit candle that smells like vanilla and lavender. A framed one-dollar bill, fingerprint smudges fogging the glass.

After *Grad Night*, I had a successful career run. I was in a few romantic comedies and did six seasons of a television show that had a loyal following but, regardless, wasn't picked up for a seventh season. My core audience consisted of teens and college-aged girls, which was fine by me; statistically, their parents put out the most money. By Hollywood's standards, I'm not rich but, for a Bedford native, I did all right.

In between my various career accomplishments, I had numerous opportunities to reprise my role in *Grad Night*, but I always declined. I never wanted to make another horror film. Gus, my agent at the time, said I didn't want to be typecast, but that was never the reason I refused to return to the franchise.

And then Mom got sick. I left my career behind, returning to Bedford to take care of her. Mom thought she was a burden— that it had somehow all come full circle and I was now sacrificing my future to better hers. Truthfully, I'd been struggling in the business for years, only able to keep it quiet because there was an army of people around me, safeguarding my secrets.

It was the one secret they didn't know about that kept eating me up inside.

A few years after we'd returned to Bedford, Mom told me she was done. She didn't want to fight the battle anymore, didn't want to keep trying new medicines. Despite her excuses, I believed she was tired of holding me back.

"I'm here by choice," I told her.

We were sitting on the front porch of the house we called home. Might as well have been a mansion, considering the small apartment where we started. No more mac and cheese for dinner. Now it was all organic greens and grass-fed meats, and if we didn't feel like cooking, takeout was always an option. In some ways, I thought we were living in our own little version of heaven, minus the fact that Mom was withering away by the day.

"You're too young to be someone's caregiver," she said, her eyes on the orange sunset in the distance. "You're too talented."

"I've been in a handful of successful movies. I'm not exactly an Academy Award winner."

"But you could be." Her shoulders tensed, and she faced me. "You're a graduate of the Performers Academy. Not some floozy in *Tiger Beat*."

"I don't even know what that means."

"It means you have something most actresses don't. You have what I didn't have." Her gaze returned to the sunset, the glow on her face so beautiful, it should have been memorialized in a picture. "And you don't need to be wasting it here in Bedford, watching me die."

I didn't know what else to say after that. She'd revealed all the truths I was reluctant to confront. Her impending death. My stalled career. What my future would look like if both of those things disappeared forever. More important, I didn't want to tell her I didn't deserve the illustrious success she described. Even if I was a good actress, I wasn't a good person.

"If you don't want to be an actress, then don't," she continued. "Be a teacher. A painter. A lawyer. I don't care. But don't stay in Bedford and throw your future away. You deserve more."

After that conversation, Mom told her medical team she was no longer seeking treatment. She said her decision was about extending her quality of life, but deep down, I knew she was making yet another sacrifice, just as she had when she gave up her dream and became a single parent. She wanted me to start living again. When she died a year later, peacefully in her sleep, it was the second greatest pain I'd ever felt.

It took another six months for me to wipe away the tears and put my plans in motion. In that time, I used some industry references to put me in touch with a few different agencies. That's how I found Fiona, an avid fan of my work beyond just the *Grad Night* franchise. Given her clientele, I thought she would be too highbrow to consider repping me, but she jumped at the chance to help me revamp my career.

Fiona.

That's the name lighting up my phone screen right now. I've done nothing but kill time since our lunch at Pendulum's, and she's already calling to check in.

"Long time no see," I answer.

"My flight is about to leave, and I wanted to touch base. I won't have time to reach out until tomorrow evening at best," she says. "If you're willing to do the reunion, I have to let them know soon."

"I still don't have an answer."

I hear her exhale, and beyond that, the frantic buzzing of the airport.

"It's your career. More important, it's your life. But I think this movie role is the best thing for you, and if you have to do the *Grad Night* reunion to get it, I think you should."

But she doesn't know, my subconscious screams.

"The earliest I can come is Saturday, but I'll be there if you think you'll need me," she continues. "Think about what this will mean to the fans who took a chance on you in the first place. Better yet, think of what this could do for your career from here on out. I'm talking Winona Ryder, Brendan Fraser–level comeback."

I doubt my return to the industry will be that dramatic. Then again, Fiona knows more about the inside than I do. She knows what people say about me. Whether it's rumored I left the spotlight to take care of my ailing mother, or because I couldn't handle the pressure.

The reunion would mean a lot to the fans, and as the Final Girl of the film, I have to be involved for it to hold the same punch. I mean, freaking *Leo* is going, and he was up for a Golden Globe last year. And then I think of my biggest supporter, Mom. On the nightstand is a framed picture of the two of us, the only personal memento displayed in this rented home. In this fake life I'm living. I want something to feel real again, even if I must confront my biggest demons to make that happen.

"Book the flight," I blurt out before I change my mind. "I'll do it."

3

Now

My flight from JFK lands in Knoxville on Friday morning. I've packed two bags, which already hold the majority of my belongings. Clothes, toiletries, a few personal items. Fiona told me not to fret about what to wear—makeup and wardrobe teams would be available with several options, making sure I look my best by the time cameras start rolling.

"Everything is going to be fine," she told me over the phone before I boarded my flight.

Yet, now that I'm forty-five minutes away from Blackstone Cottage, I wish I could retreat, board another plane that would take me far away from here, away from the memories I've spent decades avoiding.

I exit the lobby, standing behind a group of smokers trying to consume long-awaited nicotine postflight. I scan the cars and buses waiting in the circular pickup area until I spot my name on a white poster board. The man holding it—in his early thirties, heavyset, with a thick beard—stands in front of a black SUV.

"Ella?" he asks when I approach.

I nod.

When he speaks, he sounds nervous and unsure. "I'm Victor, hired by The Golden Group. Help you with your bags?"

"Sure."

I wonder then if Fiona, or someone else at the agency, warned him I might get cold feet. I take one last look at the airport, my final glimpse of civilization before embarking on the rural roads that lead to Blackstone Cottage. I turn, walking on shaky legs to the open car door, and sit in the back seat.

Blackstone Cottage isn't far away from neighboring towns, but it's not one of the popular destinations for reprieve, either, like some of the other area attractions in the Great Smoky Mountains. I don't think many people knew about it at all, until *Grad Night* came out. After we get away from the initial traffic, it's an easy drive, moving closer to the mountainous backdrop that soon surrounds us. I lean my head against the window, staring at the brightly colored trees as we pass. Glossy greens and deep emeralds swirling together in kaleidoscope fashion as we move closer to the country.

"You okay back there?" Victor asks. "Need some air?"

The partition has remained open the entire drive; I didn't even think to ask him to shut it.

"I'm fine, thanks."

"It took me a minute, but I recognize you," he says, his eyebrows raised in the reflection of the rearview mirror.

I lean deeper into the backrest. "Oh, yeah?"

It's usually best not to confront people with their own celebrity, but Victor strikes me as someone who doesn't fool around with formalities. I never want to come off as cold and rude, like the actress at Pendulum's the other day.

"I'm not supposed to know what this is about," Victor continues, "but I think I can figure it out. You're making another *Grad Night* film, aren't you?"

He sounds excited, and I realize it's been a while since I interacted with a genuine fan of the franchise. I'm averse to *Grad Night* as a whole, but never to the people who admire it. It's because of them I had a career to begin with, and it's up to them if I ever get it back. So, I play along, appreciating his admiration. After all, he knows nothing about my real reasons for hating the film.

"Not exactly, but close."

"Man, a remake would be awesome. I watched some of the others, but they weren't as good. No offense."

"None taken."

"Like I said, I am a fan. Me and some of my high school buddies even camped up here for a few of the festivals before they shut the place down."

He must have been a hardcore fan if he came to the festivals. The last weekend in October, horror enthusiasts would settle in the woods surrounding Blackstone Cottage for Grad Fest, where everyone would camp out. Every year, they tried to get an original cast or crew member to come, a keynote appearance of sorts, but I never did. As far as I had known, it was still an annual tradition.

"Shut the place down?"

"Yeah. Grad Fest only lasted a couple of years. Then somebody else bought the land. It's private property now."

That must have happened after I moved back to Bedford, and it's fortunate. Grad Fest always made me nervous because I worried that eventually some drunken fan would stumble upon something they didn't need to find. It's safer for me—for all of us—if the land isn't open to the public. Whoever owns it now must have given permission for us to film the reunion on-site.

"So, can you tell me what you're doing?" he asks.

"I'm not supposed to."

"Okay, okay. Don't want you getting in trouble." He pauses. "Can you tell me this? Is it related to *Grad Night*?"

"It is."

"Sweet." His shoulders hunch as he squeezes the wheel tighter. "I like all horror, but *Grad Night* has always stood out to me in the genre. It's the right amount of gore mixed with comedy. And I thought it was so cool how you all used your real names in the movie."

"That was the director's idea," I say. Cole thought it would raise the stakes, make us more in tune with our characters.

"And the cast! Man, y'all were the perfect group. You still keep in touch with the gang?"

"No."

"Everyone does their own thing now, I guess. Leo is on fire." He pauses again. "It must be cool to be part of something that means so much to people."

"It is." My chest swells with a sensation that's hard to define. Pride? Concern? There's a vast difference between what *Grad Night* means to the average person and what it represents to me.

"Can I ask you another question?"

Hiding my annoyance becomes more of a struggle. Victor seems like a nice person, but he's flaring the apprehension I already have about returning. Still, I humor him.

"Shoot."

"Is it true the set was haunted?"

My stomach tightens. Outside the window, the vibrant forest seems to have morphed into something ominous and dark. The foliage blurs together like roaming phantoms as we pass. I look down into my lap and turn on my actress voice, trying to sound playful instead of scared. "You've stayed on the grounds before. You tell me."

"Nah, I never saw anything. Well, that's not true. There was some spooky stuff, but nothing that can't be explained by a bunch of drunk people spending too much time in the woods," he says. "One of my buddies almost drowned in the lake once, but we got to him in time."

Details of his own experience stay with me, a reminder that the area's beauty is deceptive. Danger lurks around every dreary turn. I envision a person struggling in the water, some unseen force below the surface, refusing to let them leave. Just the thought of it makes it hard for me to breathe.

"I'm talking about the shoot itself," he continues. "All those rumors about what happened back then."

He's refusing to drop the subject, and it's making me antsy. I try to deflect. "A lot of that is hyped up by the production company, trying to make press."

"Yeah, I figured that, but there's got to be some stuff. Like that camera guy who died on set. And that person who went missing."

"The cameraman didn't die," I say, my voice sterner than it needs to be. "The other stuff is all rumor."

He finally registers the edge in my voice, and the car goes silent. I close my eyes, listening to the sound of tires crunching against gravel. We left the smooth tarmac of civilization ages ago.

When Victor speaks again, he says, "Good luck out there."

"Excuse me?"

"We're here."

The car has stopped. I gaze out the window, my heart beating faster as I take in the sight of Blackstone Cottage.

The eyelike windows stare back at me, reflecting my own secrets. The front door—red, like a tongue—is open, daring me to enter. The surrounding wilderness is a maze of mayhem and mystery. Notorious murders took place here, moments memorialized on cinema screens for millions to enjoy.

And yet it's not a set. Before me stands a real house, with real secrets. *My* secrets.

And at least one death happened here that wasn't caught on camera.

I shouldn't have returned. I shouldn't tempt fate by confronting the past. And yet what choice do I have?

I stare at the house, just as it stares back at me, peering into my soul. We're testing each other. Who will be the first to break? To shatter into pieces? Who will be the last to survive?

SCENE 1

FADE IN

EXT. BLACKSTONE COTTAGE—NIGHTFALL

SUPER: Grad Night

A two-story cabin sits in the center of a clearing, surrounded by forest. The coming night makes the area appear dark and sinister.

Silence is broken by the ROAR of an approaching car. Loud music and squealing tires echo through the wilderness. The Jeep brakes, coming to a halt in front of the cabin.

The back door opens, and RILEY (18, cool, floppy-haired, glossy-eyed) exits the car. Behind him, pulling on his waist for support, is ARIES (18, glamorous, spunky, voluptuous). Both are wearing black floor-length graduation robes. They stare at the house before them, begin hollering.

          ARIES (shouting)
  This is what I'm talking about!

          RILEY (to Aries)
  I told you Dad hooked us up. This is
  going to be epic.

The couple share a sultry kiss.

The driver's door opens, and LEO (18,

jock, strong-jawed, handsome) exits. A smile spreads across his face.

                LEO (to Ella)
What do you think?

ELLA (18, fresh-faced, beautiful, bookish) exits the car, stares ahead at the house, arms crossed.

                ELLA
It's beautiful.

                RILEY
Four years of high school hell, we deserve this, eh?

                ARIES
Yeah, we do, baby.

INT. BLACKSTONE COTTAGE—NIGHT

Ella sits in the armchair beside the fireplace. Aries is twirling around the living room. She plops down on the couch, kicks her feet onto the table.

                ARIES
This place is badass. There better be a hot tub.

The front door swings open, hitting the wall with a loud thump. Riley drops the bags to the ground, scoots them over to the far wall. Leo walks in behind him, gently putting his bags next to the pile.

                    RILEY
          You already know there's a hot tub. I
          told Dad it was a necessity.

Riley walks into the kitchen, opens a cabinet. He pulls out four glasses and starts pouring drinks.

                    ARIES
          Let's get more comfortable first.

Aries stands and unzips her gown. She shimmies out of the robe, giving the garment a playful kick before it hits the floor. She's wearing a silver mini dress, revealing and flashy.
   Riley walks over to the sofa, carrying the drinks.

                    RILEY
          Very nice, babe.

Everyone's gaze lands on Ella. Self-conscious, she unzips her gown. She's wearing a black dress. Classy and understated.

                    LEO
          You look beautiful, Ella.

Aries stands in the center of the group, holding up her glass.

ARIES
Lions for life!

                    ALL
Lions for life!

They drink.

INT. LIVING ROOM/BLACKSTONE COTTAGE—LATER THAT NIGHT

The group lounges on the sofa, noticeably more comfortable with one another. They are midconversation. The fire across the room is blazing.

                    RILEY
Your speech was good, Ella.

                    ARIES
It was perfect. What was that one thing you said about (she's thinking, trying to remember) two roads and taking the one less traveled?

Ella seems to be drifting away from the conversation, but this comment pulls her back in.

                    ELLA
Thanks. That's a quote from Robert Frost.

                    LEO
What about Principal Shultz? What was that poem he recited?

                    RILEY
Lame. Why do they even make time for the
teachers at something like that? I mean,
it's supposed to be about us, right?

                    ARIES
You noticed who wasn't there? (She
arches an eyebrow, waits.) Mr. Rhodes.

                    RILEY
Fucking douche canoe. Good thing that
old quack wasn't there.

                    ELLA
Don't you think it's sad what happened
to him? I mean, the guy lost his job.

                    RILEY
You saw the video. The dude was cussing
like a sailor. You can't go on a rant in
front of your students. I mean, we're
kids.

Riley chugs the rest of his drink.

                    ELLA
Still, it's pretty invasive that someone
stuck a camera in his room without him
knowing. Everyone in the school saw that
video, and he lost everything. I think
it's sad.

ARIES (to Riley and Leo, toying with them)
Yeah, guys. Don't you think it's *so*
sad?

An awkward moment passes. Ella looks at each person's face, can't shake the feeling they know something she doesn't.

                    ARIES (CONT'D)
          Come on. You don't know? Riley and Leo
          are the ones who made that video.

Ella turns to Leo, looks at him with genuine disgust. He avoids her gaze, ashamed.

                    LEO
          Riley made the video. I was only there
          with him when he sent it out.

                    RILEY
          And I'd do it again. Serves him right to
          think he could cuss out a classroom full
          of kids and get away with it.

                    ARIES
          That and he was threatening to fail you.

                    RILEY
          Sure, it was nice to avoid that. Then we
          wouldn't have this awesome cabin to cel-
          ebrate my graduation!

He falls back on the sofa, kisses Aries sloppily. Leo turns to Ella, his voice lowered.

                    LEO
          He really was a jerk. He had it coming.

                    ELLA
The man got fired. I heard his wife was sick. That he needed that job for insurance.

                    RILEY
Enough talking. Let's check out the bedrooms.

                    ARIES
Sounds delightful.

The couple climb the exposed staircase. Leo follows, then Ella. We look at the expansive living room, now littered with beer bottles and empty glasses. We pause at a window overlooking the dark forest beyond. Standing among the trees is a MAN wearing a lion mask and a graduation robe.
   He's watching.

4

Then

The car slows once we get off the highway, turning onto the winding roads leading to Blackstone Cottage.

I thought I'd had my share of wilderness living in upstate New York, but the woods here are different, more dangerous and rugged, the entire landscape rising upward, as the SUV escapes farther into the mountains. We pass a house with a caved-in roof and splintered gray deck. Rusted cars with missing wheels litter the front yard. The home looks abandoned, until I notice a blond child playing with dolls on the front porch. She waves as our car passes.

"Can you imagine living in a place like this?" says Gus, my agent. I'd almost forgotten he was sitting beside me in the back seat.

"Parts are charming," I say, turning back to the window.

"This area is described as the armpit of America for a reason." He stares at his BlackBerry, swiping through emails. "That's what makes the cost of shooting so cheap. This film is getting made for a fraction of the normal cost."

Gus can be brash, but he has worked with some of the biggest names in the industry. He was a great agent to land, and the fact that he's carved out time to accompany me to my first gig proves he values my talent.

Grad Night is a four-week project, all the scenes being shot at the same location. Gus plans on staying the first couple of days, although he has a hotel booked in the center of town. The rest of the cast and crew are supposed to be staying on-site, in the various rooms of Blackstone Cottage.

The car careens over a steep hill that finally levels out to a flat surface. In the middle of the landscape sits a two-story house surrounded by a thick wall of trees. The entire cabin is constructed of honey-colored wood and has large windows outlined in dark metal.

I stand beside the car and take in the complete view of where I'll be living and working for the next month, excitement bubbling in my stomach.

"Gus! It's about damn time."

I recognize the man coming to greet us instantly. Cole, the director. He's wearing faded jeans and a band T-shirt, his brown hair tangled and dangling above his shoulders.

"There's our director," Gus says, reaching for a handshake. "How's the old man?"

"Good, good." Cole turns to me, appraises me like I'm a piece of valuable jewelry. "Thanks for getting our leading lady here safely."

"Thank you for offering me the role," I say, putting on my kindest, most professional smile.

"We made a great choice. I think you will be . . . perfect." Cole seems to chew on that last word, savoring the flavor. He looks at Gus. "I wanted to talk business."

"Sure thing." Gus nods and puts his hand on my lower back. "I'll catch you before I leave?"

A woman strolls over wearing a baggy shirt and cargo shorts, boots tied tight around her ankles. Her light brown hair sits atop her head in an undone bun. She carries herself like a real woman. Confident, understated.

"This is Jenny Cruise," Cole says before walking off with Gus. "She'll show you around set and introduce you to the cast."

"I'm the AD. Assistant director, that is. Pretty much anything Cole doesn't want to handle gets left to me," she explains, initiating a quick but firm handshake. "How are you feeling about the big movie?"

"Good. A little nervous."

"At first, you'll have a lot thrown at you. Lots of names and things to remember, but that's why the crew is here. We try to set up everything so by the time you're on camera, you're ready to shine."

Instead of entering the front door, we walk around back.

"Blackstone Cottage is playing double duty," Jenny says. "Most of the rooms have been blocked off for sets. That's why we're avoiding the front door, for now. Two of the bedrooms upstairs, too. The rest of the bedrooms are being used as designated sleeping quarters. Everyone else is staying over there."

She points a few yards away to a series of buildings, what look like wooden gardening sheds you might find in the backyard of a suburban home. It might be an ideal place for storage, but the space seems small and stifling for living quarters.

"Don't worry," Jenny says, reading my mind. "You're staying inside the house. Most of the crew are stuck in the outdoor cabins."

"Anyplace is fine with me."

Jenny smiles, a look that says, *That's cute*. This isn't her first project, the exciting elements long dulled by now. As we climb the back porch steps, a call comes over Jenny's radio. She stops walking and listens.

"I need to take care of something," she says. "I'll be right back."

I survey the house's massive back porch. Across from the covered hot tub stands a group of crew members, flipping pages on clipboards and tinkering with various film equipment. A few of them stop what they're doing to introduce themselves. Most are men with forgettable names. Carlos, a gaffer. Hank and Dale, cameramen. A few sound guys and editors.

A blond girl in a tie-dyed shirt with a Mickey Mouse design skitters over, placing a large duffel bag on the deck beside her feet. The way she comes up for air, I imagine whatever is inside must be heavy.

"You must be the lead," she says.

"I'm Ella Winters," I say, smiling nervously.

"Petra Adamos." She holds out a hand, wrists covered with small tattoos and bohemian bracelets, then nods at the woman behind her. "And the little worker bee behind me is Monica Abbott."

A curly-haired brunette in a flowy, black maxi dress is bent over rummaging through a cardboard box. She doesn't raise her head to acknowledge me.

"In addition to hair and makeup, Monica and I will assist you during filming," Petra continues. "We're a small group, so we're sharing a lot of the same titles."

My eyes bounce from one person to the next, in awe of all the moving parts that bring one project to life.

"It's all a little overwhelming," I say eagerly. "But I can't wait to get started."

"What's your story?" Petra asks.

"Excuse me?"

"How'd you get in the industry? That usually tells me a lot about a person. I'll go first." She rests her hands on her hips and puffs out her chest. "When I was a kid, I never even knew a job like this existed. I mean, I watched movies and television like everyone else. I guess I was naive enough to think people looked that beautiful without help. A lot of my housemates made connections in the industry. Wannabe models and all that. I started taking odd jobs on different sets, and the rest is history."

I am bombarded with the amount of information Petra's thrown at me all at once, but I gather that's just her style. A complete open book. "Housemates?"

"I was a resident of Miss Claude's Group Home until I aged out."

"I'm sorry," I say, already worried that's not the right response.

"It's not as bad as people make it seem. My extended family couldn't take care of me after my parents died, so it was the best option at the time. Like I said, the friends I made there got me here," Petra says. "So, what about you?"

"I graduated from the Performers Academy—" I stop speaking when I clock Petra's expression. She's nodding along, likely picturing one of the pampered upbringings that belonged to my former classmates. My alma mater alone doesn't convey the entirety of who I am or why I'm here. My story. Petra's been so earnest and open that I feel like I should reciprocate.

I begin again, telling her about my childhood in upstate New York and my acting experiences before I entered the academy. I tell her about how much Mom and I struggled to get to this very moment.

"Sounds like it's been a long road to get here," Petra says when I finish. She gives me an encouraging smile. "Make sure you soak it all in. I can already tell this project will be a fun one."

Jenny appears behind me, headphones hanging around her neck. "I see you've met Petra. Let me guess. She's already told you her whole life story."

"I'm just trying to get to know her," Petra says.

Behind her, I watch as Monica moves one box out of the way and starts digging through another. I find it odd she's still not come over to introduce herself.

"What about your partner?" I ask. "What's her story?"

Petra and Jenny share a look, the former rolling her eyes. "It's a long one. You're probably better off not hearing it."

"Ready to meet the cast?" Jenny asks, sliding her radio into her pocket.

"Sure."

"If you need anything during the shoot, find one of us." Petra grins, her infectious spirit making my stomach flutter.

Jenny opens the sliding glass doors leading into the living area of the house. There is a black leather sofa across from the stone fireplace, two plaid armchairs on either side. Above the mantel is a large deer's head.

"Creepy, huh?" A muscular young man with wavy blond hair nods to the beast overhead, then holds out his hand to greet me. His grip is firm but welcoming. "I'm Riley."

"Ella. I'm—"

"The star of the show," he says, smiling. He hollers over his shoulder at the others gathered in the kitchen. "Guys, the group is finally complete."

Next to enter the room is Aries, the bad girl yin to my virginal yang. I recognize her from the kid shows she used to star in a few years back. Even if I didn't know her, I'd be drawn to her. Aries is striking, oozing confidence and sexuality. The kind of girl who makes you blush from being in the same room as her.

Instead of offering a handshake, she waves; her perfectly painted black nails catch my attention. "Aries," she says coolly.

A tall man, much older, with a balding head and thick black glasses approaches next. "Benjamin Rhodes," he says, his voice deep and husky.

"I'm Ella," I say, trying to place where in the cast he belongs.

Riley notices my confusion. "Ben here is our very own killer. The man in the lion mask."

"Of course, it's nice to meet you." I shake his hand enthusiastically.

Ben has been in the business longer than the rest of us put together, including Cole. He has one of those faces you recognize from a half dozen roles, but when put on the spot, you can't recall a single one by name.

"And I'm Leo," says a voice from behind.

I turn, getting my first in-person look at the actor who will be playing my boyfriend for the next four weeks. He's tanned and tall, but not intimidatingly so. His light blue eyes almost disappear when he smiles, a charming trait.

"Ella," I say, taking his hand. His skin is warm and soft, sending a curious shiver through my body.

"Here we are," Cole says, descending the stairs from the second floor. "The entire movie in one room. I can't express how grateful I am to have all of you involved on this journey."

Looking around, I see the crew have entered the living room from off the back porch. Monica and Petra, the sound guys and cameramen. Even Gus. They lean against the wall, listening to Cole like parishioners thirsting for a Sunday sermon.

"People keep wondering why, out of all genres, I'm determined to make a slasher film," Cole continues. "To me, the answer is simple. What's great about the horror genre is its ability to reinvent itself, all while harnessing the tropes we know moviegoers love. I don't think there's a finer art form in the entire industry."

He looks at Aries. "We have our vixen. Sassy, sultry."

He turns to Riley. "Our spoiled rich guy. You can't decide whether you want to punch him in the face or down shots with him."

Moving across the room, he continues, "We've got the creepy old guy. No offense, Ben."

"None taken," Ben quips, signaling a round of laughs.

"The handsome hunk," Cole says, tapping Leo's back as he passes. Then he stops right in front of me, places both of his hands on my shoulders. "And most important, we have our Final Girl. The character to give the audience hope after a solid ninety minutes of paranoia and bloodshed."

He's looking at me with fierce intensity. Everyone in the room is. I feel myself blushing, my body tingling. But it isn't from embarrassment. Cole's speech works on me. For a moment, I believe we're doing something brave and important. I believe every person in this room is living his or her purpose, and that certainty is intoxicating.

"Now that everyone has met, you better rest up. We start shooting tomorrow night," Cole says, taking his hands off my shoulders and turning to face the rest of the group. "It's going to be one hell of a ride."

5

Now

The house smells different. Newer, like candles have been brought in to burn out the musty scent of disuse I remember so well. The foyer of the house is filled with equipment, black and metal clusters sitting in every corner. There are no people. It's me and the house together again after all this time.

Seconds later, a petite woman descends the stairs. Her hair, which is covered by a headset, is dark with hot pink ends. She holds a clipboard and wears a smile.

"Ella Winters?" she asks.

"Yes."

"I'm Dani, the assistant director." She pauses, waiting for me to speak. "I worked on the original set, twenty years ago."

"Right. Sorry." I hold out my hand to shake hers as though that'll make up for my forgetfulness. "It's been a long time."

"It has. I was a measly errand runner back then. I'm not the only familiar face around here, though." She says it like she's trying to spare me from future embarrassment. "Austin insisted we bring back as many of the original crew members as possible. There's only one or two who are new."

Austin is the director of the documentary. Fiona told me who he was. More important, she told me *why* he mattered. He's made a big name for himself as a talented director. The studios have rewarded him by giving him a string of upcoming blockbuster films, treating him as Cole's very own protégé. Because he's a fan of the franchise, the reunion is his passion project before he makes it big-time.

"Where is everyone?" I ask, my eyes scanning the surroundings. It feels like we're the only two people in the house, but again, that's the home's mystique. It makes you feel isolated, even when someone else is in the next room. The ideal setting for a horror flick.

"Most of the crew are upstairs. You're only the second cast member to arrive."

"Who else—"

Before I can finish my sentence, Dani is already darting upstairs, talking into her headset.

Time slows as I stand alone in the foyer, memories of the past overlapping with the present. I walk into the living room, amazed that everything looks precisely the same. The mounted deer head above the stone fireplace ornaments the wood-paneled walls, although pictures have now been added on either side. They're framed photographs taken on the original *Grad Night* set, and I wonder if they've been brought in specifically for the documentary, or if they're always here, a testament to the cabin's cinematic history.

One photo shows the entire cast and crew gathered on the back porch. I remember smiling for this picture shortly before we started filming our first scene. The second photo is of the core cast—Leo, Aries, Riley, Ben, and me. Beside it is a smaller photo of the film's signature villain in costume: Mr. Rhodes.

The killer wears a lion mask, the fictional high school's mascot, and a long black graduation gown, reminiscent of the garb from *Scream*. Cole wanted to acknowledge as many horror franchises as possible. The ending is an homage to *Friday the 13th*, except there's no Jason Voorhees rising from the lake at the end. In fact, the ending makes it clear Mr. Rhodes is dead . . . although his character returns again and again in the later films. I stare at the haunting image now, thinking of the real actor behind the mask.

"He's the only one missing."

I turn in the direction of the familiar voice behind me. It's Riley. What amazes me the most is how much he looks the same. He's filled out in some areas, but he still has that boyish face. He wraps his arms around me as though holding me in place. The embrace is comforting, his scent a heady mix of cologne and cigarettes.

"I didn't know if you were going to make it," he says.

"I didn't know if I would, either," I answer honestly.

"It's weird being back," he says, "but it's even weirder knowing Ben isn't here."

Ben is the actor who played Mr. Rhodes. He had very few lines in the film, spent the rest of the time terrorizing victims, his face obscured, but his character was expanded, sometimes irrationally, in the subsequent films. Now Ben's face is as central to the franchise as the lion mask itself.

He died of cancer a few months ago.

"I wasn't always open to the idea of a reunion, but I wish we would have done it before Ben died," Riley says. "It would have been nice to see him again."

The way Riley says this, I wonder if he blames me. It's no secret I was the holdout. "I hadn't seen him in years."

"We kept in touch. He was in good spirits up until the end." Riley rubs the back of his neck, forcing himself to switch subjects. "So, how have you been?"

"Not bad," I lie. "And you?"

"Fifteen months sober."

That's Riley, no bullshit. And I'm instantly happy to hear he's making progress.

It's no secret Riley has had the toughest time since shooting wrapped. He was in several popular films after *Grad Night*, but he was always more famous for his personal life than anything he starred in. The tabloids hounded him like he was a male version of Paris Hilton or Britney Spears. They reported every time he entered a new rehab facility, and twice as much when he left. Like me, his name hasn't been in the media much for the past few years. I hope that means his sobriety will stick this time.

I know what pushed him to abuse his body so much in the first place.

"I'm happy for you," I say. "Working any?"

"I've got a small role in a Netflix series that comes out next year. My agent seems to think participating in the reunion will help get my name out there again."

"My agent says the same thing."

"Are you still with Gus?"

"Gosh, no," I answer. "I'm at The Golden Group."

"Nice. Yeah, I've changed agencies, too." His voice is hopeful, holding no hint of a troubled life. Like me, he's here looking for a new start.

Our intimate conversation is interrupted by commotion at the front door. There are footsteps, several, giving me the mental image of a stampede. And voices, each talking over the other, a buzzing of high-pitched squeals.

I don't recognize the first two people who walk inside, but the third is a hard one to forget. Aries, in the flesh. She's talking on her phone, an enormous water bottle dangling from her right wrist. She's wearing white flare-leg trousers and a khaki coat. Sunglasses cover half her face.

"It's starting to feel real," Riley says under his breath. I can't tell if he's excited or, like me, nervous.

It takes several minutes for us to catch Aries's attention. She walks over, pushing her sunglasses into her platinum-blond hair, and gives me a hug.

"How long has it been, Ella?" She turns to Riley. "And you? Looking good."

"You do as always, love," he says, giving her a kiss on the cheek.

Up close, I can see the subtle changes to Aries's face. She

looks like she's aged and gotten younger all at the same time, a strategic plan of fillers and Botox having changed the shape of her face. There's not a single crease, and her makeup is expertly blended, giving her a very literal glow.

"Who are all these people?" Dani says, coming down the stairs. "It's supposed to be a closed set."

"Don't worry," Aries says, barely looking over her shoulder. "They're with me."

"Closed set means only cast and crew."

"They are *my* crew. I never go anywhere without them."

Aries hasn't been in many films lately, but other than Leo, she's the biggest celebrity in our group. She has a following of over two million on Instagram. Every post she makes on TikTok goes viral, and every product she sponsors sells out. Some in the industry say she's the sellout, but I infer from the entourage and the Birkin bag on her arm that she's probably okay with it.

"Your contract was clear. Only one handler per cast member," Dani says. "They can help you take your things to your room, but then they have to leave."

"Are you serious, Dani?" Clearly, Aries remembers her. "Don't be such a little rule follower."

"This is coming straight from Austin. And Cole. In ten minutes, it better be a locked set."

Aries looks at us, rolling her eyes. "I don't miss this shit. Nothing like being your own boss." She turns back to Dani. "All right, where are our rooms?"

Dani starts climbing the stairs again. "Second floor."

"It's only two days," Riley says before I step onto the staircase. It's like he senses how anxious I've been ever since I walked in. He lowers his voice even more, so only I can hear. "Don't be a diva like Aries."

"Did you bring anyone with you?" I ask Riley as we mount the stairs together. "Your manager or agent?"

"Um, yeah. My sober coach, Leroy, is here. He went outside for a run. He's into nature. What about you?"

"Just me for now. My agent flies in tomorrow."

When we get to the top of the steps, Dani turns around, her arms pointing in various directions down the hallway.

"Aries, your room is the first on the left. Ella, you're at the end of the hall. Make yourselves at home but stay close. We'll be meeting downstairs once Austin gets here."

With that, she takes off, talking into her headset as she walks away. Aries turns in to her room, her entourage coming up behind me to deliver her luggage.

Alone, I make my way to my bedroom, a room I remember clearly. It's the same place I stayed the last time I was here. A small rocking chair on my right. The sights, the smells, the coarse feel of the quilt beneath my fingertips—every inch of this room pulls me closer to the past. To my left, there's a window overlooking the forest. I stare outside, longing to escape. I imagine the trees with their gnarled branches and spidery limbs holding me hostage.

"I wondered when you were going to give in," someone says.

When I turn around, a woman is standing in the doorway. Her hair is pulled back; chic clothes hang loosely from her thin frame.

"Petra?"

"Welcome back, stranger." She smiles, effortless beauty exuding from every feature on her face. It's hard to imagine someone so striking chose a career behind the camera instead of in front of it. She leans against the doorframe. "Can you believe I made the cut? It was a lot bigger set back then. More people running around. Now there aren't so many."

"Dani said the director wanted to include as much of the old crew as possible. I didn't know you were still working in the industry."

She rolls her eyes playfully. "Some days it feels like I never left."

It's almost worth coming back just to see Petra again. I think of all the late nights we had together, the laughing between takes. It's like I'd forgotten not everything that happened here was bad. Before I know it, my eyes are brimming with tears.

"Hey, are you okay?" She reaches for my arm as I'm going to wipe my cheeks.

"It's a lot being back here."

"I know. I feel the same way." She was with us back then. She knows what we did, and why I'm so emotional now. "Have you seen any of the others?"

"Aries and Riley."

Her cheeks blush. "Yeah, I saw him arrive."

"Did you talk to him?"

"Haven't worked up the nerve." Her lips form a straight line, and she shakes her head. Leo and I weren't the only ones to have a romantic fling on set. "We haven't spoken in years. You know how it is."

"It's easy to lose touch."

"What about you?" Her eyes narrow into a knowing stare. "Are you nervous to see Leo?"

"Yeah, I am."

Already, it's easier to be honest with her than with anyone else. I look at the open bedroom door, hear footsteps in the hallway. Someone is leaving, or maybe they're arriving. It could be him.

"It's only a weekend." She offers another smile. "We'll get through this together."

And for the first time since I arrived, I think I might.

6

Now

Food is being served on the back porch, a meet and greet of sorts for old and new crew members. Sliced meats and soft cheeses and baked breads cover the tables. You'd think it was for an army, not our small reunion crew. Some people are in line making plates; I wait my turn, deciding on only a small baguette to settle my rolling nerves.

"Ella."

When I turn, it's Cole. I haven't seen him in twenty years. Gone is the frizzy, shoulder-length hair, replaced with a sharp cut. He has swapped his concert shirts and faded jeans for a collared shirt and dark pants.

"How've you been?" he asks without giving me time to answer. "I can't tell you how happy I am you agreed to do this. It wouldn't be the same without our shining star."

His eyes search my face, then trail my body, and it's like I can read his mind. I'm not shining anymore. My looks are still there but hidden beneath years of not caring about them. And I'm nearing forty now. Basically, a death sentence for a woman my age in Hollywood.

"We owe it to the fans," I say through gritted teeth. It would still be unwise to say anything that might upset Cole. His career has only grown since *Grad Night*. He's now an influential Hollywood player. While I'm willing to bet he's still an asshole, probably an even bigger one, he maintains his power to make or break a person's career. My new career, if I can get it off the ground.

"Oh, man, they're going to love it. I've been checking Reddit nonstop. Shooting this reunion now, while the gang is still around, can introduce the franchise to a whole new generation. Not to mention, it could open more doors for all of us."

It shouldn't surprise me that Cole is incapable of picking up on my uneasiness. He's immediately gone back to his brilliance, the darling firstborn that is *Grad Night*. I wonder, if anyone was to take a poll, how many directors would be considered narcissistic? Sociopathic? And what did he mean by the gang is still around? Ben is clearly gone. Does he even care?

"Ah! There she is," Cole shouts. He's no longer looking at me; his gaze is on Aries as she exits the house through the sliding glass doors. He holds out his arms for a hug. "Sweetheart, it's been too long."

Aries accepts the embrace cautiously. She's always been much better at playing the game than I am, which is why she's still in it.

The door opens, and hushed silence falls over the group as Leo walks outside. I suspect that often happens whenever he enters a room. Not only is he handsome, but he's now mega-famous, which means mega-rich. The definition of success.

Despite his cemented celebrity, all I see is the person who stole my heart all those years ago. My insides feel a familiar flicker of adoration. Leo was my first love, first everything. I'm almost dizzy at the thought of interacting with him again.

He claps a hand on Cole's shoulder, then leans in to give Aries a hug. His eyes lock with mine, and there I am again, holding my breath. Every hair on my body standing at attention, my thoughts swimming. I walk into the living room, away from the humid heat and swarms of people, where I can have a few minutes to compose myself.

After all this time, I can't believe I'm seeing him again. His presence brings back emotions I'd rather not confront, but Leo was an important person in my life once. I can't forget how he defended me when no one else did. How he protected me, even when I didn't deserve it.

I hear the swooshing of the sliding glass door opening, then being pulled shut. Leo follows me into the living room. We're alone, the rest of the cast and crew outside.

"Ella," he says, a soft longing in his voice. "I can't believe you're here."

"I could say the same to you," I say quickly, afraid to meet his eyes. "I figured you'd be busy making another hit."

"The schedule is pretty tight these days, but I had to make time for this. *Grad Night* is what put me on the map. I can't forget that."

He's still humble, which makes me swoon even more. It amazes me how some people, like Cole, can develop an enormous ego after a small taste of success. Leo isn't like that, and when I look at his face, I'm seeing the young man from twenty years ago, not *People*'s Sexiest Man Alive.

I remember our last day on set when I was at my lowest, overcome with disgust for what we'd all done. Once in the car, Leo put his hand over mine and squeezed. "It's going to be okay," he said. "It's over now."

I looked up at him, accepting the magnitude of what we were leaving behind, and what we were carrying with us.

"I don't know if I can do this," I told him.

"We'll get through this," he said. "Together."

Together.

That word was what kept me going for the next two years. Looking back, I'll never know why we continued our relationship that long. Was it the sincere bond we'd forged between takes and beneath a clear blue sky? Or was it the secret that cleaved us to each other? Leo was fully aware of the blame I carried, and he tried to ease my guilt.

It became easier once the press tour for *Grad Night* began. We were around each other every night, and while we were all smiles in front of the cameras, dropping witty one-liners and anecdotes in interviews, behind the scenes, I was still a mess. Gus stayed busy fending off reports that I was an emotional liability, while Leo coped by working as much as possible.

"I have to stay busy," he said after he'd booked his first leading role in an action film that was scheduled to start shooting in Australia. "Acting is the only thing that keeps me from thinking about that night."

We broke up not long after he took the job.

"I tried getting in touch with you a while back," he says, pulling my thoughts away from the past. "I've lost your number."

Leo tried to get in touch with me? "I've been out of the spotlight. This is my first time on set in . . . I don't know when."

"I know. It's like trying to hunt down a ghost." Our eyes meet for only a moment, then he looks away. "I wanted to offer you my condolences about your mom."

Maybe he does still think of me from time to time.

"She was in a lot of pain at the end," I say.

"It's real big of you to do what you did, taking care of her," he says. "The few times I was around her, she seemed like a nice lady."

"It was always the two of us. It's what I needed to do." I push away the memories of Mom and try to focus on something lighthearted. "What about you? How've you been?"

Before he can answer, I catch sight of something in the corner of the room. It's blinking and red, pulling my attention away from our conversation.

I step away from Leo and closer to the steadily flashing light on the center shelf of the living room TV console. Another moment passes before I realize what it is.

It's a camera, and the lens is angled at us.

SCENE 2

INT. GUEST BEDROOM/BLACKSTONE COTTAGE—NIGHT

The door creaks open. Leo enters the room first, followed by Ella. All the furniture is made of honey-colored wood. Deer antlers hang above the dresser, casting intriguing shadows on the walls.
   Leo sits on the bed, bounces up and down, checking to see if it's sturdy. He looks out the nearest window.

                    LEO
          Nice view.

                    ELLA
          It's night.

                    LEO
          I know. I'm just saying it will be nice.
          In the morning.

An awkward moment passes.

                    LEO (CONT'D)
          You okay?

                    ELLA
          Yeah. It's . . . been a long day.

                    LEO
          Feeling sad about all you're leaving be-
          hind?

Ella laughs at this, her stiff posture beginning to ease.

ELLA

No. That's not it.

Playfully, Leo starts singing "Graduation" by Vitamin C. He crawls across the bed, taking her hand and pulling her to him. Ella joins him on the mattress. She laughs.

ELLA

You're a goof.

LEO

And you're a bad liar. Tell me what's bothering you.

ELLA

I'm just thinking about my parents. I feel guilty for cutting dinner short.

LEO

We wanted to get on the road before dark.

ELLA

I know.

LEO

Do you wish we hadn't come here?

ELLA

It's not that. I think it's hitting me this is the last time for everything. A year from now . . . who knows where we'll be.

                    LEO
Well, I'll be storming the fields at UT. And you'll be learning about biology or brain matter, whatever premed students like you study.

She laughs again but still seems unsure.

                    LEO (CONT'D)
Just think about this weekend. It'll be fun. Hiking in the morning. Hot tub in the afternoon. I have my best friend, my girl. What else could a guy need?

                    ELLA
I guess I feel out of place. I mean, they're your friends.

                    LEO
Our friends now. We could have done a dozen different things this weekend but we're here together. It's going to be fun.

                    ELLA
Yeah. You're right.

They kiss. Slowly, then with more passion. A voice from off-screen interrupts the moment.

                    RILEY (O.C.)
Want to get in the hot tub?

LEO
In a minute. (He shakes his head.) That guy is crazy.

A pause. Ella stares out the window, seeing nothing but her own reflection in the glass. She is reluctant to share her true thoughts.

ELLA
Were you really part of that whole Rhodes scandal?

The question comes out with urgency, like someone gasping for air after being caught in a current. It's clear this is what is bothering her.

LEO
I wouldn't call it a scandal.

ELLA
He lost his job. I was working in the office the day he got fired. It was a huge scene.

LEO
Of course you were. They only pick the best of the best to work in the office.

ELLA
I'm serious. The guy was really broken.

LEO
He'd been messing with people for years. Maybe he deserved to get fired. The guy was a creep.

                    ELLA
    Or maybe getting fired pushed him over
    the edge.

Leo leans back on the bed, fingers laced behind his head. He stares at the ceiling, thinking.

                    LEO
    You're right. It was a messed-up thing
    to do, but everything snowballed. That's
    what happens with Riley. It starts as
    one thing, turns into something else.

He pauses to look at Ella. She agrees with what he is saying.

                    LEO (CONT'D)
    For years, it's been the two of us playing around. But now I have you. You make
    me want to be someone better.

Ella leans in for a kiss. Soft, romantic. Then she kisses him with more desire, puts his hands on her body. She straddles him, pulls off his shirt. She rubs her hands over his strong torso.
   Leo leans up, pulling the dress off her. Still kissing, he flips her around so she's lying on the bed. We move away from the bed, where we see the rest of the clothes land on the carpet. Leo's jeans. A bra. Then panties.
   Leo and Ella are under the covers. They stop kissing.

                    LEO (CONT'D)
          Are you sure you want to do this?

                         ELLA
          I'm sure.

                         LEO
          We don't have to—

                         ELLA
          I want this. I want you.

She pulls him in for another kiss. They
begin to have sex. Leo remains focused. Ella
looks as though she is in pain, then pleasure takes over. She moves in rhythm with
him. She is a woman now, leaving her girl-
hood behind.

EXT. BLACKSTONE COTTAGE—NIGHT

We move away from the cabin, back to the
original view we saw in the beginning. The
house is darker now.
   In the woods to the left, we get a glimpse
of the MAN wearing the lion mask. He walks
in the direction of the cabin.

7

Then

I eye the set like a gladiator before entering an arena. A four-post bed stands in the center of the room, decorated with a plaid quilt and embroidered pillows, the exact type of kitsch you'd expect to see in a secluded cabin.

"You ready for today?"

Leo stands beside me, undeniably handsome. I wouldn't be surprised if he landed the part on his looks alone, but courtesy of Gus, I'd seen snippets of his screen test before I accepted the job. Leo is talented, too.

"Yes," I say, wondering how I can be a successful actress when I am such a shitty liar.

The Performers Academy taught me a lot about form. The proper way to faint on command. How to channel my own experiences for on-screen emotions. Those lessons gave me skills, but not confidence. As much as I want this career, there is a part of me that wonders if I'm good enough.

Not only is it my first day of filming, but Cole wants to begin with the scene where my character loses her virginity. I knew there was a sex scene in the film. I've read the script over and over, memorizing every line. I even predicted I'd feel antsy before the cameras rolled. The only situation I hadn't prepared for was that this would be the first scene I'd shoot.

Cole arrives, commanding the attention of everyone on set. There's something intimidating about the way he watches over us, like a great hawk assessing his selection of prey. It's not his appearance—unkempt hair that falls into his eyes and an all-black ensemble. Maybe it's because we all know he's a member of Hollywood royalty, his father being the esteemed Daniel Parks. We all do what he says, without question or thought. Jenny and Cole are behind the camera, deep in conversation, when Leo approaches them.

Petra comes over wearing black overalls atop a striped shirt. She pats the bulky fanny pack around her waist. "I'll be touching up your makeup in between takes, and I'll handle your wardrobe while, you know . . ."

The sentence trails off.

"While I get naked?"

"I guess so, with this scene. But really, anything you need to make you more comfortable, let me know."

"Any tips would help."

Petra puts on a bracing smile. "Can't help you with any of the on-screen stuff, I'm afraid, but this is my third feature, so I'm starting to get a feel for things. I can tell you everyone is nervous in the beginning." She leans in closer, like she's sharing a secret. "Especially when it comes to the sex stuff."

I exhale a sigh of relief. "Good to know it's not just me. I mean, out of all the scenes to get us started. It's like, 'Hi. Nice to meet you. Here's my bra.'"

She laughs, an endearing cackle. "Look at it this way, get the hard part over now. The rest of the shoot will be a breeze."

"Remind me of that when I'm covered in corn syrup."

"Will do."

"Places," Jenny shouts from across the room, taking a seat beside Cole. I lock eyes with Leo. He gives me a sheepish smile.

"You got this," Petra says, squeezing my shoulder.

I walk toward the bed, pulling my robe tighter with each step.

A few crew members are still on set, making sure every prop is placed and every light is poised. I recognize Petra's partner from yesterday, Monica. She's leaned against the wall wearing another floor-length skirt, a bottle of water in her hands.

"All right, now," Cole says, obvious irritation in his tone. "Get on the bed."

I scan the room again, waiting. I'd been told the sex scene would be a closed set, and yet there are still almost a dozen crew members standing around, hovering behind Cole in a nameless posse.

"Are we starting now?" There's a quiver in my voice I wish wasn't there.

Cole makes a dramatic gesture, turning his head from left to right. "Yes, Ella. If it's all right with you, I thought we'd shoot the scene."

Jenny looks away, as does Petra. From somewhere around the corner, I can hear a man sniggering. Dale, from yesterday. He's a cameraman, I think, but he's not holding any equipment now. Why is he still here?

I tune out the sounds, blur out the faces staring at me, and remove my robe. My breasts are covered with nude pasties, and a neutral thong covers my lower half. I slide beneath the plaid quilt. We've not even shot the dialogue for this scene, yet here I am, waiting for Leo between the sheets, desperate for Cole's approval.

Leo takes off his robe, too, tosses it to someone off set. He's wearing boxer briefs, which seems like an entire uniform compared to what I'm wearing. Not wearing, rather. He climbs on top of me, getting into position.

"Are you ready?" he whispers, his voice gentle.

For a moment, I think he's reciting a line from the script. Then I realize he's talking to *me*, making sure I'm okay.

"Yeah."

"Now that we're in place, I'm going to tell you what to do. Make sure you listen," Cole says. "Kiss."

Leo leans down and kisses me, his lips soft and gentle, his

breath minty as though he prepared by downing half a bag of Altoids.

"Kiss her for real," Cole shouts. "You're supposed to be having sex."

Leo sticks his tongue in my mouth. I open wider, taking him in. At the same time, he starts grinding more ferociously, simulating sex beneath the covers. We continue kissing, our hands tracing each other's bodies in conjunction with Cole's orders. It feels like we continue doing this for hours, but it must only be a few minutes. I feel Leo's groin against my leg, hardening, and try to ignore it.

"Stop!"

Just like that, the passion is switched off. Leo raises himself, like doing a push-up, and looks in the direction of the crew.

"Ella, you're flopping around like a dead fish over there," says Cole. "Can you act like you're at all interested?"

I'm trying, I want to say. Truth is, I have no idea what I'm doing. This is my first time on a major movie set. My first sex scene. And although I'm ashamed to admit it, much like my character in the film, I'm a virgin. It doesn't matter how great of an actress I am. All I can pull from are different love scenes in other films I've seen; I have no experiences of my own.

Nearby, another crew member breaks into laughter. Carlos, I think, is his name. He's standing beside Monica, the two of them whispering. Jenny gives them a threatening stare, but she remains quiet as Cole instructs us on what to do.

We start again. Leo kisses me, harder this time. When he starts moving his hips again, I try to follow his rhythm. I think of it as choreography, nothing else. And it's easy to forget about the awkwardness of the situation with Leo's lips against mine, this person I met little more than twenty-four hours ago. His caresses begin to feel genuine, not staged. I'm starting to think we've made progress when—

"Cut!" Cole shouts. When I look over, he's staring into the monitor, likely rewatching the shot we just took. He rubs his hand against his chin, never taking his eyes away from the screen. "The sheets keep sliding down and showing the thong. You're going to have to take it off."

"What?" My ribs feel as though they're squeezing together, forcing the question out.

Cole looks up, his stare lethal enough to spear through me. "You can't have sex with underwear on. Don't worry, the camera won't capture your twat."

I don't say anything, but the look on my face is enough. I'm mortified.

"We could pull the sheets up higher?" Leo offers. "Then it won't matter."

"Or we could get a phone so you can call Ella's dad and ask for her hand in marriage." Cole snickers. "We're shooting a scene, Leo. Let's get it over with."

My chest is rising, falling, and I'm afraid everyone on set can see. I'm afraid Leo can smell the sweat covering my body in a slimy film, puddling beneath my arms. The undergarments you're allowed to wear are strictly stated in the contract. I shouldn't have to take off anything that makes me uncomfortable.

But I'm scared. Cole could have me kicked off the set in no time, replace me with a dozen different girls who would gladly take off their underwear for this role.

I inhale slowly, turning back to Leo. I slide my hand beneath the sheets until my finger finds the dainty fabric of the thong and begins to tug. Then there's another hand. Leo's hand, holding mine in place.

"Wait," he whispers. We make eye contact, and it's like he's seeing right through me. Reading my thoughts and fears. I'm a virgin, but I feel like that stare is a more accurate glimpse of what sex is like than anything else we've done. His gaze is so intimate.

"We need a break," Leo says. He stands, making sure not to expose me with the raised sheet. Oddly enough, Cole doesn't appear frustrated when Leo gets off the bed and marches toward him.

"Take ten, everyone," he says, and it amazes me how quickly the entire crew seems to disperse. Jenny doesn't make eye contact as she stands and moves across the room, reaching for a bottle of water.

"This shoot might take longer than we expected," Monica says, and I can't help feeling her volume is intentional. She locks eyes with me, only for a second, before ambling out of the room. There's an unmistakable cruelty in her stare that makes me feel like I'm being pierced with a dozen little daggers.

Petra joins me on the bed, carrying my robe. I pull it on as though it were a life jacket that could save me from drowning.

"That was humiliating," I tell her. The intensity of the moment has passed, and yet the emotions linger. My throat is raw from trying not to cry. If one single tear falls, the entire set will know, and it'll add another ten minutes for makeup to fix it.

"Cole's being a dick." She looks around, making sure no one can overhear our conversation. "That was harsh, especially for the opening scene."

"I need a little time to get into my character," I say, even though the excuse is useless. "It would be easier if there weren't all these men standing around."

"It's definitely a sausage fest around here." She smiles at me genuinely. "But I'm here with you."

"Your partner. Monica. She was openly laughing at me with the rest of the crew."

Petra sighs and shakes her head. "Don't worry about her. She's a miserable person and tends to take it out on others."

"What about Jenny?" I ask, my voice a whisper. "She's AD and didn't speak up once."

"Her role is a lot more assistant than it is director. Even if she did say something, I doubt Cole would listen."

Petra said she was here to handle my robe and retouch my makeup, but I wonder if there's a deeper purpose. If she had reason to believe Cole might be this brazen.

"You've worked with other directors. Have you ever worked with Cole?"

"This is his first feature. The only time he's ever called the shots. I was a handler on one of his dad's films. It was my first gig, actually. Cole was there, and he was—"

"Difficult?"

"*Pig* seems to be the better word."

I laugh.

"There you go. Lighten up. Try not to think about the icky stuff."

Raised voices erupt from the hallway. Petra and I turn, trying to see what's going on. At first, I think it's Cole throwing a tantrum, but as I listen, I realize it's Leo, going head-to-head with the director. Jenny stomps through the doorway, trying to defuse the drama between them.

"That's a new one," Petra says, unable to peel her eyes away. "Can't say I've ever heard anyone talk to Cole like that."

"What do you think they're talking about?" I ask.

"I don't know," she says.

Their conversation remains a mystery, but when Leo returns, Cole empties the set, and my underwear stays on for the rest of the shoot.

8

Now

I stand still, watching the blinking light in front of me.

"Ella, are you okay?" When I don't respond, Leo stops staring at me, then follows my gaze. "Is that . . . a camera?"

He sees it, too. The house isn't playing tricks on my mind. I'm not crazy.

I bend down to get a better look at the camera. I'm close enough that I can see my own warped reflection in the lens.

Aries enters the living room from outside. She halts when she sees me bending over in front of the console. "Um, what are you doing?"

"There's a camera hidden in this room," I say, glaring at the lens. "It was capturing my entire conversation with Leo."

She strides over, a skeptical expression on her face, like my hysterics aren't to be believed. When she sees the camera, she marches to the back door and shouts outside.

"Cole, could you kindly come here and tell us what the fuck is going on?"

Aries's outspokenness makes me want to close up more, like back then. I turn away from the camera and walk toward Leo.

He's leaning against the foyer wall, his arms crossed, his face as confused as mine.

A few seconds later, Cole strolls into the room, followed by Dani, Petra, and two other crew members I don't recognize. Riley comes in soon after.

"What's the problem?" Dani asks.

Aries has her hands on her hips. "Can you tell me why—"

Before she can finish, Cole raises his hand to silence her. It's then I notice his earpiece. He's on the phone.

"Uh-huh, okay. Bye." He's smiling as he takes the device out of his ear and slides it into his jacket pocket. When he looks back at Aries, the smile is gone. "What's wrong now, love?"

"Ella found a camera hidden in the living room."

She points, and Cole comes closer to get a better look. He doesn't say anything for a while, but it's clear he's not confused; rather, he's contemplating how he should address its discovery.

"We're still waiting on an explanation," Aries says, tapping her foot against the hardwood.

He exhales in frustration. "It's part of the reunion."

"We didn't sign up to be filmed without consent," says Riley, shaking his head.

"Don't get mad at Cole," says a voice from the other end of the room. "It was my idea."

A man walks forward. He's wearing baggy khaki pants and a concert tee over a long-sleeved shirt. I recognize him from my frenzied Google searches before boarding this morning's flight.

"Austin McKinty," he says. Standing closest to Leo, he holds out his knuckles to initiate a fist bump. "I'm the director."

"Leo." He watches him with suspicious eyes.

"I'm well aware of who you are." He walks to the center of the room, taking time to look at each one of us. "I'm familiar with all of you. And *Grad Night*. The entire franchise. I can't tell you what an honor it is to be working with you all."

Cole claps a hand on Austin's shoulder. "This guy's an up-and-comer. He's got an impressive list of credits, and I've had the pleasure of working with him on some of my own films."

"None of this explains why there are hidden cameras in the living room," Aries says, her arms crossed. "And who knows where else they're hidden. Outside. Upstairs. In the bedrooms?"

Austin smiles, taking his time answering. "There aren't any cameras outside, or in the bedrooms. Those are your private quarters. But I have placed several cameras around the communal areas of the house."

"Why didn't you tell us?" Leo asks. There's a quiver in his voice as he tries to suppress his anger.

"I planned on it," Austin says. "I was hoping to introduce myself first. I didn't think you'd spot it right away."

"So, you were trying to record us without our knowledge?" I ask.

"It's not as mischievous as you're making it sound. I wanted to capture some candid moments, yes. That's what I'm trying to do with this entire documentary. I want the audience to get the feeling that they're right here with us, that they're a part of this film."

"We're sitting down for interviews in the morning," Riley says. "It can't get more real."

"There's something forced when you know you're being filmed, even if you're only being yourself. I wanted to capture the subtleties of a reunion like this. What it's like to return to a place that played such a significant part of your life. What it's like interacting with the crew and cast after years apart." Austin pauses, fixing his gaze on me. "What it's like seeing your former lover again."

My head turns toward Leo. He's staring back at me. My cheeks burn, and my throat is sore with anger, making it difficult to speak.

"I didn't sign up for this. This is supposed to be a reunion, not a reality show."

"Come on, Ella," Cole says. "It's not like he's going to show anything incriminating. Most of the candid shots won't even play audio. You have to trust this guy. I've seen his work. He knows what he's doing."

"I want nothing more than to produce a film all of you can be proud of. The four of you, especially," Austin says. "You've played such an important role in the lives of the fans, mine included."

The original cast. I realize this is the first time all four of us have been in the same room in twenty years. The others notice, too, and we acknowledge one another before turning our gazes to the floor. Are we all thinking the same thing? That this place was much more than the set of our first blockbuster. It was also the setting of something much darker, an event we've each spent the past twenty years trying to forget in our own ways.

"From now on, be up-front with us about what's going on," Leo says at last, "even if you are trying to get the best shot possible."

"Will do." Austin taps his forehead with two fingers. "And I want to thank each of you for being part of this."

Austin's gaze once again falls on me. My cheeks blush, whether from anger or something else, it's hard to tell. I bite my lip. I hadn't realized until now, but the entire crew has assembled, watching his address to the cast. Petra is leaning against the staircase banister. When she catches my attention, she mouths, *Sorry*. I make a beeline for her, hurrying to get out of the room before any of the others can catch me.

"Did you know about this?" I ask her once we're out of the house, heading in the direction of the lake.

"I didn't know you were being filmed without permission," she says, walking in stride beside me.

"It's so unnecessary. They already have us here. Why do they have to keep pushing?" I inhale a deep breath and puff it out, but it does little to settle my aggravation. "Austin might think this is his idea, but it has Cole written all over it."

"Cole does have a knack for rubbing people the wrong way." She looks at me. "You okay? It seems like something else is bothering you."

"I never thought we'd be back here. It's like slipping through time." We're closer to the water than the house, but I still survey the scene to make sure no one can hear us. "It's hard being here with the same people who were there that night."

The sadness washing over her is uncomfortable to witness. Petra was with us that night, too, and has carried the same secret all these years. Whenever I thought about reaching out to anyone from set, it was this reaction that kept me from doing so. It's painful to confront the past.

"We all agreed to move on. Try not to think about it," she says. "Besides, not all reunions are bad."

I force myself to smile. "I'm happy to see you again."

"What about Leo?"

"Time will tell." I inhale more crisp mountain air. "I need to cool off. Clear my head before I head back to the cottage."

"It's an early start time in the morning," Petra says, walking back in the direction of the house. "Don't stay up too late, okay?"

I sit alone at the lakeshore for several minutes, until the sky turns a stormy purple. Nightfall at Blackstone Cottage is like another world. Nature grows louder, tree leaves rustling, creating a whooshing noise that sounds like whispers. The water, still from a distance, licks the sandy banks. Birds caw at random intervals, a reminder there's life all around.

And yet it's dark, so dark. If you wander too far away from the house, you won't be able to see what's in front of you.

I realize how isolated I am, and head back the way I came. The only thing worse than being stuck inside Blackstone Cottage with the cast is being stranded in the wilderness alone. Along the trek back, it sounds like the forest is collapsing around me, branches and twigs creaking with every step. Then another sound grabs my attention. A voice.

"It's bullshit, and you know it." It's Aries's voice, carried through the trees, but I can't see her.

The second voice I recognize as Cole's. "It's creative freedom. That's important to a new director."

"What about our freedom?"

I stop, still unable to see anyone, and listen closer.

"I know it goes against your nature, but you need to relinquish some control," Cole says. "Austin isn't out to get you. What is it you're so worried about?"

A pause. I imagine Aries scrambling for a response. She can't let on that she has anything to hide. "You can't force me back here without telling me the truth about what's going on."

"No one is forcing you anywhere," he says.

Aries's reply is grim. "It didn't feel like I had much of a choice."

What does that mean? Aries and Cole have always had a complicated relationship; I remember that from when we were filming. But why did she say she didn't have a choice?

The voices cease, replaced with the sound of someone trampling through the underbrush. The sound comes closer. A jolt of panic shoots through me, and I pick up my pace in the direction of the house. By the time I see lights from the back porch, Aries comes into view.

She hears me coming and jumps.

"Damn, Ella." She gasps, a mixture of fear and relief on her face. "I thought I was alone."

I know that's not true because I overheard their conversation, but at least she didn't catch me eavesdropping.

"After that introduction from Austin, I needed to clear my head," I say, looking back in the direction of the lakeshore. "I'm not comfortable with the hidden cameras."

"Yeah, I talked to Cole about that. He reminded me that if I don't follow through with my commitment, none of us will get paid."

"What?"

"The reunion was only green-lit if all the members of the core cast agreed to participate. If one of us bails, they'll scrap the whole thing. Push off our pay and whatever else has been promised to us by saying production stalled."

"I didn't know that."

Aries kicks at the dirt with the tip of her boot. "I can't believe after everything, I'm back here at this stinky cabin, with Cole telling me what to do."

"I always got the idea the two of you were close."

She looks at me, trying to unravel the true meaning behind my words. "If I was close to Cole back then, it's because I was desperate to kick off my career. Back then, no one believed me when I said he was a creep," she says. "At least now the truth is starting to come out."

"What are you talking about?"

"All the allegations." She stares at me, but I shake my head. "Wow, you have been living under a rock."

"What allegations?"

"Three different women have come forward claiming he drugged and assaulted them."

My stomach roils. "When?"

"They spoke out in the last few months, but the attacks happened years ago."

"And you think it's true?"

"Of course it is." She stares ahead, stone-faced. "Women don't make that up."

"Then why is he here? Sounds like he has way bigger issues than shooting a reunion."

"As usual, the whole thing is being swept under the rug, courtesy of Daniel Parks. The women talked to a journalist, but eventually settled out of court. I'd bet that's why Cole's production company was so insistent about shooting the reunion now. They need some good press to outshine the bad."

"Has Cole said anything about it?"

"Not to me. Probably not to anyone," she says. "The rumors are out there now. He might not get what he deserves, but there will always be some people who give him the side-eye based on the accusations alone."

Cole might have his own reasons for filming the reunion, but the stakes waged against us are higher. I'm afraid our secret could slip out, especially if we don't know when we're being filmed.

I step closer to Aries, my voice a whisper. "I'm worried about a hidden camera catching a conversation about that night."

Her eyes widen as though my mentioning that night will invoke some type of curse. She recovers quickly, darting her eyes from left to right before speaking. "We've not talked about it in twenty years. I'd say we can make it another weekend."

"Aren't you anxious about being back here? That someone might—"

"If you don't want people to find out, then stop talking." It's a warning, a dangerous expression on her face. Just as quickly, her demeanor changes, and she's the light, carefree Aries the world loves. "I'm heading over to craft services. I could use a drink."

She takes off in the direction of the crew cabins, which I assume are stocked with expensive booze. I consider joining her, continuing our conversation, but her reaction to my last question made it clear that she no longer wants to talk. Plus, I'm exhausted. My emotions have been all over the place today, and I need rest.

This weekend is already shaping up to be more than I bargained for.

9

Now

Mom is at Blackstone Cottage.

She's standing in the same spot I was in last night, down near the lakeshore, her white nightgown blowing in the wind.

When I see her, my chest fills with joy and hope and love. I rush forward, but before I can touch her, some silent realization takes over.

She's not real.

She turns now, still beautiful but paler than I remember. There's a grimace on her face. I can't decipher whether it's anger or fear.

"You shouldn't have come back," she says.

The sky turns dark, heavy storm clouds moving in at warp speed. Pressure builds between my ears, signaling the rain to come. My shoulders clench as I feel the cold air approaching.

"You shouldn't have come back," Mom repeats. She faces me now, her back to the water. That's when I see the crimson stains on her white dress. On her hands, too. Blood. There's a tightness around my neck, like I'm being strangled, and then . . .

My eyes pop open. The hands around my neck are my own. My chest rises and falls rapidly as I try to catch my breath.

Night terrors. I had them for months after *Grad Night* wrapped. They returned after Mom's diagnosis, but quickly retreated once I realized there was no amount of worry or medication that could save her.

This is the first time I've had one since she died, and it's no coincidence that it arrives once I'm here.

You shouldn't have come back. Mom's ghostly words follow me into wakefulness. I roll onto my side, my scalp damp and itchy from sweat. Whenever I close my eyes, I see the bloody image of my mother standing by the lakeshore.

I slide on a pair of sandals and pull a hoodie over my head. It's almost time for me to report for hair and makeup. The group interview is listed first on the call sheet, and I can't decide if that comforts or intimidates me. No one seems to appreciate the memories being back here stirs up—not even the people, like Aries and Petra, who were there.

Outside, the darkness is dimming, the sky a gray-blue wonder with dense clouds. Mornings here are beautiful; I remember that. I'd always hear people talk about the great outdoors, like it was some kind of passageway into another dimension. I couldn't care less about the wildlife roaming the woods or the gar in the water, but there is an unmatched cleanliness to the morning mountain air. A rare, crisp quality that's long been eradicated from the city. The sound of the lake water in the distance is comforting, far removed from the horrifying presence it seemed to represent in my dream.

The porch door opens. Petra and Dani come outside, Austin trailing a few steps behind them.

"Good," Dani says when she sees me. "You're up."

"How was your night?" Petra asks.

"I didn't get the best sleep," I say. "Trying to enjoy the calm before the storm."

Petra smirks. "Feels just like old times, doesn't it?"

"You should head over to hair and makeup," Dani says. "The group interview is first on the schedule."

"I'll walk with you," Austin says, scuttling to me as Petra and

Dani take off. "I didn't sleep well, either. Too excited about today."

My shoulders rise. I can't help feeling guarded around him considering how yesterday went. "How'd you get roped into the *Grad Night* universe?"

"I've always been a huge fan of the franchise," he says. "I couldn't pass on this project. Not only does it give me the chance to work with Cole, but I also get to finally meet all of you."

A fan. Austin must be ten years younger than me, and he carries an enthusiasm that mirrors my own when I first arrived on this set. It's a vibrancy I didn't notice during yesterday's introduction.

"I want to apologize," he says as though reading my mind. "The cameras were installed before anyone arrived, but I'd planned on telling the cast about them. Honest. I'd never want to make any of you feel uncomfortable."

"I'm not used to cameras recording my private conversations."

"I'm sure. I wish I could have told you about them," he says. "I thought it would be cool to get as many candid moments as possible. The fans are so excited about this project. It took years to get it off the ground, but I guess that was a blessing in disguise. Now I get to be involved."

"What do you love so much about *Grad Night*?" I ask. "I mean, it's a good film as far as horror movies go. I guess I still have trouble wrapping my head around the fandom."

"I just love the nostalgia of it. The first time I watched it, I was at a sleepover. I remember trying to act tough around my friends, but inside I was scared shitless. Every time I'd catch it on cable, all those same feelings came flooding back. That's what people love about it more than anything, I think. It's one of the films that made me want to enter the industry."

When I accepted this job, I hoped for a reaction like this. I hoped that my work would inspire others. My dreams have come to fruition, but at a cost.

Austin, still lost in his own thoughts, laughs. "I thought all of you guys were the absolute coolest when I was a kid. I even had a poster of the cast in my room. It's surreal we're all here together."

"I just hope you do the reunion justice," I say. "And no more surprises."

"I promise," he says, shaking his head. "And you know, after this I start work on another feature. If you'd be interested, I'd love to get you involved."

As flattered as I am by his offer, I'm skeptical it could be that easy to book another job. Can I ever pursue my passions without desperation hovering over me? I can have talent and experience, beauty and dedication, but it's never the right combination. It's never enough.

"Are you in search of middle-aged women for your next project?"

Austin scoffs. "I loved *Grad Night* growing up, but I'm not interested in sticking with the tropey stuff for the rest of my career. I want to tell compelling stories that will resonate with people." He locks eyes with me. "I think someone with your experience would be perfect for that."

"The whole reason I'm here is to get more exposure."

"The reunion will definitely provide that." He stops walking once we arrive at the cabin. "Looks like we're here. I'll see you on set?"

I remain standing, watching as he takes off toward the main house, suddenly energized by the possibilities of what could happen once this weekend ends.

These aren't the same crew cabins, even if Cole and Austin put them on the same spot. This time, it feels much more like a cross between a makeup trailer and a tiny home, far less like a space used for a half dozen purposes.

Inside Cabin One, there are racks with multiple outfits, and a lighted mirror in the corner of the room. A petite woman with short black hair and thick glasses stands in front of it. She has a tattoo of a hibiscus flower climbing her left arm.

"I'm Ella," I say, holding out my hand.

The woman is stuffing different tubes of makeup in her apron. She looks at me for a long while before turning around. "Sit."

I follow her instructions. Not every crew member enjoys small talk, and this isn't like last time, when the same group of people were around one another for several weeks. We're only here for the weekend, and it's likely I won't see most of these people again.

"Do you know what you're wearing?" the woman asks without looking at me.

"No idea," I say. "Dani said there would be different options."

The woman turns around again. She drops her chin, taking a long, hard look at my appearance. I watch through the mirror as she walks over to the clothing rack and pulls back a curtain.

In the reflection, I see the familiar lion mask and graduation gown staring back at me. I gasp, fidgeting in my seat. It's been years since I've seen the costume in person, and I wasn't expecting it. The way it's positioned, it almost looks like someone is wearing it, waiting to pounce.

"You a little jumpy?" the woman asks.

I laugh nervously. "It caught me off guard."

"Austin and Cole want to get some candid shots of someone wearing the original costume," she says, pulling back the rack to show three or four replicas of the same mask and gown combo. She riffles through the other wardrobe choices, pulling out a black pantsuit. "How's this?"

It's not my style, but after spying the other options, I believe it's the one I'd find most comfortable.

"Works for me," I say.

She puts the outfit to the side and returns to the mirror, carefully selecting which products to use on my face.

"Are you happy to be back here after all these years?"

"It's a job," I say hesitantly. "I've never done a reunion before, but we owe it to the fans."

There's a strange feeling in knowing your success is indebted to thousands of people you've never met. Millions. Over the years, I've caught snippets with rising stars and directors citing *Grad Night* as one of their inspirations; those are the people who give me the will to keep going, the knowledge that my work has inspired them just as I was inspired by so many actors before me.

Then there are the other fans. The ones who don't care much about art, only like another excuse to watch women get hacked to pieces. Once at Comic-Con, a fifty-year-old "fan" offered me five thousand dollars if I'd give him a pair of my sweaty socks. I'm not sure which disgusted me more, the offer itself or that I could still remember the days when I would have taken him up on it.

"You know what they say." The makeup artist looks back at me. "This place is haunted."

"Yeah." I squirm in my seat. If she knows about the rumors surrounding Blackstone Cottage, she must have some deeper connection to the film. "Did you work on the original set?"

"Close your eyes," she says, dodging my question. She's holding a fluffy shadow brush in front of my nose. I listen, and she starts dusting the powder across my lids. "I don't like horror movies. Never seen it."

"It's not everyone's cup of tea."

"Suck in your cheeks," she says before swiping bronzer along my cheekbones. "I almost didn't accept this job because of the rumors, you know. I'm superstitious like that."

This is now the second time she's brought up the *Grad Night* set being haunted. I wonder if she's more enamored with the franchise than she lets on, or if she's trying to mess with me.

"Why did you accept the job?" I ask. "You know, if it's not your thing."

"Cole and I go way back," she says.

Cole. He has a connection to everyone, it seems. He did back then, and again now. Sometimes I wonder how someone so unlikable can have so much control over other people. It must come with the territory of being Daniel Parks's son.

"Close your eyes," she orders again.

Wetness spritzes across my face, the shock of the sensation

making me flinch. Setting spray. When I open my eyes, I'm met with my reflection in the mirror. Years have passed since I've sat in the makeup chair preparing for a day on set. It's like slipping through time and glimpsing my future all at once. If I can hold it together for a few days, keep my fractured memories and whispers of hauntings at bay, I might be able to have a career again.

The cabin door opens.

"Ella, are you almost ready?" Dani asks, holding a clipboard close to her chest.

"She's all done," the makeup artist says. Her eyes fix on me. "Good luck out there."

I don't say anything else as I exit the cabin, following Dani the short distance back to Blackstone Cottage.

It's showtime.

SCENE 3

INT. BEDROOM/BLACKSTONE COTTAGE—NIGHT

We see the corner of a headboard slamming against the wood-paneled wall repeatedly. Riley moans on the bed. Aries is on top of him, her long hair falling in front of her face.
   She leans back, writhing in pleasure, breasts exposed. She climaxes, rolling to the left beside Riley. Both are panting.

          RILEY
That was amazing.

          ARIES
I think I want a cigarette.

          RILEY
Not inside the cabin. Dad will kill me.

          ARIES
Let's head out to the hot tub, then. I'm sick of waiting on them to join us.

          RILEY
Maybe Leo is finally getting laid. Can you think of a more romantic place to lose your virginity?

          ARIES
More romantic than the back seat of your Volvo? Come on, don't tell me you got

this place just so Ella would put out for your best friend.

                    RILEY
          I mean, it's not the only reason.

Aries smacks his chest playfully. She hops out of bed, looking around the room for something to cover her exposed body.

                    RILEY (CONT'D)
          You can't say the guy hasn't been pa-
          tient. They've been together, what, a
          year?

                    ARIES
          Sometimes a girl needs time. You can't
          rush it. Especially when Leo is going to
          be banging girls left and right come
          rush week.

                    RILEY
          Don't think that. I mean, he's been with
          lots of girls. I've never seen him go
          nuts for someone like Ella. Maybe
          there's something to that whole playing
          hard to get thing.

                    ARIES
          Always seemed like a boring strategy
          to me.

Across the room, her phone rings. She marches to the dresser, looks at the screen, and ignores the call. She starts sifting through her open suitcase.

                    RILEY
Who was that?

                    ARIES
Carly. I think she's bummed I didn't invite her up here.

                    RILEY
You understand, right? I mean, Dad was cool with the four of us coming, but the last thing we need is some rager who damages the place.

Aries tightens the back of her string bikini, shimmies over to Riley, still on the bed.

                    ARIES
I more than understand. In a few years' time, you'll be running your dad's business. I want you to make as much money as possible so you can provide for me and the vanload of kids we're going to have.

She kisses him.

                    ARIES (CONT'D)
Oh babe, we've got our whole lives ahead of us. We can do whatever we want to do. Go wherever we want to go.

                    RILEY
Let's start with the hot tub.

EXT. BACK PORCH/BLACKSTONE COTTAGE—NIGHT

Steam hovers above the water, the jets whirring. Aries dips a toe into the water before sinking the rest of the way in.

> ARIES
> Ah, this is amazing.

Riley is wearing his graduation gown, unzipped, over his swim trunks, like a bathrobe.

> RILEY
> I'm grabbing a beer. You want anything?

> ARIES
> Cigarette.

Riley walks over, puts it between her lips, then lights it for her. She smiles approvingly.

> ARIES (CONT'D)
> I'll take another drink, too.

> RILEY
> Coming right up.

Riley goes inside. Aries inhales the cigarette deeply, leans back. It's difficult to tell the difference between the smoke in the air and the steam coming off the water. She closes her eyes and smiles. In this moment, she is content, happy.

Her phone rings again. She wades through the water to the other side of the tub, and reaches for her phone. This time, she answers.

>ARIES (to Carly, on the phone)
>Carly? Hiiii. Happy graduation. You're drunk. No, everything is fine here. Yeah. No, I haven't heard. What?

Riley returns. He puts both drinks on the table beside the hot tub and gets in the water. He moves closer to Aries, wrapping his arms around her, but she pushes him away, annoyed. She's wholly invested in the phone conversation.

>ARIES (CONT'D)
>You've got to be fucking kidding me. When? Are you sure? My God. That's crazy. Yeah, you too. Bye.

>RILEY
>What was that? Let me guess, Carly caught Brad cheating on her. Again.

Aries still looks bothered. Whatever conversation she had, it was far more serious than that.

>ARIES
>No. She told me . . . you know Rhodes? That teacher you got fired?

                    RILEY
Yeah.

                    ARIES
She said he murdered his wife. It's all
over the local news.

                    RILEY
What the fuck?

                    ARIES
I mean, I thought the guy was a creep,
but I didn't think he'd do something
like that.

                    RILEY
What a psycho. Why would he do that?

                    ARIES
Didn't Ella say something about his wife
being sick? That he lost his insurance?

                    RILEY
Hey, don't do that. What we did had
nothing to do with this.

                    ARIES
I can't believe it. I've never known a
murderer before.

                    RILEY
Hey, when they get down here, don't say
anything about it. I could tell Ella was
freaked out earlier. I don't want to get
her started again.

                    ARIES
          Yeah, don't want some poor woman's mur-
          der to cockblock your friend, right?

                    RILEY
          Aries, baby, that's not what I'm saying.
          I don't want this to spoil our night,
          okay?

Aries nods but is still visibly shaken. He
pulls her closer to him, kissing her forehead, her shoulder, then her lips. When he
pulls away, she's smiling.

                    RILEY (CONT'D)
          Speaking of Ella and Leo, I'm going to
          check on them. They need to join us. The
          night is young.

Riley towels off and puts the graduation robe
back on. Aries is left alone in the hot tub.
She takes in her surroundings. Gone is the
world of possibility; now all she sees are
potential threats.

INT. LIVING ROOM/BLACKSTONE COTTAGE—NIGHT

Riley walks back inside. He looks overhead
at the staircase.

                    RILEY
          Ella? Leo? You up there?

He's about to climb the stairs when something catches his eye. The front door is
slightly ajar. He stands still for a moment,

thinking, his mind playing through scenarios.

He walks to the front door and slams it shut. He twists the lock with a CLICK.

                    RILEY (CONT'D)
Fucking wind.

10

Then

It's almost two o'clock in the afternoon, but I'm still struggling to wake up.

Last night, Leo and I shot more scenes together, the ones where the two of us are talking alone upstairs. My stomach flipped when we returned to the bedroom, but my nerves subsided once I remembered we wouldn't be taking off any clothes. Just dialogue and acting. The job is far less intimidating when sex is out of the equation.

Unless you're Aries, that is. This afternoon, she's shooting her sex scene with Riley. Because the rooms are so small, the intimate scenes must be shot with the doors open, which makes it easy for me to hear every sigh and moan from where I stand at the bottom of the staircase.

I hear Cole, too, praising her performance.

Just right. Perfect.

Arch your back a bit.

Beautiful, Aries.

I'm not sure what emotion is worming through me. It isn't jealousy, per se. It's desire. I wish that whatever magic is being displayed in front of the camera right now belonged to me. I wish I could have received that reaction from Cole on my first day.

I start walking up the steps. Several people crowd around the door, watching. No one seems to be leering; rather, they're appreciating the art taking place before them. The delicate choreography each scene entails, especially intimate ones. I sneak closer to the doorway, catch a glimpse of a topless Aries straddling Riley, the sheets pulled around the lower halves of their bodies.

Shame shoots through me, hot and biting. I turn to go back down the stairs when I feel something collide with my lower back. As I turn to look, I nearly miss my step. My body lunges forward, my hand grabbing the banister just in time to prevent me from stumbling down the staircase.

I remain motionless, still trying to catch my breath after the near miss.

"Watch it!"

Monica is standing at the top of the staircase, a mug of steaming coffee in her hands.

This is the first time we've spoken. Unlike Petra, Monica hasn't made any attempts to get to know me. Her sneers behind the camera during my sex scene with Leo are the most attention she's given me since I arrived. She wasn't standing there a moment ago, I'm sure of it. Was it her hand I felt hit my back, or did I bump into the railing accidentally?

"What are you even doing?" she says, watching me closely. "You shouldn't be up here."

"I was just . . ." Spying. Doing the exact thing I didn't want other people to do during my own sex scene. "I was curious. Wanted to see how the scene was going."

"And?"

"Let's just say I'm happy I don't have to follow that." I toss my head in the direction of the open doorway, right as another moan rings out.

"Aren't we all," she says, her mouth pinched. "You're needed downstairs. Your agent is here."

"Gus?"

Monica ignores me as she pushes past, bumping my hand on the railing in the process. A round of applause erupts from the crew members crowding the doorway as Cole yells, "Cut!" I hurry downstairs before anyone else sees me.

Outside, I find Gus sitting in a rocking chair on the front porch.

"There's my girl," he says, his balance wavering as he tries to stand.

"What are you doing here?"

"I thought we'd have a little chat," he says. "See how things are going."

We walk along the trail that runs between Blackstone Cottage and the lake, and I begin rehashing the first day on set. How Cole was insistent about pushing boundaries, contractually and otherwise. I was hoping Gus might say something to him, remind Cole that he has an obligation to treat us respectfully, even if we are starring in *his* movie.

"Look, he's one of those directors. Artsy, in the moment, passionate. And he's worse because he comes from Hollywood royalty," Gus says, twisting his hands together. "Everyone knows Cole will never be as good as his father. Even Cole knows that. It's a heavy burden for a young director."

"If Leo hadn't said something, he would have kept messing with me," I insist. "What he did was wrong."

"You made it through. That's all that matters in this business. You're going to have scenes, hell, sometimes entire movies, that make you uncomfortable. What's important is that you finish the job. Move on to the next. Some of the best performances of all time were the hardest to film."

I know he's right. Mom and I used to sit around reading stories about different Hollywood starlets. About the mishaps and mistakes and fateful moments that sparked a career. This could be my chance, but at the same time, I don't want to feel like I'm compromising myself to achieve my dreams.

"I don't think *Grad Night* is going to earn me an Oscar nomination."

"But the next role might. Or the one after that. You never know what will happen." He dips his head closer to mine. "But I can tell you this: if you get a reputation for being difficult on Cole's feature film, it won't be easy for you to land your next part."

I exhale in frustration. He's right, and I hate it. "At least there are no more sex scenes."

"There you go! Silver linings." He reaches into his pocket. "This might help, too."

He hands over a pill bottle. No label is glued to the orange plastic.

"What is this?"

"Something to help calm your nerves."

"I'm not going to start taking drugs, Gus."

"Do you think I'd give you something that would harm you? I'm trying to look out for you, kid. Next time Cole, or anyone else, gets under your skin, pop one of these, and you won't feel as agitated."

I stare at the bottle in my hands. The emotional and physical demands of shooting a film can take their toll. Some actors rely on medication to get them through the late nights and early morning calls, but I've never been one of them. Of course, I've never taken on a project this big.

"Call me next time you're feeling overwhelmed," Gus continues. "I'd rather hear from you than the director."

I halt, my posture suddenly slumped. "Cole called you?"

"He was as flustered with how the scene went as you were." He puts his hand on my shoulder. "He only needed a little convincing that you're the right girl for the job."

Within the hour, Gus's car arrives, and he leaves. I remain at the front of the house, hands crossed over my body, watching as the taillights fade and disappear. Today's visit felt more like a threat than a moment of reassurance, a reminder that I could lose this role as quickly as I got it. I look down at the pills Gus gave me, give the bottle a rattle before slipping them into my pocket.

I stroll aimlessly toward the back of the house, closer to the woods. The forest feels different when you're exploring it alone. Peaceful, yet fiercely alive, its own life source making itself known with every crying bird and cracking branch. The walking path becomes less defined, bulging roots and scattered leaves covering the ground. I'm afraid I've gone too far, so I backtrack, making my way toward the row of crew cabins, when I hear voices. They're coming from the trees behind Cabin Six.

I take another look at Blackstone Cottage up ahead before moving closer, listening. I hear laughter.

"Don't be such a tease," says a man's voice. "We have to do something to pass the time."

"What about Jenny?" It's Aries. Her sultry drawl is easy to recognize.

A dry laugh escapes. "I'm not worried about Jenny. You shouldn't, either."

"Guys like you don't have to worry about a thing," Aries says, her voice playful, flirtatious, "but your girlfriend might feel differently."

Is Jenny in a relationship with someone on set? The last thing we need is some kind of love triangle between Aries, Jenny, and another crew member.

"Jenny's doing a job like everyone else," the man says. "Besides, all work and no play . . ."

"I've seen *The Shining*," she says, snickering. "There's plenty of fun to be had around here. Give it time."

The conversation stalls, and I hear footsteps approaching. I jump back, hoping whoever walks around the corner won't think I was listening. A few seconds later, Cole emerges, adjusting his pants before walking back to Blackstone Cottage.

My thoughts whirl inside my head, trying to piece everything together. Are Jenny and Cole in a relationship? Is that why she remained quiet as he berated me during my sex scene? She didn't want to have a fight with the boss, her boyfriend.

The conversation I overheard sounded like Aries and Cole might have a tryst on the side. Or perhaps something happened between them before. I wonder if Aries talks to all men that way, bordering between flirtation and aggression.

A few seconds later, Aries comes around the side of the crew cabin. She's wearing the same plush white robe I wore after my own bedroom scene, her long hair draped over one shoulder.

"Enjoying the fresh air?" she asks, seemingly unaware I eavesdropped on her conversation with Cole. "I know I needed it after this afternoon."

Again, she's referring to her sex scene with Riley. From the glimpse I had, it looked like it was hot and heavy.

"It's a shame we haven't shot any scenes together yet," I say. "So far, I've only worked with Leo."

"I think Cole does it that way on purpose." She looks in the direction Cole took, then turns, walking alongside me. "He likes to jump straight into the sex stuff because, well, he's a guy. I think separating the women is part of his strategy, too."

"What do you mean?"

"He thinks the crux of every horror movie is the sex and the violence. Sure, that might be why people buy tickets, but the heart of every horror film lies in the women on-screen. He forgets that."

We walk past the row of crew cabins, closer to the lakeshore. With each step, the relaxing sound of water lapping against the shore grows louder. Above, a flock of birds zips through the sky.

"It's funny," she continues, smirking as she speaks, "Cole thinks he's an expert because his father is part of the Hollywood elite, but I have more experience than he does. He didn't really have to work to get here."

"How old were you when you got started?"

"Only ten. My mom did what she could to raise three whiny kids on her own. On her off days, she'd parade us around talent searches." Aries has a bitter finality in her tone. "Those small gigs led to the kid shows, and it became clear that my mom would only get a break if I became the new breadwinner."

"Is that why you still do it?"

"I don't know." She raises her head, like she's never really thought about it. "I'm a leopard now, I guess. Not interested in changing my spots. *Grad Night* is my chance to shed my old image and create a new one for myself."

"You're doing a great job. Cole is always singing your praises," I say, hoping to get a better sense of their connection with each other. "Have you worked with him before this?"

"I've seen him around L.A. He requested me for the part. Of course, he wasn't going to give me the lead. I'm much better suited for the slutty sidekick." She looks me directly in the eyes. "He intimidates you, doesn't he?"

"I think any director would intimidate me."

"You've got to shake that. These guys can smell it on you." She pushes back her shoulders, raises her chin. "The need for approval, the need to be liked. They feed off it."

"How do you do it?" I ask. "Have such confidence?"

"I didn't at first. You have to *act* like you have it. Eventually, it becomes real. Now I have the mindset that if someone doesn't want me, whether it be a man or an agent or a director, another person will. I'm the prize here, not them."

"And you think I need to be more like you?"

"I think you're talented enough to get away with it." She unwraps the sash hanging around her waist and tightens it. "Monica told me you were spying on me during my sex scene with Riley."

My cheeks flush, and I look away. "I wasn't—"

"It's okay. I don't mind. I was spying on you last night, too. During your scene with Leo. You were great. Vulnerable, endearing." Turning, she faces the lake, holding her hands out at her sides as a breeze whips past. "My tits might bring the guys into theaters, but your performance is what's going to make this movie a hit. Your character. The sweet, innocent girl who emerges on the other side a total badass."

"Thank you." My chest swells with pride. Aries is an industry veteran, so her words carry value. Then I remember the awkwardness of running into Monica on the stairwell, my irritation that she snitched to Aries. "I wish Monica hadn't said anything. She's ignored me since I got here, but when I ran into her today, she was a total bitch. I think she tried to push me down the stairs."

Aries laughs, brushing the hair away from her face. "You know why she's doing that, right?"

I shake my head, clueless.

"She auditioned for your role." Aries narrows her eyes. "She's an actress, too. Half the people working on crews are. Or models. Or singers. They're no different than we are, taking a shitty job, hoping it will lead to something better."

"I never knew she auditioned."

"She didn't have a chance. Cole would never cast her as a leading lady. She's not his type. Too cold." She turns on her heels, walking back the way we came. "The makeup artist who had originally signed on dropped out last minute. He probably hired her because she was cheaper than finding someone new, and she took the job thinking she might have a chance of being onscreen."

"That explains why she doesn't like me," I say, following her. "It's not like I took the part from her."

"People in this industry are petty. And they're always looking for ways to get ahead. That's why she's being nice to me. She's hoping I'll put in a good word for her to my agent."

"Do you think I should say something to her? Explain I didn't know—"

"No. Don't let on that you know anything." She stops and turns to face me. "Just don't take any shit from her." After she starts walking again, she adds, "And maybe watch your back."

Aries said Monica likely took the job on the off chance they needed a new leading lady last minute. Combining that fact with Gus's visit leaves an empty feeling in the pit of my stomach.

"You don't think she'd do anything to me, do you?"

"Monica landed a small role on a television pilot with one of my friends. The show never got picked up, but Monica only got the part because the original actress had a gnarly case of food poisoning." Aries pauses. "Rumor is Monica spiked her food."

"Are you serious? Just so she could take her part?"

Petra had warned I was better off not hearing Monica's backstory, but I'd thought that was merely an expression; I never imagined her history was so sinister. I recall standing on the staircase, the sensation of something sweeping across my back. Maybe she did try to push me.

"People always say they'd do anything to be famous. Some people mean it." She stares at me, her eyes unblinking. "I wouldn't chance it."

Aries's warning is understood, although I don't know if she's someone I should trust. It's odd she's befriending me now. She said it herself; Monica is only nice to her in the hopes she can get something in return. Which begs the question, what is Aries hoping to get out of me?

11

Now

I'm the first cast member to enter the living room, where our formal group interview will take place. Austin is sitting against the far wall, behind his camera.

"You're the first to arrive," he says, his gaze scanning my body before returning to a clipboard. He grins. "You look great."

Petra, beside him, smiles. "Love the outfit."

I look down at what I'm wearing. I hadn't realized when I picked it, but there is a bandeau top beneath the blazer. A little too hip for my tastes, but when I'm sitting, the audience won't be able to see much of my torso. My hair is pulled away from my face, curled inward, falling below my chin.

"Thanks." I flex my fingers, trying to release my nervous energy. "So, how's this going to work?"

"We're just having a conversation." Austin stands, handing his clipboard to Dani. "I'll ask you about your experiences filming and the impact of the movie as a whole."

"Sounds easy enough," I say, but my voice is unsure.

"The fans are going to love it." His hand squeezes my shoulder as he walks past.

Dani steps forward and nods at the five chairs in the center of the room. "Sit in the middle."

I follow her instructions, taking the middle seat.

"Not that one," she says. "I meant the right middle. Cole will be in the center."

"Cole is being interviewed with us?"

"Yes. The core cast and the original director."

I sit, crossing my legs, and lock eyes with Petra.

"You've got this," she whispers before taking off after Austin.

As she's exiting, Leo enters. He's wearing an expensive black suit. His hair is thick and tousled and looks blonder than it did yesterday. The sight of him makes me catch my breath. When he sees me, he smiles.

"We must share a stylist," he says.

I laugh. "We were going for dark and mature."

"Looks good on you."

His eyes linger a second longer before Dani addresses him.

"Take the left middle chair," she says. "Where are the others?"

Before anyone can answer, Riley enters wearing distressed jeans and a navy crewneck, a combination that would make anyone else appear underdressed. On him, the ensemble is effortlessly chic, and when he smiles, his expression contains the same boyish charm that wooed audiences all those years ago. He takes a seat next to me, and Dani doesn't object.

Aries arrives next. Everyone in the room pauses when they see her, admiring her dress, low-cut and bright red. Her ice-blond hair is curled and styled over one shoulder.

"Everyone waiting on me?" she says before taking her seat, basking in a few more moments of attention.

"Now we only need—"

"I'm here!" Cole bursts into the room, sunglasses pulled over his eyes. He pauses momentarily to leer at Aries, then he takes his spot in the center seat.

We take turns looking at each other. It's still strange, the fact that we're all back here after so much time. Within a matter of minutes, the cameras begin rolling.

"This is truly an amazing opportunity," Austin says. "I'm sitting here in the famous *Grad Night* cabin with the cast of the original film. Tell me, when is the last time the five of you have been in a room together?"

"Not since we wrapped the press tour," Aries answers.

"After all this time, how does it feel knowing audiences still care about the franchise?" Austin asks.

"What's great about *Grad Night*, or what's great looking back," Cole says, "is that the film was a sleeper hit. We didn't have as much press as other movies because so many people were convinced it would fail."

"It didn't, though," Austin says. "In fact, it ended up being one of the highest-grossing films of the year. What was supposed to be a two-week theater run turned into two months. Many credit the film with renewing the horror genre. Did any of you know it would be such a success?"

"I did," Leo says. "I mean, we certainly weren't set up for success. As Cole said, the studios pretty much wrote us off, didn't give us the financial investment they give to other films, but being on this set, with this cast, working under Cole's direction, I knew this project was special, and I'm happy audiences felt the same way."

A warm sensation spreads through my chest. Leo has made more films than the rest of us combined. I can't say much in terms of comparing *Grad Night* to other projects, but I agree with him about believing this film was special. I felt the same way once.

"Let's talk about what it was like filming. You were on set for a total of twenty-nine days. What was it like being here that long?"

"Boring. No phones, no internet," Aries says. "It felt like we were isolated from the rest of the world."

"I loved it," Riley says. "I grew up in the mountains, so I found it refreshing to be out in nature. We were forced to find ways to entertain ourselves."

"I was ecstatic to be part of something," I say. "It was a unique experience. I've not worked on any other project like it."

"How would you entertain yourselves?" Austin asks.

"Fishing. Hiking," Riley says.

"And pranks," Leo adds.

The group laughs. Cole says, "Yes, a few pranks."

"Like what?" Austin asks.

"Well, Aries got us good one day," Cole says.

"Let's skip over that one," Aries says. For once, she seems embarrassed, eager to move the conversation along.

"It provided quite a shock for everyone on set," Leo says. "Carlos and Aries got us good."

"Who is Carlos?" Austin asks.

I jump in, eager for a simple question to answer. "He was a gaffer who worked on the original set." I look back at Leo. "But Riley is the one who did that. Not Carlos."

"No, it was definitely him," Aries says. "I wanted to surprise them. Shake up the tension. Turns out it caused more trouble than it was worth."

I look at Riley, confused. "It was you, wasn't it?"

"Sorry, Ella," he says, his eyes bouncing from me to the camera. "That was all Aries and Carlos."

"It's been twenty years," I say, shrugging. "I guess your mind plays tricks on you after all that time."

And yet I remember it like it was yesterday. What was intended as a lighthearted moment morphed into something overwhelming, became an omen of the tragedy to come. I was certain Riley was the one involved, and yet everyone else is convinced it was Carlos. How could I be wrong about something that appears so clear in my mind?

"A lot of people attribute the success of the movie to the cast," Austin says. "Cole, you've referred to this group of people as your Dream Team. Tell me, what about this group works so well?"

"Every actor in this room was a nobody—"

"Speak for yourself," Aries pops in, and we all laugh. It's almost like the banter is scripted.

"Yes, Aries had a few small roles on television," Cole starts again, his voice wavering with laughter, "but no one was a big star. This was their first major project, as it was mine. There was something refreshing about starting a film like that. Scary, too. None of us knew what we were doing, but we came to set each day with an enthusiasm to learn. Once we started, each person played their part perfectly. It's almost like every character was tailor-made for the actor.

"We had the heartthrob, Leo. Obviously, the guy is good-looking, but he brought this sensitivity, this courage. Then, we have Riley. Funny and clever. He's at the height of confidence that night, having bagged the most beautiful girl in school. Aries brings this sensuality to the film, represents all the classic horror-movie sexuality without ever once being grotesque. A little bit *Mean Girls,* a little bit Ginger from *Gilligan's Island.*

"Lastly, we have the star of the film. Our Final Girl. She's the most powerful person in the room, but she doesn't know it. And everything that happens prepares her to recognize that power, so she can overcome the very real monster tracking her down. It's up to her to avenge the deaths of her friends, and Ella handled all that responsibility brilliantly. In my opinion"—he pauses as we lock eyes—"it's the best performance in any horror film. Ever."

My cheeks burn with a mixture of bashfulness and pride. Cole's praise is flattering, even all these years later. I don't believe Cole sees greatness in anyone other than himself, but he's allowing us each a small win in front of the cameras, especially me.

"There was another core member of the cast who isn't here with us today," Austin says. "Benjamin, the infamous Mr. Rhodes. What's it like being back here without him?"

"There's an obvious absence," Leo says.

"Yeah. It's tough," Riley says. "We remained close throughout the years. We didn't see each other often, but he'd always message and call to check in."

"Same with me," Aries says. "Every time I had a new project, he'd drop a line to congratulate me."

For the first time, I register that Ben kept in touch with everyone on set except me. Or did I push him away, as I did the others? Another beat passes, and I realize everyone is looking at me, waiting for a response.

"Ben was a real pro, and we learned so much about the industry by working with him," I say. "I wish he could be here with us."

Rather, I wish we would have done this sooner, before he died.

"Let me add," Riley says, "I don't think there is anyone, aside from Cole, who was happier with the film's success. Ben loved being part of the *Grad Night* fandom. He never shied away from interviews and autographs and pictures. He kept attending horror festivals up until his most recent diagnosis. A lot of people try to disassociate from a franchise, but Ben was never like that."

A calming energy blankets the room. It's a shame Ben couldn't be here, but I'm happy that everyone remembers him so fondly, and simultaneously, overcome with regret that I let the past push me away from so many people. Across the room, I lock eyes with Petra. She smiles and nods for me to keep going as though she can sense I'm beginning to crumble.

"A lot happened during filming that resulted in some of the biggest moviemaking legends of all time," Austin says, sitting up straighter. "Many say the film owes its success to some of the rumors that were started."

"The film owes its success to the hard work we put in," Cole says, his pretentiousness starting to leak through in his tone. "But yes, some of the lore surrounding the film certainly helped."

"There are rumors that Blackstone Cottage is haunted."

"Well, local legend says these woods became a place of refuge for people during the Civil War," Cole says. "Eventually, the location was found out, and a lot of people died here. I was always fascinated with the tales of hauntings."

Austin and Cole are, unknowingly, steering the conversation into dangerous territory. A nervous chill tremors through my entire body. I shift in my seat, begin fidgeting with the hem of my blazer, trying to appear at ease.

"So, is it true?" Austin asks. "Do you think the place is haunted?"

"Personally, I don't believe in the supernatural," Cole says. "It's society's obsession with ghosts and legends that I find entertaining."

"You're telling me you don't believe in ghosts?" Aries says to Cole playfully.

"There's a reason I directed *Grad Night* and not *The Conjuring*," he answers. "Mr. Rhodes was a real character. A real evil. Some people want to blame demons and ghosts and vampires for the atrocities that man has committed. I'm not interested in letting man off the hook. So, no, despite my fascination with the macabre, I don't believe in the supernatural."

"What about the rest of you?" Austin asks the group.

"I saw some weird things happen," Riley says, his tone carrying a hint of amusement that defuses the tension brewing between the directors.

Austin leans forward, intrigued. "Like what?"

"Nothing major. Strange sounds in the night," Riley says. "This feeling like I was being watched."

"You were on a movie set," Leo says, his voice laced with skepticism. "You likely were being watched."

"You're right, but there's no denying there's an eerie feeling to this place," Riley says. "It's because we know it's so isolated."

"I totally think it's haunted," Aries says. "I packed a duffel bag full of crystals before coming back."

The group laughs, but I can't. It's as though there's a wall between me and the rest of them, and as much as I'd like to join in their merriment, the nervous sensations inside my own body take over.

Cole looks at me. "Ella?"

"I don't know if it's haunted, but I agree with Riley," I say, straining to smile. "The place gives off a weird aura. The perfect place to film a horror movie."

"It's not just ghosts," Austin says. "People say this place is cursed, and they point to a lot of the mishaps on set as proof."

An awkward pause. None of us know whether to chime in or let Austin continue. I'm unsure whether I'm being too quiet or if I need to say more, change the topic. I recross my legs, trying and failing to keep my body still.

"A cameraman was injured during filming," Austin continues, reading from his clipboard.

"Not true," Cole says vehemently. "There was a medical emergency, but it had nothing to do with filming."

"Another member of the crew is rumored to have gone missing," Austin continues, almost talking over Cole. "Jenny Cruise, your assistant director. Her last known job was on this set."

My stomach drops, a strange heat starting at my feet and rising upward.

"Another rumor, I'm afraid," Cole says, his tone relaxed. "There's nothing to suggest anyone went missing. We can't keep track of everyone who worked on the set."

"Her aunt insists no one has seen her since *Grad Night* wrapped," Austin continues. "When she filed a missing person's report, it made national news at the time, although it didn't result in any leads."

I look around at the others. Their faces are still as stone. I wonder what they're thinking, if their thoughts are racing like mine.

"It didn't go anywhere because nothing happened," Cole says curtly. "Every member of our cast and crew, including Jenny Cruise, left our set, safe and sound."

My heart beats hard against my rib cage. Flashes from that night resurface, memories I thought were long forgotten. The roaring music. The pelting rain.

I rise from my seat, the abrupt movement startling the room into silence.

"I'm sorry," I say when I realize everyone is staring at me, their gazes a mixture of curiosity and concern. "I need a moment."

Without waiting for permission, I rush out of the room, the standby crew members watching me with confusion. Petra is waiting by the door. She tries to touch my shoulder as I pass, but I lean away. I don't need to be around anyone right now, even her.

I need to get as far away from people as possible. Away from this conversation. Away from the memories.

I need to get away from Blackstone Cottage.

12

Now

Outside, the air is cool and slightly damp. A storm is gearing up.

I gulp down the air, trying to steady my breathing. Each step calms me, takes me farther away from the cameras and memories, but I don't have much time to appreciate the break. Within seconds, Dani is calling after me.

"Get back here," she shouts. "We're in the middle of shooting."

"I need a moment," I say, my words rushed and stilted, like I've run a marathon. I'm running away from my problems, from the past. Another thought settles into my brain, Mom's warning in my dream last night: *You shouldn't have come back.*

I continue my march to the lakeshore, and once I'm alone, I sit on the damp sand, not even caring that the grime will ruin my outfit, this stupid, ridiculous outfit I would never select for myself. It's something a washed-up actress would wear in an attempt to get her career back.

I've not felt so unlike myself since the last time I was here. Since we—

"Are you okay?"

Riley's voice is calm and hesitant. I turn, seeing him standing several feet away. His hands are tucked into his front pockets, sweat starting to seep through the heavy layer of powder on his forehead.

"No," I answer honestly. "I'm not."

He takes a step closer. "Want to talk about what happened back there?"

I don't want to talk to anyone, but the words have been stifled since I arrived, and I'm longing for a release. Riley is, perhaps, the best person with whom I can share my feelings; it's no secret he's battled his own demons over the years, and I'd be willing to bet most of them link back to twenty years ago.

"I can't stop thinking about it," I say. "About what we did."

Riley was there, too. All of us bound together by this soul-crushing secret.

He moves faster now, desperate to reach me. He sits beside me in the sand, hands still in his jeans.

"It's hard for me, too."

"Is it? It doesn't seem like it's hard for anyone except me," I say. "Everyone is sharing memories about fun times on set. That line of questioning was getting dangerously close to the one event we all choose to ignore."

"Cole doesn't know—"

"He said her name! *Jenny.* What was Austin going to ask next?" I pause, catching my breath. "I couldn't hold it together anymore."

"Don't think about Jenny," Riley says, his voice low. His expression is a mix of confusion and concern. "Or any of it."

"How could I not?"

Silence. Only the tinkling of water before us. Then Riley exhales.

"No one knows, Ella. Being here might bring back memories, but that's all they are." He pauses, looking out as the falling sunlight casts dazzling diamonds over the lake's surface. "I hate myself for what we did. At least, I used to. I've forgiven myself and everyone else involved. It's the only way forward."

"Forgiveness isn't going to erase what happened."

"Forgiveness gives us the tools we need to carry on with our lives."

"Maybe we don't deserve to carry on," I say. "Maybe what we need is punishment."

"I can't think of anything worse than carrying this secret for twenty years," he says. "If you ask me, we've been doing time since the moment she died."

All the anxiety building inside me shatters, sadness and regret piercing through me. A person died, and we covered it up. Why? To protect some stupid movie? To protect ourselves?

There's silence again as I process what Riley said. Time has hardened the barrier between my feelings and that night, but nothing can ever erase the guilt I carry. Maybe Riley's right. That guilt—this horrible, gut-wrenching feeling—is my penance. Sometimes, I don't think it's enough.

"I shouldn't have come back," I say at last.

"I felt the same way. I'd been turning my agent down for years."

"Why did you finally agree to return?"

"This is the longest I've been sober since . . . well, ever. I'm not sure what's different this time around, but I'm more determined than ever to get my life back." He picks up a wad of sand with one hand, letting the granules fall between his fingers. "Before I got clean, there was an incident at a bar. I got into a fight with these guys, and someone recorded it. Turns out, the tabloids got their hands on it. My agent worked out a deal with the magazines. They'd hand over the tape if I agreed to participate in the reunion."

"Why?"

"You know how the industry works. Someone knows someone who will benefit from my involvement. The tabloid kills the tape, they get some good press from my agent's other clients. The reunion gets made, the studio makes a ton of cash."

"So, they're blackmailing you into doing the reunion?"

"The word *blackmail* is a little extreme," he says, reaching for another fistful of sand. "I'm willing to do anything to keep that video under wraps. One more scandal, and I'll lose the only chance I have left in this business."

His desperation to recapture his career mirrors my own, but I'm beginning to wonder if it's worth it. "This industry just takes and takes. Maybe it's not worth giving any more. Have you ever thought of doing anything else?"

"I grew up in a small town, and my goal was always to get out. I can't go back now and start over. It would be too humiliating."

Again, his motivations strike a chord within me. Bedford is a quaint community, and I enjoyed living there with Mom by my side, but I can't imagine being there for the rest of my life. What would I even do? And now with Mom gone, the memories are too much to handle. I've never considered another career. Acting allows me to try on the personas of countless characters, all of whom are more exciting and powerful than my normal self could ever be.

Being Ella has never been enough, and now my desire to act is even stronger. I'm not just trying to be someone else; I'm trying to forget the horror of what we did all those years ago.

"I can't stop thinking about that night," I say. "Being back here makes it worse."

"Why do you think I brought my sober coach with me?" He laughs. "It's a tough two days, but we're almost halfway through. I can make it one more night, then leave this memory in the past where it belongs."

"How are you able to do that? File it away like it didn't happen."

"Learn to accept the things you can't change. It's a corny line from the program, but it's true. In fact, the whole process has made it easier for me to accept all the messed-up things I've done in the past. The drugs and alcohol, those masked the pain. The program heals it."

"What about the making amends part?"

He exhales and smiles. Clearly, Riley has had this debate with himself numerous times.

"We can't tell the truth about that night without ruining everyone else's lives in the process," he says. "I'm not comfortable doing that. Are you?"

I think about it. It's been twenty years since our group marched out into the forest and did something terrible. By some miracle, no one ever uncovered our crime. The most that's come out are jumbled rumors and lore. Would anyone benefit from learning the truth now?

"No," I answer at last, "I'm not."

I already ended one life.

It's not in me to ruin four more.

SCENE 4

INT. KITCHEN/BLACKSTONE COTTAGE—NIGHT

Riley has his back to us. He's standing in front of the kitchen countertop, pouring vodka into a short glass. We hear his phone begin to vibrate. He fishes it out of the pocket of his graduation robe, looks at the screen, and answers the call.

> RILEY
> Dad? Hey, yeah, we got here fine. The place is great. Thank you so much.
> (Pause. He nods.) I know, Dad. It's only the four of us. We'll be okay.

He stops talking, listening to his father. His expression changes, serious and somber.

> RILEY (CONT'D)
> Yeah. I heard about that. It's crazy.
> (Pause.) I have no idea why he did it. The guy is nuts.

He's trying to appear more relaxed, but it feels false.

> RILEY (CONT'D)
> Look, I'll call you first thing in the morning. Yeah, have a good night. You too.

He hangs up the phone. He stares ahead blankly, takes a long sip of his drink.

                    RILEY (CONT'D)
          Fuck.

He slams the drink down and walks in the direction of the stairs. As he walks away, we follow him, taking notice of the fire still blazing. There's an axe leaning against the fireplace.

INT. HALLWAY/BLACKSTONE COTTAGE

Riley rests against the wall and sighs. He knocks on the bedroom door.

                    LEO (O.C.)
          Just a minute.

                    RILEY
          Yep.

He waits impatiently.
   The door opens, enough for us to see Leo's face. He is shirtless.

                    LEO
          What's up?

                    RILEY
          Just checking in on you guys. You ever
          planning on coming down?

                    LEO
          Yeah. Ella is hopping in the shower.

Riley thinks about this. He takes in Leo's appearance, turns his head to try to get a look behind him.

                    RILEY
          Did you?

Leo shrugs in a way that seems to confirm Riley's suspicions.

                    RILEY (CONT'D)
          Way to go, man.

                    LEO
          Look, I'm not trying to make a big deal
          about it—

                    RILEY
          No, it's cool. I'm cool.

A pause. Riley cocks his head, insisting that Leo leave the room and join him in the hallway.

                    LEO
          What's up, man? You're acting weird.

                    RILEY
          I need to tell you something. Aries got
          a phone call. You know Rhodes? Turns out
          he went crazy and killed his wife to-
          night.

Leo's jaw drops. He's shocked, appalled.

LEO

Are you serious?

RILEY

Yeah. I mean, I don't know all the details, but it happened. Dad called about it, too.

LEO

Does he know about the video? That we—

RILEY

No, I don't think anyone knows besides some of the guys and Aries. And now Ella.

LEO

Fuck, man, you don't think he did that because of us, do you?

RILEY

Killed his wife over some beef with a couple of high school kids? No. No. (He's unconvinced.) I mean, he did it because he's a sick creep. We knew that all along, but I didn't think he'd do this.

LEO

Fuck. That poor woman. I mean, did they arrest him?

RILEY

I don't know. I'm sure they will.

                    LEO
          And do you think he'll tell them about
          the video? Say that's why he did it?

It's apparent this is exactly what Riley believes will happen.

                    RILEY
          No, no. Everything will be fine. Even if
          it did come to that, we'll be okay. My
          dad has connections. And we didn't do
          anything wrong. (He's clear about that
          point.) I wanted to give you a heads-up.
          I noticed Ella acted weird about it ear-
          lier. I didn't want you two to be caught
          off guard.

                    LEO
          Yeah, I'll break the news to her. Maybe
          in the morning. I need some time to pro-
          cess.

                    RILEY
          Yeah, come join us outside in the mean-
          time. The water feels great.

                    LEO
          We'll be down there. I promised her we'd
          take a walk by the lakefront. We'll
          probably do that first.

Riley cups Leo's shoulder, the tension
around them beginning to melt. He smiles.

                    RILEY
          You romantic son of a bitch.

                    LEO
          Yeah, yeah. See you in a few.

The door shuts, but Riley doesn't walk away.
He stares ahead at nothing, lost in thought.

INT. KITCHEN/BLACKSTONE COTTAGE

Riley reaches the bottom of the stairs. He
looks out the window to his right, and we
get a glimpse of Aries relaxing alone in the
hot tub.
   He looks at her longingly, but decides he
needs another drink. He walks back to the
kitchen. As he passes through the living
room, we get another look at the fireplace.
   The axe leaning against the wall is gone.
   Riley doesn't notice. His mind is on other
things. He goes to the counter, pours another drink. He walks over to the sink and
looks out the dark window, staring at his
reflection. We see the car parked outside,
surrounded by dark trees.
   He looks down at his drink, contemplating
his life, his choices. When he looks back
out the window, we're able to see a reflection of the MAN standing behind him wearing
the lion mask.
   Riley turns around.

                   RILEY
          What the fuck?

The MAN is motionless, then he turns his
head to the left, toying with his prey. The

bizarre mystery infuriates Riley, who believes himself to be invincible.

                RILEY (CONT'D)
    Have it your way. Fight me, freak!

Before Riley can say or do anything else, he is struck in the throat with the axe. The MAN pulls the weapon away. A spray of blood spurts from the wound. Riley, in shock, puts a hand to his neck. He tries to scream, but no sound escapes his open mouth. His larynx has been crushed. All that comes out is a weak gurgling sound.
   The MAN strikes him again, this time in the shoulder. Riley slumps to the floor. In the reflection of the window, we see the MAN strike again. And again.

13

Then

It's surprising how enjoyable filming a horror flick can be. Our throats are sore from screaming, our skin agitated from layers of fake blood and latex bruising, but in between takes we're laughing, rolling our eyes at how predictable and corny the script is.

We're all sitting on the back porch, an overhead lamp illuminating the night forest. Riley stands and yells for what must be the tenth time tonight, "Fight me, freak!"

That's the cringey line he shouts at Mr. Rhodes before he almost decapitates Riley in front of the kitchen sink. Every time he says it, we burst out laughing.

"I mean, who would say that if they were in danger?" Aries says, her feet propped up on the porch railing. "Why don't these people ever run out of the house?"

"He doesn't think the guy's a threat." Petra sits on the railing, her feet dangling.

"It makes sense Riley would try to fight him," Leo says. "His character is a total douche. No offense."

"None taken," Riley says, puffing out his chest. "Besides, my character dies first. He has no reason to be afraid."

"I'm saying, if some guy confronts me wearing a graduation gown and a lion mask, I'm turning the other way," Aries says.

"That type of common sense is why you're the second to die, not the first," I say.

Riley slides a navy blue Razr phone out of his pocket, holding it from a distance to snap a selfie. "The guys back home are going to love this," he says. "If we ever pick up enough service to send messages."

"What do the hillbillies back in Kentucky think about you starring in a horror movie?" Aries asks.

"They think I'm the luckiest guy on earth," he says. "Most of my high school buddies are either on probation or factory zombies by now. If I play my cards right, I could build a whole new life for myself."

"Probation?" Aries asks, a look of disgust on her face. "How rough was your childhood?"

"You don't want to know."

"Not everyone grew up on the set of a hit television show," Leo adds, seemingly in defense of Riley.

"I wish my housemates could see what I'm doing right now," Petra says.

"Do you stay in touch with them?" I ask.

"Not really. I made friends when I was there, but we've lost touch. Sometimes I wonder where they ended up," she says. "The world loves to gobble up young girls with no opportunities."

Part of me wants to know exactly what she means, where her peers are now. Trying to afford the Performers Academy required sacrifices, but my upbringing appears to have been a breeze compared to hers. Compared to Riley's life, too.

"Here," Riley says, handing over his phone. "Snap a picture. I'm sure someone would get a kick out of seeing you on a horror set."

"My family isn't really worth a flip. That's how I ended up at Miss Claude's in the first place," Petra says. "It feels like I've been on my own for a while."

"Family is overrated," Aries says. "My brothers only use my stardom as an excuse to get laid and take drugs. They couldn't give two shits about what I'm doing."

Cole walks outside, headphones hanging around his neck, and says, "Riley, we're ready for you."

Riley stands and pounds his chest with two hands, like a gorilla. "Fight me, freak!"

We burst out laughing again, even Cole.

"You need to head to wardrobe," Petra tells me, hopping off the rail. "Figure out what your character is going to wear for the rest of the movie."

As we walk in the direction of the crew cabins, Petra looks over her shoulder to see if anyone is following. "I ran into Riley last night. I couldn't sleep so I left my trailer to go for a walk and saw him sneaking down to the lake to fish."

A laugh leaves my chest at the image of Riley parading around set at night, looking for mischief. "What? Why would he want to go fishing?"

"Apparently, he's done it his whole life. He said one of the perks of this job is it's near a great fishing area." She laughs. "I ended up joining him."

"You didn't! Do you even know how to fish?"

"He showed me. And there were no poles involved. When you're fishing for catfish, you use your hands."

"That. Is. Disgusting."

"I thought the same at first," she says. "But it actually ended up being fun."

I laugh again. "Did you catch anything?"

"No fish." She thinks on it. "Feelings, though. I might have caught those."

I nod my approval. "Look at you. Having a little fling on set."

"Hey, we're out here for a month in the middle of nowhere. Might as well have some fun."

When we enter the wardrobe cabin, Monica is standing in front of a clothing rack. "What are you doing here?" she asks Petra, completely ignoring me.

"Ella is here for her final fitting," she says.

"I know that. You're supposed to be with Cole on set." Finally, Monica's cold stare finds me. "Stand by the mirror."

My eyes land on Petra, silently pleading with her to stay, but all she does is shrug before taking off. I don't like the idea of being alone with Monica, especially after what Aries told me about her. If she was capable of poisoning a rival once before, what might she consider doing to me?

Thankfully, she doesn't talk much as I slide into the jeans and tank top I'm meant to wear in the latter scenes of the movie. With a measuring tape around her neck, she picks and pulls at the fabric, pinning different parts in place.

"We'll have to hem the length," she says, finally locking eyes with me in the mirror. "Have you put on weight since you arrived?"

"I don't think so." I look down at my body. "The fit feels fine."

"This wasn't the original outfit Cole selected," she says. "We had to go up a size. You wouldn't be the first actress to pig out on craft services."

I don't think that's true. I think she's only trying to mess with me, creating another point of contention.

"We've started off on the wrong foot," I say. "Maybe we should try again."

"I'm here to do a job," Monica says, rolling her eyes. "Maybe you should focus more on doing yours and less on making friends."

One of the pins in her fingers jabs into my side, and I wince in pain. Instinctively, my hand goes to my midsection, a pinprick of blood staining my fingers.

"Sorry," she says.

I open my mouth to speak but stop when I hear the commode flushing. I'd assumed we were the only two people here, and yet Jenny exits the narrow bathroom across the way.

"Feeling better?" Monica asks her, turning away from me.

"Yeah," she says, wiping her mouth.

"Are you sick?" I ask.

"Too many days in a row of poor sleep, late nights, and shitty food."

"Ella and I were just talking about that," Monica says. Now she's just patronizing me.

I exhale as I pull the tank top over my head. "I think we're done here."

"I'll walk with you back to the main house," Jenny says, waiting as I wiggle back into my original clothes. Once we're outside, Jenny looks back at the cabin and says, "Don't let her get to you."

"It's fine," I say, resenting how everyone is picking up on the tension between me and Monica. Considering how passive she was during my sex scene with Leo, I'm surprised Jenny's coming to my defense now. Maybe it's easier for her to speak her mind when Cole isn't around.

"Every set has a Bitter Betty, and Monica is ours," she says. "Just shake it off."

"You've been in the business awhile," I say, preferring to change the subject to something other than Monica.

"Growing up, movies were my escape." She pauses as though considering the question further. "I didn't have the best childhood. Raised by an overbearing aunt. Never around kids my age. I majored in film studies at college but eventually dropped out and started taking odd jobs on sets. Figured I'd earn more experience that way."

"Is that how you met Cole?"

Jenny falls silent. Several seconds pass before she says, "Yeah. I owe a lot of my success to him."

"I might try to catch a glimpse of Riley's death scene," I say as we approach the cottage. "Want to tag along?"

"I'm calling it a night. Just have a few more things to pack up." She moves toward the front of the house, then stops. "If Monica or anyone else gives you a problem, all you have to do is tell me."

"Sure," I say, appreciating the offer, even if I'm not convinced.

Inside the main house, Riley is shirtless, his taut middle covered with corn syrup and artificial wounds. He's lying on the kitchen floor, an overhead camera scanning his body, making sure to capture each gory detail.

"You ready?" Cole is behind the camera speaking to Ben, who stands beside him.

"Just a second."

Ben is holding a wad of tissue against his lip, trying to stop the very real blood that started spewing three minutes ago. The kill scene between Riley and Ben got a little too real, and his upper lip paid the price. Riley's character is taken down quickly with an axe to the neck, but the camera lingers longer, catching blow after blow to his mangled midsection.

"Are you okay, man?" Riley asks Ben, coming to life.

"These things happen," Ben says.

"Come on, Ben. You're wearing a mask," Cole barks. "Pull it down and let's get back to work."

Most people would exhale in frustration or downright refuse Cole's callous demands, but Ben doesn't. He walks across the room, tosses the bloody tissue in a wastebasket, and returns.

"Okay. Places," Cole shouts, thrilled to get back to work. "Three . . . two . . ."

Riley is flat on the floor again, spurts of blood pouring out of the artificial wound in his neck. The masked menace hovers over him. He raises his arm, holding it in place for a few seconds before slamming the axe toward Riley's torso.

"Perfect," Cole shouts. "Let's try it again."

"If it's perfect, why do we have to do it again?" Riley asks.

Cole stands and walks over. "Will you just do what I tell you to do?"

I feel the presence of someone standing behind me, and it's not long before my senses pick up on Leo, his musky smell flirting with my nostrils. The heat of his body, so close to mine.

"What Cole doesn't understand is that each time he reshoots, Riley gets slammed back on that hard floor," he says.

"Why not use stunt guys?" I ask.

"Cheaper without them. Riley insisted he wanted to do his

own stunt work," he says. "He'll be black and blue before this week is over."

"Are you doing your own stunt work?"

"Hell, no. My double arrives on set next week." He smiles widely. "Can't risk messing up my face."

Coming from anyone else, that sentence would appear cocky, but coming from Leo, it sounds surprisingly vulnerable. I smile.

"Can we cut the racket back there?" Cole hollers.

Leo and I look behind us. Several other people crowd the living room, trying to get a glimpse of the shot. It's impossible to know whether Cole is directing his anger toward us, them, or everyone.

"In fact, unless you're part of the scene, get out of here," Cole continues. "I want to work in peace."

Funny he didn't have this same reaction when Aries and I were naked, shooting our respective bedroom scenes. His thoughts were likely elsewhere.

"Why is he always hot and cold?" I ask Leo as we walk outside.

"I think a lot of directors are that way."

We leave the set and wander away from Blackstone Cottage, following the path toward the lake. A breeze rustles the leaves in the trees, carrying with it the faint scent of pine.

"I thought this was your first film."

"It is. That I'm acting in, anyway," he says, kicking at the ground. "I've been on loads of sets ever since I was a kid."

"I didn't know your family was in the industry." I'd assumed Leo was like me, a nobody fighting for their place in the business. Thinking back to my first conversation with Petra, I ask him, "What's your story?"

"I grew up in L.A. Everyone in my family has worked in the industry at some point or another. My aunt's a composer. My dad helped build sets. That's where he met my mom, a production assistant. My uncle is a character actor. Walter Stone. Heard of him?"

"Don't think I have."

"You'd recognize his face. He had a lot of small parts in different nineties sitcoms." He smirks. "A few turns as the gas station attendant and Party Guest Number One on the big screen."

I sense Leo is trying to be funny, so I laugh, but his connection to the industry reminds me of how big it really is. Getting into the Performers Academy was hard. Only the best of the best are granted entry, and even then, not every graduate makes it once they leave. The seclusion of the academy shielded me from how broad the industry is. You're lucky to get your foot in the door, even if that door is different from the one you intended. I doubt Leo's family members set out for those particular jobs; it's likely where they landed after they missed the bigger parts.

Leo is different. He has that star quality about him.

"What do your parents think about the movie?"

"My mom cried. Dad stayed silent so he wouldn't." He smiles, kicking at the ground again. "I told them not to get their hopes up. For all we know, this could be a flop, but it's still the male lead in a studio-produced movie. That's further than either of them ever got."

"They must be proud."

"What about your family?" he asks.

"Mom is always my biggest supporter. She hounded my drama teacher into giving me special lessons after school. After that, she worked countless jobs to make sure we could afford the tuition at the Performers Academy." I smile, thinking back. "I know a lot of people thank their parents, but I really wouldn't be here without her."

"What about your dad?"

"Not in the picture."

A tree branch cracks in the distance, the sound grabbing our attention. I hadn't realized how far we'd ventured into the forest. I was too distracted by Leo, listening to his stories, imagining what kind of life he's lived. Blackstone Cottage is no longer visible, hidden by the thicket of trees, their trunks covered with fuzzy moss, their tops blooming with vibrant green leaves in the rising sunlight.

"It is beautiful here," I say, staring up at the patch of sky visible between the treetops. "I always thought my town was in the sticks, but it's nothing compared to this place."

"What time is it?" Leo says, looking at his watch to answer his own question.

"Do you have a scene this morning?"

"No, but if we hurry, I might be able to show you something."

He grabs my hand and picks up his pace down the trail. The path is dissolving, blending in with the unmarked forest floor.

"What is it?" I ask.

"It'll be better if we keep it a surprise."

We move deeper into the forest until we're hiking uphill. My calves tighten with every step, and I wonder where he is taking me. I've never ventured this far away from set before. I can no longer hear the lake's constant, tinkling presence, its sound replaced with the crunching of our feet against earth, the crackling of tree branches and cawing of birds overhead.

Leo stops, checking his watch again.

"Okay, now close your eyes," he says.

"Tell me what we're doing, please."

Being this far away from civilization makes me feel exposed and unsure.

He walks behind me, placing his hands on my shoulders. "Trust me."

As I exhale, I close my eyes, the vivid forest turning black. Leo gently nudges me forward. I can feel his grip guiding me.

"No peeking."

"I won't."

I'm too afraid to look. I'm not adventurous like Petra or confident like Aries, and with the two of us out here alone, I'm afraid he'll finally see it, too. That I'm not like the rest. I'm a fraud.

We stop walking when the slope of the ground levels out. I reach out my hands, expecting to steady myself against a tree, but there's nothing around me. My fingers fall through the air. The only sensation that keeps me in place is Leo's hands on my shoulders. He squeezes.

"We made it just in time," he says. "Open your eyes."

All I can see is baby blue sky and the mist of clouds, but instead of their being at a distance, the clouds are around us, stopping below my chin. With the forest at my back, I feel almost like I'm soaring through the sky. Flying. I take a step forward.

"Careful," Leo says, pulling me back. "I've got you."

That's when I see that we're standing on the edge of a cliff. It's not jagged, like I might expect. There's plenty of room for the two of us in this spot, and it's high enough for us to be enveloped by the early morning sky.

"Pretty neat, huh? Riley showed me this spot on our first day here. It's called Cloud Tops Rock. You have to wait for the precise time of morning, when the clouds are low enough that you can be right there with them."

"It's amazing."

His palms on my shoulders grow warmer as I listen to the soothing sounds of his breathing. We're so close, I can feel his chest swell with every deep inhale. I turn to face him, my heart beating faster. Something about the view and the forest and this moment together gives me the strength to act on how I feel.

I lean forward until my lips are on his.

We continue kissing until the clouds disappear, taking with them the rest of the world.

14

Now

It doesn't matter what Riley says. I can't stay here one more night.

I almost completely broke down on camera.

The others are able to compartmentalize. Maybe they've found forgiveness or inner peace. Hell, maybe they're just better actors.

"You can't just leave," Dani says, standing at the foot of my bed, watching as I stuff clothes into a duffel bag. "You signed a contract."

"I don't care about a fucking contract."

"You haven't even sat down for your one-on-one interview. You're the Final Girl! The reunion won't be complete without you."

"All the others are here," I say. "Finish it without me."

"The reunion only works if you all participate."

"I'm sorry, Dani," I say. "Austin will have to figure something out."

The one piece of advice that sticks with me is what Riley said about bringing the others down. Leaving might put the reunion in jeopardy, could possibly get the whole project scrapped, but at least none of us will end up in jail. I can't let my guilty conscience spiral into some confession.

"Even if you want to leave, you're not getting off this mountain until the crew transport arrives at the end of the day." She's getting frustrated, raking her hands through her black-and-pink hair. "The bus won't be here for hours."

"Call an Uber."

"Service sucks. You know that. There's not even a landline."

"We'll figure something out," I say. "You can't just keep me hostage."

Someone knocks at the door. I ignore it, hoping whoever it is will go away. I'd bet money it's Petra, hoping to talk me out of leaving. Knowing Riley, he made a beeline for her after talking with me. He knows she's the one I'm closest to on set, and the two of them have history.

There's a second knock.

"Go away," I shout over my shoulder before Dani can let them in.

The door creaks open. "I just got here."

The voice catches me off guard. It's not Petra standing in my doorway. Or Riley or Aries or anyone else from set.

It's Fiona, my agent.

I blink once, twice, as though she's a mirage that will disappear. When it sinks in that she's here, I throw my arms around her.

She taps my shoulders cautiously. "Okay, okay. I'm here. No reason to get all emotional."

I'm not crying, but I very well could. Seeing Fiona's face is the most normal part of the last two days. She reminds me of the world outside Blackstone Cottage, that if I can make it through this, my life can continue where it left off.

"Thank God." Dani looks at Fiona before exiting the room. "Maybe you can talk some sense into her."

"It took two flights and an Uber to get here. I still wish I could have come sooner," she says, pushing her Dior sunglasses onto her forehead. "I know you were hesitant about participating in the first place. After hearing about the group interview this morning, it looks like you need some backup."

"You already heard?"

"I ran into Cole downstairs." She sits on my unmade bed, pulls my hand, urging me to sit beside her. "He told me you stormed off the set. What's going on, Ella?"

I refuse to look at her. I keep picking at my ragged cuticles. "I wasn't comfortable with the line of questioning."

"What was he asking you about?"

I can't tell her the truth. I won't.

"Austin kept asking questions about what happened during filming twenty years ago."

"It's a reunion, Ella. What did you think he was going to ask you about?"

She gives me a look I've never seen from her before. Somewhere between sadness and worry.

"I've tried to steer clear of talking to you about what happened back then. Maybe it would be better if you opened up," she says. "I've been in the industry for a long time. I know things are hard for women . . . were harder before MeToo. If someone took advantage—"

"My goodness, Fiona. Nothing happened to me." I turn away from her, hiding the disgust on my face.

"Cole has a reputation for hurting women—"

"He didn't do anything to me. Nobody did." I recall what Aries said earlier, about the allegations against Cole, and how the documentary is supposed to remedy the situation. It's understandable why Fiona might assume he's at the center of this, but my trauma cuts much deeper. "It's harder being here than I thought. Seeing how everyone else's lives have turned out. It reminds me how much I've given up."

"Don't compare yourself to them. You took some time away to focus on your mother. That's admirable. Nothing is more important than family," she says. "You still have a shot in this business. I'm only here to help you see that."

"And if I leave, all my dreams of reviving my career go with me?"

"I never said that, but it would be easier if you stayed. Make the studios happy. They'll return the favor," she says. "Cole told me they have enough material to splice together the group interview. No one will ever know you stormed off. That means you only have to make it through your solo interview."

"And Ben's memorial ceremony tomorrow morning," I remind her. The reunion won't be complete without that, and they'll want all the cast members involved.

"It's only one more night." She says it like it's so simple.

I can already feel myself racing for the exit, but Fiona's presence has grounded me, reminds me that toughing this out for a few more hours will make all the difference for my future.

"It means a lot that you came."

"Does that mean you're staying?" She looks hopeful.

I nod and smile, my optimistic expression dropping as soon as she exits the room.

15

Now

I enter the main house with Fiona by my side. We're able to catch the tail end of Leo's one-on-one interview. His charm is evident, not only in the eloquent way he speaks in front of the camera but in the reactions from Austin and everyone else on the crew watching him. Their smiles speak to the fact that Leo is a natural charmer.

"He's pretty cute," Fiona says, whispering so only I can hear. "You shouldn't have let that one get away."

"Ancient history," I say, watching him.

At one point, Leo and I might have been able to make our relationship work, but the secret we share tore us apart, another casualty of that horrible night. We've both had numerous partners in the years since our breakup. Most of my relationships have been with people outside the industry, never lasting for more than a year or so. Leo has dated a handful of young starlets and industry veterans, his love life chronicled by the likes of Page Six and *Us Weekly*.

"And cut," Austin says, standing. "Great job, mate."

"Thanks."

Leo stands and stretches, nodding and grinning at everyone in the room. When he sees me, his smile widens more.

"I'm going to have a quick chat with Austin," Fiona says, ducking away before he approaches me.

"You're up next, I guess?" Leo says.

"Yep." I look down at my second outfit of the day. A red blouse and black slacks, Fiona's wardrobe of choice. "Figured it would be best to get this over with."

Leo steps closer, his face only inches away from mine. I catch a whiff of his cologne. "Are you okay? You know, about earlier?"

I was so flustered when I stormed away from set, I didn't even think about how embarrassing it was for Leo to have seen the whole thing.

"I'm fine. Riley talked to me, and my agent is here now. I can get through this."

"I know you can," he says with confidence. "You're strong."

It feels like my cheeks are burning. I wonder if he truly sees me that way after all these years, after all the mistakes I've made.

"Ella?" Austin calls from across the room.

"Guess it's showtime." I squeeze past Leo, our chests touching as I do, shooting fireworks through my body.

"Good luck," he says, and I can feel his eyes on me as I cross the room. It's flattering to know I can still capture his attention.

Austin and Fiona are huddled around the monitor. They raise their heads when I approach.

"Are you ready?" Austin asks.

"I think so."

"I wasn't trying to upset you earlier," he says, looking at me and then Fiona. "I'm not even sure what I said."

"She said she's ready," Fiona says with complete confidence. "Forget about earlier. Let's start rolling."

He leans forward, puts his hand over mine. "If it's getting to be too much, all you have to do is tell me." There's a level of concern in his eyes I'm not used to seeing from directors. His bedside manner is far different from Cole's and others' I've worked with throughout my career.

"I'll be fine," I reassure him before sitting in the chair Leo left, the cushion still warm.

I try not to focus on Austin's opinion of me. Even if he did have a childhood crush on me, after the stunt I pulled this morning, his perception is likely no different from what other people in the industry believe. Before I stepped away from my career, rumors had started to swirl that I was emotional and unpredictable, but it wasn't for the reasons people think. The problem was, I couldn't tell anyone the truth. Not my co-stars or new directors or Gus. I didn't even tell Mom. The only people who know the real source of my freak-outs, like the one I had earlier, are the people here this weekend—Leo, Petra, Riley, and Aries. I need this interview to go well so I can prove to Austin, and everyone else on set, that I'm capable of getting a job done without letting my emotions take over.

The woman with the hibiscus flower on her arm stands in front of me, powdering my forehead. "Your makeup is smudged."

"It's all this humidity," I say, reluctant to admit I'd been crying between interviews. "Can you touch it up?"

"No time." She sounds irritated, dipping her brush back into the compact. "Another layer of powder will have to do."

When she steps away, Petra is behind her.

"Don't worry. You look great," she says. "I'm looking forward to this."

"I'm glad *you* are."

"You'll be fine. Remember, you're the star of the movie," she says, always capable of a good pep talk. "You're the one people want to hear from."

"That makes me more nervous."

"Fuck your nerves," Petra says with a laugh. "You got this."

"Places!" Austin calls out.

Petra moves away, finding a spot along the back wall with the rest of the crew. Fiona stands nearby, giving me a thumbs-up. I smile back nervously.

"All right, Ella," Austin says, and I cringe at the delicate nature of his voice, like he's talking to a small child. "Tell us what attracted you to *Grad Night*."

"The script grabbed me from the first page," I begin before going into the tried-and-true story of how the role ended up being my big break. After participating in dozens of press junkets, I've learned that the appeal of a good interview is the relatability factor. People enjoy hearing about the journey to success more than witnessing the success itself.

After a few minutes of telling the same story I've told many times before, I feel my voice easing, becoming more comfortable and confident. I'm shedding the insecure person I was in my first interview, stepping into the role of a new character, a new Ella, one who has nothing to be ashamed of.

"Any memorable moments from set?" Austin asks. Even his voice sounds more at ease, as though he's impressed with my performance thus far.

Several images flash through my mind. The embarrassing sex scene with Leo—an on-set foul that would never be allowed today. Watching the other cast members shoot their death scenes.

That night in the woods . . .

I squint my eyes closed, forcing my thoughts elsewhere.

"I loved shooting the final scene with Ben," I say. "It was a powerful moment, both for my character and for me as an actress."

We talk about that scene a bit longer, Austin addressing me with more direct questions. I answer each one without flinching. Before I know it, the interview is over, the entire crew, including Petra and Fiona, applauding when I stand.

When I walk over to meet them, Fiona says, "See? Nothing to worry about."

"I knew you could do it," Petra says.

Dani hands me a bottle of water. "Good thing you decided to stay. The audience is going to love your take on what it was like back then."

"She's right," Austin agrees, walking over from his director's chair. "All those details you provided about working with Ben . . . I felt like I was right there with you. This is the nostalgia I wanted to bring to life."

"You think you have enough material?" I ask.

"Totally," he says. "We'll meet up later this evening, and I can show you some clips."

"I'd love that," I say.

He lowers his voice so that the others standing around can't hear. "We can talk about my next project, too. I think you'd be perfect for it."

I exhale in relief. Maybe I can make it through this weekend after all.

SCENE 5

EXT. BACK PORCH/BLACKSTONE COTTAGE

Aries is still in the hot tub. She wades over to her phone and starts playing music. She raps along with the lyrics.

INT. BEDROOM/BLACKSTONE COTTAGE

Leo and Ella are sitting on the bed. They wear different clothes. Ella's hair is wet from the shower. They hear the music from downstairs and lift their heads.

                    ELLA
            What's that?

                    LEO
            Guess the party is starting back up. You
            want to head to the hot tub?

                    ELLA
            Maybe in a minute.

                    LEO
            Let's take that walk by the lake. I bet
            it's beautiful at night. We'll sneak
            away, hit up the hot tub when we get
            back.

                    ELLA
            Sounds good.

They stand and slide on sandals. Leo hands Ella his letterman jacket to keep her warm.

INT. STAIRCASE/BLACKSTONE COTTAGE

Leo and Ella creep down the stairs. They peer out the window to the right. Aries is rapping along to a different song now. She's smoking a fresh cigarette.

Leo puts his finger to his mouth, makes a *shush* gesture. Ella giggles. They slide against the wall to the front door and walk outside.

The partitioning wall prevents them from seeing into the kitchen, but we catch a glimpse of Riley's dead body on the floor.

EXT. BACK PORCH/BLACKSTONE COTTAGE

Aries is growing bored of the music and the hot tub. She turns off her phone, takes a moment to soak in the quiet surroundings. She realizes she's been alone too long.

> ARIES
> Riley?

She exits the hot tub, wrapping a towel around her body.

INT. STAIRCASE/BLACKSTONE COTTAGE

Aries looks up the stairs first.

> ARIES
> Riley?

EXT. LAKESHORE—NIGHT

It's completely dark except for the houses across the water. A wooden canoe is tied to a dock jutting out into the water.

          ELLA
Do you think people live here or are there more rentals?

          LEO
Probably both. (He pauses.) You okay about earlier?

          ELLA
Yeah. I'm happy we did it. I feel, I don't know, different.

          LEO
I think that's normal.

          ELLA
Graduation night is getting to me. It's a lot of change.

          LEO
I love you, okay? Don't worry about anything else.

He pulls her in for a kiss.

INT. UPSTAIRS HALLWAY/BLACKSTONE COTTAGE

Aries is standing in the doorway to their bedroom. It's empty. She walks down the hallway to the second room.

                    ARIES
        Leo? Ella?

No response. Aries seems annoyed, slightly unsettled. Behind her, a shadow passes in the hallway.
  She walks downstairs, through the living room, and that's when she sees Riley's body. She screams.

EXT. LAKESHORE—NIGHT

Leo and Ella are still kissing when they pull away from each other. They look back in the direction of the house.

                    ELLA
        Did you hear that?

                    LEO
        They're getting wild. Good thing there
        are no neighbors.

Another scream rings through the night. This time, it's clear that this is not a game. Leo and Ella sprint back to the house.

INT. LIVING ROOM/BLACKSTONE COTTAGE

The front door bursts open. Leo enters first, then Ella. Leo runs straight through the living room to the back patio door, the place they'd last seen Aries. Through the window, we see the empty hot tub.
  Another scream.
  It's Ella. She's standing in the kitchen,

staring at Riley's body. Leo runs to her, wrapping his arms around her. He stares at the body, in shock.

A hand grabs Ella's shoulder. She jumps and screams again.

It's only Aries. She has a finger to her mouth, begging them to be quiet. She pulls them to a small laundry room to the left of the front door.

Once inside, Aries locks the door.

              LEO
What the fuck happened?

             ARIES
I don't know, but there's someone inside the house.

             ELLA
How do you know?

             ARIES
After I found Riley . . . (She pauses, the memory too painful.) I thought I saw someone upstairs, watching me from the landing.

             LEO
Why didn't you leave?

             ARIES
Because we're in the middle of nowhere and I didn't know what to do. We need your car.

                    LEO
          The keys are upstairs in my—

Ella remembers she's wearing the letterman jacket. She feels inside the pockets, pulls out the keys.

                   ARIES
          Fuck, yes. We need to get out of here.

                    ELLA
          What if the person is out there?

                   ARIES
          There's a window. We'll go out that way.

     ELLA (trying to make sense of an insane
                    situation)
          Who would do this?

                   ARIES
          I think it's him. He's the only person
          who would want to hurt Riley.

                    ELLA
          Who?

                    LEO
          Not now, Aries. We need to get in the
          car and go back to town. Ella, you go
          first.

EXT. BLACKSTONE COTTAGE

Ella crouches and climbs through the window, then Aries. Leo is the last one to make it outside. The trio look from left to right, surveying the scene. They sprint to the Jeep, which is a few feet away.

                    LEO
        Fuck. Someone slashed the tires.

                    ELLA
        What do we do?

                    ARIES
        Drive it anyway. Till the fucking wheels
        fall off. We have to get out of here.

It's the best option available to them. Leo gets in the driver's seat, Aries in the passenger seat, and Ella slides into the back.
  Leo tries to crank the engine. The music from earlier begins blaring again. He slams the radio until it stops. The car isn't moving.

                    ELLA
        What's wrong?

                    LEO
        It won't start. Someone must have messed
        with the engine.

                    ARIES
        If the car won't start, how will we—

Aries is cut off by the sound of shattering glass. The axe breaks through the window and cuts her right shoulder. Blood splatters against the dashboard and interior windshield.

Leo and Ella scream. Aries is in shock. The passenger door opens, and she is pulled out onto the ground.

Leo and Ella exit the car, careful not to turn their backs on the attack. Aries is on the ground. Standing over her is the MAN, the lion mask pulled down to cover his face.

                    ARIES
        Please, no. Don't.

The MAN slams the axe down onto Aries's chest. He raises it high in the air, preparing for another hit.

Leo and Ella are horrified, frozen with fear. Finally, Leo snaps out of his trance and locks eyes with Ella.

                    LEO
        Run!

The couple take off toward the house. As they run past, we see the MAN continuing his attack on Aries, swinging the axe over and over again.

16

Then

Aries closes her eyes and inhales deeply through her nose. She waits for Cole's cue, then lets out a ferocious scream.

She's shooting her character's death scene. Leo and I have spent the past two hours filming the short pieces of dialogue that take place inside the car, before Rhodes's deadly axe cuts through Aries's body, but Cole insists on getting some extra close-ups before the inky night sky gives way to sunlight.

This kill scene is the most important, Cole says. The first girl to die in a horror film must be memorable. Casey Becker in *Scream*, gutted and hung from a tree. Marion Crane dripping with blood and shower water in *Psycho*. Even the brief appearance of Michael Myers's sister in *Halloween*, her death occurring before the opening credits finish their roll, sets the tone of the film.

Aries is the undeniable vixen of our film. It's important to capture all the anguish and terror and desire this scene represents. Her character deserves a little more screen time, plus it allows the audience a few more moments to appreciate her voluptuous physique as she prances around in a bikini. The unnecessarily prolonged torture of Aries's character makes my stomach turn, but Cole—and audiences—can't get enough. He's spent hours now whetting his appetite for more eroticism, more bloodshed. More, more, more.

"She's good."

Leo stands beside me wearing a bloodstained tank (not sure if the blood belongs to Aries's character or Riley's at this point) and distressed jeans. We're watching behind the monitors as Cole tries to perfect his shot.

"She is," I agree when I realize it's been almost an entire minute and I haven't said anything. Aries does an excellent job of conveying all the emotions this scene requires, but what I deem truly mesmerizing is the confidence she has while doing it.

She doesn't get flustered between shots. When Cole criticizes her—*That sounds too screechy . . . Your hair is in the way*—she shrugs it off and moves on. For more than an hour, she's been in her bikini, surrounded by an entire crew of ogling men, and she doesn't seem fazed. She even laughs between takes before belting out another fear-filled scream.

"I can't believe this is her first horror film," Leo says, his eyes still watching her.

I wonder what he thinks of her acting compared to mine. I was so uncomfortable when shooting our love scene that he had to break rank and confront Cole. Aries is a total pro, and it shows.

"Gosh, it's hot out here," Leo says. "You'd think without the sun it might cool off, but it's even worse."

At times, the thick air makes it hard to breathe. My clothes stick to my body, and I'm desperate to take a shower. "You're right. I figured I was out of breath from the shoot."

"It's the South," he says. "I can't wait to get out of here."

"I thought you liked being in the middle of nowhere?"

A slideshow of our time together plays through my mind. Leo and I, walking together by the lakeshore. Our first kiss by the rock. We've been inseparable since that day, each sector of this property a backdrop to a new romantic moment. Experiencing this location with him makes it all the more special.

"I do. Or, I did. I think I'm getting cabin fever, no pun intended," he says. "It was nice the first couple of weeks, but I'm missing the city. The chaos and the noise and the endless take-out options."

"Ten more days," I remind him, but I'm not as happy when I say it. The experience of shooting this film has been challenging at times, but I've quite enjoyed being here with him. I'm not sure how things will change once shooting wraps.

"All right, Cole. I think that's enough," Aries shouts. She sits up and Ben offers his hand to help her stand. "I don't know how much more I have to give."

"This is an important scene," Cole argues, hovering by her with a camera.

"We've been at this for almost two hours," she says. "Whatever you're looking for, I'm sure you've got it."

Beside him, Jenny reaches out to hand Aries a towel, but he blocks her.

"I'm the director," he says. "The scene isn't over until someone says 'Cut.'"

Aries bends down and palms Rhodes's axe on the ground. Playfully, she slides the blade inches away from Cole's neck and says, "Cut."

Behind me, some of the crew begin to snigger. Even Jenny has a smirk on her face.

"Fine," Cole says, dropping his hands and equipment at his sides. "Let's call it a night."

"Thank you," Aries says defiantly as she stomps away.

"How does she get away with that?" I ask, perplexed by yet another strange interaction between Aries and Cole.

"I'd say she has a few tricks we don't know about," Leo says, watching her leave. "I'm going to hit the showers. Want to meet outside the main house in twenty? We could do some more exploring."

"I thought you were tired of the great outdoors," I say playfully.

He steps closer so that no one else can hear. His hot breath tickles my ear when he speaks.

"I'm not tired of time with you."

Leo heads toward Blackstone Cottage, along with a few crew members packing up equipment. A smile spreads across my face, and I bite down on my cheeks to make it go away. I'm completely smitten, and anyone would have to take only one look at me to see.

I walk toward the lake, planning to spend a few minutes on the dock before heading back to meet Leo. To my surprise, I see that someone is already there. Aries stands at the water's edge, the moon shining on her like a spotlight, revealing her bathing suit and the fake gore still on her body. I would have thought the showers would be her first destination. Instead, she dips into the water and washes herself clean.

A second later, I see that she's not alone. Cole walks behind her, taking off his shirt before joining her in the lake, their on-set disagreement already behind them. Is this one of the tricks to which Leo had been referring? Aries's cackle bounces off the lake water, echoing in the night, as Cole swims out to meet her.

I look around, thinking I might spy Jenny or Carlos or another member of the crew, but it's only them. Once again, I'm trying to decipher the meaning of their relationship. Do they dislike each other, or is it the opposite of that? Is it something more?

They keep a safe distance in the water. For now.

I turn away before I witness anything I might not want to see, and walk back to Blackstone Cottage.

I'm getting used to working long hours on little sleep. Most people my age are in college, cramming their brains with knowledge or partying with friends until the wee hours. I'll never experience that life, but I'd like to think the path I'm on mirrors the traditional track in that one respect. It must be something about youth. The young try to avail themselves of every single moment before they get too old to appreciate what life has to offer.

This afternoon, we're sitting around the living room—Leo, Riley, Aries, and me—our makeup and wardrobe already complete. We're shooting the opening scene today, the one where we arrive at the cabin. It's bizarre to think we've been working together this long and are just now shooting a scene with all four of us. The entire cast, sans Ben, although in the *Grad Night* universe, he's technically here, watching us from afar.

The crew is setting up equipment, ignoring us as usual, as we wait for Cole to arrive. We're gathered around the fireplace talking, and for a moment, I'm overwhelmed with appreciation for the people in this room. We've become real friends, some of us more. Petra has been an honorary member of our group ever since her romance with Riley heated up, or maybe it's her friendship with me that brings us all together. Either way, I'm convinced this experience wouldn't be the same without this exact combination of personalities.

"How many scenes do we have left to shoot?" Riley asks, bringing my focus back to the conversation.

"It can't be many," Petra answers, resting on the arm of the chair where Riley sits. "I know Ben and Leo are shooting their kill scene tomorrow."

"That should be fun," Leo says, rubbing his palms together.

"And Ella has her big finale," Aries says. It's hard to decipher whether the words come with resentment or admiration. Her smile could go either way. "Other than that, it's secondary stuff. Make sure they have everything we need before we head out."

"Didn't they capture all the landscape stuff before we got here?" I ask.

"They had enough time," Leo says.

"How long were you here?" Riley asks Petra.

"About a week," she says. "It was a drag. I think Cole spent half that time shooting stuff only to change his mind."

"Let's be happy he got his indecisiveness out of the way before we got here," I say.

"I'm not sure about that," Aries says. "I wouldn't be surprised if Cole showed up on the last day and said we need to start over."

"Good thing we're low-low-budget," Riley says. "We don't have to worry about it."

"You always have to worry when Daddy's money is involved," Petra says under her breath. "If Cole thinks this isn't good enough, Daddy will keep paying until he gets it right."

"I thought this was his big break away from his father?" I ask.

The rest of the group laughs. Aries leans closer. "Cole says that because it makes him look artsy. You wait and see. Once the promotional stuff rolls around, every interview will start off with a question about the great Daniel Parks's son's debut film."

The others nod in agreement.

A voice from outside breaches the house, rupturing the cheery atmosphere of the room. We stop talking and listen. My first thought is that Cole is having another creative tantrum, but it can't be. The outraged voice is female.

Aries, Petra, and I walk to the open door to get a better view of what's going on. Cole is involved, but he's the target of the angry voice.

The person yelling is Jenny.

It's full-throated, deep-gut shouting. It sounds like one of the shrieks that came out of Aries's mouth when she was shooting her death scene. And Jenny's face, red and swollen. The woman is clearly upset, not even trying to calm her hysteria in front of the cast and crew.

"Stop lying, Cole!" she shouts. "Stop fucking lying!"

Cole looks flabbergasted. I'm not sure if it's because the argument is taking place in front of the entire set, or if it's because he genuinely doesn't know what to say to Jenny in response.

"You need to calm down," he says. "You're overreacting."

"How can you even say that?"

Cole looks back at the house, but his eyes land on Aries. They exchange a knowing look, one I'm not sure anyone else picks up on besides me. I think back to the conversation I overheard them having my third day here. Remember their late-night rendezvous at the lakeshore. The love triangle. Could it be Jenny found out?

Cole looks beyond Aries, sees that Jenny has captured the attention of the entire cast and crew. His cheeks flush, and he grits his teeth.

"You can't talk to me like this on my own set," he says, turning back to her. There's a pompous quality to his voice. Bad acting—there isn't any other way to describe it. "Take control of yourself, or—"

"Or what?" Jenny shouts, her words tumbling out in a mix of anger and desperation. "Are you threatening me?"

"Or I'll fucking fire you, Jenny. Okay? Get your shit together."

Before Jenny can respond, Aries sprints down the back porch steps. She wraps her arms around Jenny, leading her away from the main house. I'm torn between admiring Aries's willingness to get involved and questioning her motives. If Aries is having an affair with Cole, surely she wouldn't add salt to Jenny's wounds by consoling her. Or maybe her actions are that twisted and intentional. She might get off on causing drama and gloating in the aftermath.

Jenny doesn't question Aries's action, which makes me wonder if she's even suspicious of her connection with Cole. Maybe she suspects Cole is cheating but doesn't know with whom.

After Aries and Jenny walk away, there's an eerie silence that falls around us. Cole is motionless, almost afraid to turn around. The silence lingers, only the singing birds making a sound.

"Everyone, take ten," Cole says in the most professional voice he can muster. "Let's get ready to shoot."

He stomps away in the direction of the crew cabins. He enters one, although I'm not sure which. Slowly, the cast and crew make their way back inside the house, and I return to my seat. An awkward energy permeates the room.

"What do you think that was about?" Riley asks.

"No idea," Leo says, his response suggesting he doesn't want to touch the topic with a ten-foot pole.

"Cole can be over the top," Petra says, "but he must have done something awful to make Jenny that mad."

"What do you think he did?" I ask.

Before anyone can answer, another voice enters the conversation.

"If you want to know, why don't you ask Cole?" Monica says, staring directly at me. "Better yet, ask Jenny. It's better than sitting around gossiping like a little brat."

"I wasn't trying . . ." My words fall into one another, and I'm unable to put together a coherent sentence. My cheeks blush, and I feel the sudden urge to melt into the ground beneath me. "I didn't—"

"That was a nasty fight," Monica says. "Don't be disrespectful."

"We were *all* talking about it," Petra says, standing, but Monica ignores her, keeping her focus on me.

"The only reason you have this part is because of Cole. He saw something in you that none of us see." Monica gestures around the room, and that's when I notice that, again, the entire crew is watching, everyone's attention on me. "This is how you repay him?"

"I wasn't trying to be rude."

My cheeks are burning, my eyes watering. I narrow my gaze, trying to focus on anything other than the countless faces watching me. Then I feel a hand on my shoulder. Leo's hand.

"You want to take a break?" he whispers to me.

I'm too shaken to answer. Too embarrassed.

"Don't single Ella out like that," Riley says to Monica.

"We all know the real reason you don't like her," Petra says.

But everyone *doesn't* know the real reason. Petra knows Monica auditioned for my part because I told her. Aries, too. Everyone else? The cameramen and gaffers and editors? They all believe what Monica thinks. That I'm ungrateful. That I'm not good enough.

Another wave of emotion rolls through me, and I'm afraid I won't be able to hold back my tears any longer.

"I don't like her because her shitty performance is ruining this movie," Monica says.

That comment does it, flipping a switch inside me that shifts all my sadness and humiliation into anger. My hands ball into fists as I move forward.

"I'm giving everything I have to this character," I shout, taking another step toward Monica. "Do you think Cole gave me this part because I'm a 'shitty' actress? He gave it to me because I'm the best person for the job."

Monica blanches, and her menacing eyes surrender all their power. She knows I'm speaking directly to her. She might have auditioned for my part, but that's as far as she got. This role is mine.

She tries to speak. "I am—"

"You're working behind the scenes because that's where Cole wants you," I say. "And I really don't give a damn what you think about my performance or anyone else's. This movie is going to succeed because of me and everyone else in this room."

Anger pulsates inside me, begging for release. Part of me wants to pounce on Monica this very instant, rip her to shreds. I've put up with her passive-aggressive bullshit too long. Maiming her with words isn't enough. My temper craves something more vicious and brutal. I'm out for blood.

Petra rests her hand on my shoulder, fixing Monica with a pointed look. "Well, is there anything else you'd like to address?"

Monica's eyes bounce around the room, surveying the stunned faces of the cast and crew. Her gaze shifts to the floor as she mumbles, "You all heard Cole. We're shooting in ten."

She walks away quickly, disappearing into one of the downstairs bedrooms. For just a second, the rest of the room remains motionless, waiting for any further repercussions before they get back to work.

Beside me, Petra breaks out in laughter, her face alight with glee. "That was awesome."

"It really was," Riley says, wrapping his arm around her waist. He looks at me. "I didn't know you had it in you."

"She had it coming," Petra says.

Their compliments barely register in my mind. I'm still fueled by my rage, the burning sensation in my cheeks refusing to fade.

"Are you okay?" Leo asks, reaching for me. He's the only one who seems to perceive my continued agitation.

"I need a minute," I say, brushing away Leo's hand.

I keep my head down as I climb the staircase, snaking past the crew members, trying hard not to make eye contact with any of them. I don't want anyone looking at me right now.

Alone in my room, I take several deep breaths, but nothing helps. I wonder how the afternoon could spiral into such tension, and right before we're about to shoot the scene, too. That's when I spot my purse on the wooden rocking chair. I look through it until I find the bottle of pills Gus gave me.

I haven't thought about taking one since he left. I didn't think anything could be worse than my first day of shooting, but this, being called ungrateful and untalented in front of everyone on set, being forced to defend myself . . .

I untwist the lid and pick a green oblong pill. I swallow it down and close my eyes, waiting for the feeling of relief to take over.

17

Now

People are gathered around the front of the house, waiting.

"The bus will be here in less than five," one of the crew members shouts.

Fiona turns to me, a look of disgust on her face. "A bus?"

"It's the only way to make it back to town. They bring one in for the entire crew." I look at the sky above. The clouds appear to have banded together, the sky a gray slab of stone. "Plus, Cole and Austin are particular about the rules. Only the cast and select crew members are allowed to be around when the cameras aren't rolling."

"Oh yes, I'm familiar with the rules." She looks back at the house, and it seems to me she's relieved to be leaving. I don't think she'd want to be this far out in the wilderness once night falls. "I am happy I got to see you."

"You shouldn't have had to come all the way out here, but I'm glad you did. You talked me off the ledge."

"Me too. And you were fabulous. Trust me, this was the right decision."

I'll never be convinced coming back here was the right choice.

There are too many lingering traumas surrounding this place, but if this is the necessary evil I must overcome to get my career back, I'll suffer through it.

The bus arrives a few moments later. The crew members who aren't staying overnight gather their belongings and board. Fiona takes one more look at the house before facing me.

"You'll call me if you need me?"

"I promise."

"One more night," she reminds me. "You got this."

I sit in one of the rocking chairs on the front porch, watching the crew board the bus. I spot Riley's sober coach carrying a small backpack. Behind him, I see my makeup artist from this morning and wave, but she doesn't see me before disappearing into the back of the bus.

"You know who that is, don't you?"

Petra is standing in the open doorway of the main house. She takes a seat beside me in another rocking chair.

"Shit, am I supposed to know her?" I ask. "Did she work on the original?"

"Of course she did," Petra says. "That's Monica."

I turn my head quickly to look at the bus. I spot her sitting in one of the back seats, her head against the window. Now the familiarity is clear. Her face has aged, and her hair is different, but her features are clearly there. Monica. She knew it was me the entire time we were in the makeup trailer and never let on.

"I can't believe I didn't recognize her," I say. "Why didn't she say anything?"

"It's not like the two of you got along the first time around."

"She hated me." Now I'm remembering our awkward interactions, the way she criticized my every move. All because she wanted my part. "If she's still in makeup, I guess she never made it as an actress."

"It's a hard industry," Petra says. "You know that."

Which is why it's important that I stick with the reunion until it's complete. As Fiona reminded me, it's the only way studios will consider me for other roles.

"Part of me hates being here," I say. "I wish I could jump on the bus with them and leave. I'd even sit next to Monica."

"It's not been that bad being back, has it?"

Petra may not know how fragile being here has made me. She, like everyone else, seems to be handling the reunion far better than me.

"I got to see you again," I say after a long pause. "So, no, it's not all bad. And we're shooting the memorial for Ben tomorrow. I wouldn't want to miss that."

All of us owe it to him to stick it out for that. It will be a touching moment in the documentary. Probably the only part I'll watch.

"Hey, what are you still doing here?" I ask. "Shouldn't you head out with the rest of the crew?"

"Some of us are staying behind to get things ready for tomorrow."

"At least we have a little more time together," I say. "I'll catch you later?"

I'm desperate to find Austin and see how my interview clip turned out. As I walk around the back of the house, I spot Aries standing by the trees, turning her head from left to right.

"Where is everyone?" she asks when she sees me. "I need to find Austin."

"I was going to ask you the same thing," I say. "He said he'd show me some clips of my interview."

"He told me the same," she says. "I'm hoping your one-on-one went better than the group interview."

"It did, thanks," I say snidely. "I needed to clear my head."

"What did you think of Cole's speech? Talk about a crock. The movie is popular because it has hot people having sex and getting stabbed. For whatever reason, sex and violence are forever intertwined. Box office gold."

"You really don't want to be here, either, do you?"

Aries stops and looks at me, her eyes narrowing. "Why are *you* here, Ella? You hate everything about the franchise as much as I do. Why do it?"

"I'm trying to get back in. To the industry, I mean," I say. "I'm too old to play scream queens, but I might have a shot at some bigger stuff, if I can get my name back out there."

Aries starts walking in the direction of the lake. I match her pace.

"See, you're learning to play the game. You need to be out there with your talent."

"I've not acted in years."

"Yeah, well the best ones usually take a break, then come back with a vengeance."

From what I remember on set, Aries was the one with the most talent. She gave the best performances, whether she was having sex or getting murdered. It always surprised me that Leo became the biggest star, not her.

"You work mostly on social media these days?" I ask her.

"I average five thousand dollars a post," she brags.

"Why don't you keep acting?"

"After a while, I only started to feel comfortable at home. I'm tired of the sets and the travel and the schmoozing." She pauses, and I wonder if she's going to talk about that night, but she switches gears. "Besides, I'm not sure which is worse, being cast as the mom in a teenage television drama or being advised to wear a knee brace beneath your fishnets. I'm getting too old and would rather bow out than get booted off the stage."

"We're not even forty yet," I say. "In any other field, we'd be in our prime."

"Hollywood goes by dog years, don't you know?"

"It's funny age never seems to be a concern for men," I say. "I mean, look at Leo. He's not struggling for roles. He even gets away with playing the heartthrob in those hero movies."

"Men get hotter as they age. Meanwhile we're stuck competing with girls in their twenties." She laughs. "Either way. Good for you, taking another go at it."

As usual, with Aries, I can't tell if she's giving a compliment or making a dig.

"It's not like I expect it to be easy," I say. "I'm just hoping the reunion will put me back on the radar."

"You know what I'd like to do?" she says. "I'd love to direct my own movie."

"Really? What kind?"

"I have no idea. Anything, as long as it's a badass story. Something that puts the women first. Like *Promising Young Woman* or *Blink Twice*. Lord knows, Hollywood could use more female directors."

"You should do it."

"It would take years to get off the ground." She scoffs. "Unlike Cole, my dad hasn't won an Oscar and two BAFTAs."

"You have money. Five grand a post, remember?"

We both know how quickly that would fly on a set. Still, Aries is determined. I believe she could be successful at anything, and even now, all these years later, I envy that fact.

"I'd back you," I say. "Hell, I'd audition for it."

"I'll cast you as the good-natured but pestering mom of my female protagonist," she jokes, then stops abruptly. We've reached the lakeshore, and there isn't anyone in sight. "I have no idea where Austin is. The house was empty when I came outside. Guess I'll check back at the main house. Are you coming?"

"I think I'll stay out here a while longer," I say, the serene landscape calling to me. "If you see Austin, tell him I'm looking for him, too."

"Will do."

She heads back to Blackstone Cottage. I stare ahead, watching as the setting sun dips ever closer to the endless stretch of water below.

18

Now

I often forget how beautiful it is here. How quiet. I've been alone for what feels like minutes and an eternity all at once. An endless sensation of being present in the moment.

I wander away from the shoreline, curious if Aries had any luck finding Austin. As I walk, I admire the beauty of the approaching dusk. The trees have filtered into darkness, and yet I can still see the lush foliage.

Before I know it, I'm wandering off the main trail and into the woods, my footsteps crinkling against fallen leaves and twigs. I'm not sure where I'm going. It's been so long since I've been in this forest, and yet part of me feels as though I never left. I remember the beauty of Cloud Tops Rock, that early morning when Leo showed it to me, where we shared our first kiss.

Something snaps behind me. It could be nothing more than a fallen branch or animal skittering about, and yet I'm overcome with the feeling that I'm no longer alone. I'm being watched, if not by another person then possibly by the hidden cameras Austin scattered along the property. He promised they were only in the communal areas, but who knows if that's true? I never know whom to trust.

"Austin?" I call out, wondering if, like me, he's wandered into the woods, but there is no response. Silence.

A memory flashes in my mind: filming the chase scene with Ben all those years ago. We started right around this time, when evening gives way to full darkness. I ran and ran and ran through these woods, until it felt like my lungs might give out. Ella, the character, was determined to survive; my real self was desperate to please. I picture Ben perfectly. Flowing gown dusting the forest floor, the lion mask covering his face, the bloodstained weapon clutched between his hands.

Another snapping sound distracts me, and when I blink, for a moment I think I see Ben standing there, menacing costume and all. Startled, I march deeper into the forest, farther away from where the sound originated, a budding paranoia urging me to go.

That's when I see it. A large tree, unique from all those surrounding it because there is a small carved heart in the center of its trunk. I go to it, as though in a trance, pressing my hand against the rough bark. My heartbeat pulses in my palm.

"Ella?"

I turn quickly. Leo is standing only a few feet away from me, appearing as a shadow in the approaching darkness.

"What are you doing here?" He sounds concerned as he lumbers across the overgrown vegetation to get closer to me.

"I don't know." I look back at the tree, letting my hand fall. There's a sinking feeling in my own heart. "I went for a walk, and I ended up here."

Scanning the forest, I notice that it doesn't look any different from the rest of the wilderness, and yet I know this place is special. The final resting place of all our secrets. Leo's hand reaches out to touch mine, a magnetic energy flying off his fingertips.

"It's almost nightfall," he says. Tugging on my hand, he turns me away from the tree to face him. I follow his direction, hypnotized by his touch. "Let's head back to the main house. We both know how dangerous it can be out here after dark."

We walk in silence for several minutes, taking in the cacophony of life around us. Cawing birds and cracking twigs, the whistling of the night breeze. It's not until we've exited the forest and are back on the main road that we begin to talk.

"What were you doing out here by yourself?" he asks.

"I wasn't alone at first. Aries and I were at the lake. We were trying to find Austin, and she headed back to the cottage." I pause, trying to recall what prompted me to hike deeper into the woods. "I thought I saw someone in the forest, and that's when I saw you."

"You saw someone?"

"I thought I did." I wrap my arms around my waist. "I think I spooked myself."

"You're worrying me, Ella. First, with the way you handled the group interview." Leo glances over his shoulder, wincing as though it's painful to look back. "Now I found you at the tree of all places. It isn't healthy."

"Coming back here was a mistake." I close my eyes, realizing I'm fighting back tears.

"It's almost over," he says. "Once the documentary is complete, we can go back to forgetting this place ever existed."

"Is it that easy for you and everyone else to forget?"

"It's never easy," he replies. "It's necessary."

I look at him, no longer caring about the tears trailing down my cheeks. Leo has seen me at my worst. He saved me when I was at my worst, and I can never forget that.

"If you could go back, would you have done something different?" I ask. "We could have gone for help. We could have called the police."

Leo's hands drop to his sides. He looks above at the misty clouds sailing through the sky, contemplating.

"I would have done everything differently," he relents. "But there's no use playing that game with myself. We can't change the past."

"You're right."

"I'm not talking about that night." He stops walking, forcing me to stop and listen. "I'm ashamed of the way we ended things."

The specifics of our breakup barely register. Because so much transpired before and after the demise of our relationship, I accepted a long time ago that we were doomed from the start. Still, Leo represents what could have been in my life, both professionally and personally. If I hadn't let my guilt consume me all those years ago, I could have had a successful career. I could maybe still have a loving relationship.

After our breakup, Leo's star continued to rise while my mental health crumbled. Soon, everyone around me saw the change in my person, even Gus. He didn't know why I was so emotionally unstable, only that his sure thing of an actress was slowly losing her shit.

"I never blamed you for anything," I say. "I needed the time to myself, and you had to move on."

"I should have done more to check in on you. Make sure you were okay."

"I'm better now," I say, even if that's not entirely true. This weekend has proven that. My emotions are as easily rattled now as they were twenty years ago. "Being here has brought back a lot of difficult memories, but I'm trying."

"The reason I wanted to come back was to see you." He lifts his hand, resting it on my cheek. "You deserve happiness, Ella. I need to know you're okay."

"I am."

For once, the words ring true. I place my hand on his chest, and it reminds me of how he used to bring me comfort, reminds me of our first kiss at Cloud Tops Rock, when I felt as if I was flying. I miss this. Not him, rather, what he represents. Our relationship was the last time in my life I was truly at peace before heartache and tragedy wrecked everything.

We kiss, the goose bumps on my body springing to life. The softness of his lips, the taste of him—it's all so familiar. Our bodies cling to each other, falling through time and space, to a moment in our lives when we weren't overcome with fear and guilt and—

A scream slices through the air.

We jerk away from each other, our eyes searching the area, trying to find the source of that awful sound.

SCENE 6

INT. LIVING ROOM/BLACKSTONE COTTAGE

Leo and Ella burst into the room. Leo shuts the door behind them and locks it.

                  ELLA
What should we do?

                  LEO
Go upstairs. We'll get our phones and call the cops.

INT. BEDROOM/BLACKSTONE COTTAGE

Leo and Ella run into the bedroom, slamming the door behind them and locking it. Ella wants to get as far away as possible from the door. She crouches behind the bed.

                  LEO
Where's your phone?

                  ELLA
I left it in your car.

                  LEO
Fuck.

He rummages through his bag until he finds his cell phone.

LEO (CONT'D)
I found mine. Shit, there's no service.

ELLA
Oh my gosh, Leo. What are we going to do? Who was that out there?

LEO
I don't know.

ELLA
Aries. Right before she . . . (She can't bear to finish the sentence.) She acted like she knew who it was.

LEO
I have no idea who is out there. Some fucking psycho.

ELLA
She acted like you should know.

LEO
Look, it doesn't matter who it is. All that matters is we find a way out of here. He's still outside. We need to think.

A sound from downstairs grabs their attention. Footsteps. The MAN is in the house.

ELLA
Oh shit, Leo. What do we do?

Leo takes the dresser and slides it in front of the bedroom door. He joins her on the far side of the bed.

              LEO
   The door is locked. We're safe. We'll stay here until morning if we have to, then we'll go find help.

The footsteps are growing louder. He's getting closer. The doorknob on the bedroom door begins to turn, RATTLING. Ella is using both hands to cover her mouth, trying to silence her panicked breathing.
  Leo has one finger in front of his lips, telling her to be quiet.
  The rattling stops, and they listen as the footsteps move farther away down the hall.
  Leo breathes a sigh of relief.

            LEO (CONT'D)
   He kept moving. We're safe.

The axe breaks through the bedroom door. Splinters of wood fall to the floor. The axe keeps coming, until we're able to see through to the other side. We catch a glimpse of the lion mask, streaked in blood.
  Ella screams, jumps up. Leo leaps, too, unsure. He looks behind them.

            LEO (CONT'D)
   The balcony.

They run through the open sliding glass
door, pulling it closed behind them, trying
to buy time.

EXT. BALCONY/BLACKSTONE COTTAGE

Ella is staring back inside the bedroom, too
frightened to look away.

              ELLA
He's going to break down the door.

              LEO
Ella, I need you to listen to me. It's
not a far drop. We can climb over the
edge and lower ourselves down, then
we'll make a run for it.

              ELLA
I'm not leaving you.

              LEO
One of us has to go first. The dresser
blocking the door should slow him down.

Ella is unconvinced, but she listens. She
climbs over the railing, then lowers herself
until she's dangling, but she's still several feet above the ground.

            LEO (CONT'D)
Ella, you have to let yourself fall.
Then take off running. I'll find you.

Ella takes a deep breath and drops, her body
landing against the ground with a THUMP.

She stands, inspects her body for injury. She's sore but complete. It's a miracle.

She starts running for the tree line but stops when she hears a scream. She turns around slowly, in time to see a person flying over the balcony. The body lands on the ground with a sickening, deadly THUD.

19

Then

The midday sun warms Cloud Tops Rock's slate surface. My bare skin rubs against it, rugged and raw, but the friction isn't uncomfortable. All I feel is pleasure as Leo hovers over me, his lips moving between my lips and neck, then back again.

These moments have become the highlight of the shoot. Better than knowing I'm the lead in an indie horror flick. Better than the follow-up gigs Gus believes I'm bound to get if *Grad Night* is a success. On-screen, I'm Ella the character. On set, I'm Ella the actress, timid and green.

With Leo, I feel invincible, important, seen. The chemistry between us is effortless, as though we were always destined to find each other, hold each other in this way. What is that saying about real-life connections falling flat once they get on camera? Maybe it's a blessing our relationship hasn't progressed until now; we needed that awkward meet-cute to become as close as we are.

"I'm crazy about you, Ella," Leo whispers in my ear, his voice low and desperate and genuine.

"I feel the same way," I say, trailing my finger across his collarbone, along the curve of his shoulder.

Leo's hands trail from my hair to my chest to my navel, his touch ticklish, but warm. All I want is more of him. He slides his hand beneath my skirt, and then his fingers are inside me, rubbing me in just the right way. My breathing gets heavier. He leans up, starts unfastening his pants.

"What are you doing?" I raise myself onto my forearms.

"I don't know." He pauses. "Just in the moment."

But now that moment is gone. I ruined it. Leo and I have enjoyed our make-out sessions behind the trees and fooling around on the rock, but we haven't gone all the way yet. Every time I think I'm ready, this paralyzing fear takes over. I'm not sure why. My feelings for Leo aren't in question, but my commitment to sex is.

"Did I do something wrong?" he asks, moving with caution. "The last thing I want to do is rush into anything."

"It's not you. I'm the problem." I sit up, pulling my legs close to my chest. "I'm a virgin." I cringe as the words come out, the same way every audience member does when that line is spoken in a film.

"Oh." He seems surprised. Growing up on the outskirts of Hollywood, he's probably not used to women my age being so modest. He puts an arm over my shoulders and pulls me closer to him. "Whether or not you've had sex before doesn't matter to me. I'm only happy to be with you."

We kiss again, although the passionate splendor from earlier is gone. It's been replaced with something even better, if that's possible. Something solid and real. Leo accepts me as I am.

"Want to head back?" I ask. "Odds are, someone is looking for us by now."

"I could stay out here with you all day. Cole and the rest of them be damned." He kisses my neck, smiles. "But yeah. We can go, if you're ready."

After weeks of working around the clock, Cole has rewarded us with a day of rest, and most of the cast and crew have convened around the lake. I spot Riley and Petra sitting on a towel spread across the sand. She raises her head, smiling when she sees us.

"Where have you two been?" she asks, her tone heavy with innuendo.

"We hiked up to the Cloud Tops," Leo says.

"Nice," says Riley.

Aries approaches. She's locked arms with one of the crew members. Carlos, I think is his name. "How are the little lovebirds?"

I'm not sure if she's talking to Petra and Riley or Leo and me. We've tried to be discreet about our romance on set, but it's useless trying to keep secrets from Aries.

"Enjoying a lazy morning," Leo answers for all of us. "Are you getting in the lake?"

"Not enough filtration. It's like swimming in dirty bathwater." She looks back at Carlos, a twinkle in her eye. "We're about to head into the woods ourselves. Carlos is going to teach me the art of axe throwing."

Aries and Carlos skip off behind one of the crew cabins, while everyone else takes turns diving into the water off the dock. The four of us sit, watching.

"Axe throwing," Riley says. "What the fuck even is that?"

"I'd say it's code for blow job," Petra says, and we all laugh.

"She sure is something," Leo says.

I still can't fully figure Aries out. My mind recalls how she ran to Jenny's rescue after her blowup with Cole. I'm convinced Aries is the reason Cole and Jenny are fighting, even if Jenny doesn't know it. And now she's wandered off to the woods with Carlos. Is it a ploy to make Cole jealous? It's dizzying trying to keep up.

Leo and Riley decide to join Cole and the others on the dock. Before he walks away, Leo kisses my cheek, reassuring me that our morning on the mountain meant something to him, even if it meant more to me. I scoot closer to Petra, who's fiddling with a chain around her neck.

"What's that?"

She blushes, moving her hand so I can get a better look at the necklace. It's a slender silver chain. Hanging in the center are two dark shells shaped like crescent moons, almost identical in size.

"Riley put this together for me," she says. "We've been collecting shells from the lake. He got a chain from the costume cabin and turned it into this."

"He didn't," I say, reaching out to touch the pendants. "Who knew Riley was so crafty? You must be getting serious if he's making you jewelry."

"Hard to tell. I've not had a serious boyfriend in, gah, I don't even know how long. I can barely remember what it feels like to like someone, but we're having fun."

"It's okay to admit you have feelings for someone," I tell her. Something in the way she talks makes me think she's reluctant to take down walls, understandable considering her upbringing.

"After *Grad Night* comes out, all of you will be huge movie stars. He'll drop me faster than the premiere groupies can drop their panties," she says playfully. "I'm not going to get my hopes up about a relationship."

"Or the movie could flop and we all go back to shooting Pizza Hut commercials and performing in community theater."

"Have more faith in yourself."

"Maybe you should have more faith in Riley."

Laughter from the dock echoes in our direction. A flock of birds soar and dip through the clear blue sky. This must be one of the prettiest days we've had since we arrived. She looks ahead, that effortless smile radiating across her face.

"Sometimes I think I never want to leave," Petra says.

I smile, also. "I know what you mean."

Petra stands abruptly, her expression changing from one of hope to one of confusion and . . . terror.

"Aries?" she cries.

I stand, too, looking in the direction where Petra shouted.

That's when I see her. Aries stumbling out of the woods, both her hands covering the right side of her abdomen. She's struggling to reach us, and when she gets closer, I see why. A blossom of blood is spreading across her torso.

"Aries!" I run to her, catching her before her knees hit the ground. "Aries? What happened?"

"The axe . . ." Her words trail off in a whisper, then she's falling backward, lying flat on the hard earth beneath us.

"They went axe throwing," Petra says as though she's just now remembering. She turns to the left and right, looking for Carlos.

"We need to get help," I say, pressing my hands on Aries's abdomen, which is covered in blood. She's deathly still.

"Help!" Petra shouts, running toward the shoreline. "We need help!"

Within seconds, it seems, the entire cast and crew appear around us. Most of them rush out of the lake, still dripping with water. Toward the back of the crowd, I see Leo, Riley, and Cole. They seem frozen in place, afraid to get any closer.

The two biggest cameramen come running over and prepare to lift her. One takes her legs, while the other places his hands beneath her shoulders. They only raise her a few inches off the ground when Aries lets out a bloodcurdling scream. They lower her back down.

Her head tilts to the side. She's staring at the gathering audience, her eyes open but her stare blank. Her cheeks even have a hint of blue. How much blood has she lost, and if help comes, will they get here in time?

"Aries?" My voice is quiet, on the verge of breaking. My throat feels raw, fighting the tears bound to come.

No one knows what to say, what to do. Even the birds in the trees have quieted, seem to be staring in awe at the beautiful girl before us, covered in blood.

In the next moment, life miraculously reappears in her eyes, and Aries releases a guttural laugh. She sits up abruptly, facing her audience. "Gotcha."

Even though she's moving now, talking, the panic coursing through me remains. I can feel my arms and fingers shaking, warm tears rolling down my cheeks. "What?"

Aries raises her blood-covered hands and places a finger in her mouth, licking it clean. "I think when it comes to on-set pranks, I'm the winner," she says. "Well, and Carlos. Come on out!"

I look in the direction from which she stumbled. Carlos peers out from behind the trees. He's smiling, although not with the same glee as Aries. When he walks toward us, I see he's carrying one of the portable makeup kits.

"Not too bad, I'd say," Aries says, touching her face. "I made myself look like I was at death's door, and all I had was a hand mirror."

"Very funny, Aries," Cole shouts. The cast and crew look at him before turning their eyes back to Aries. "Now, can we give her a round of applause and move on. This has been an epic waste of time."

People break into a weak round of applause, although most people still seem unsure. Her reaction had been so convincing. She is an actress, after all.

"I'm only having a little fun, Cole," Aries says, prodding him. "You know all about mixing business with pleasure."

This comment invokes a livelier reaction, some of the cast members beginning to laugh and even hoot, until another scream rings out. I'm not sure whose voice it is, but suddenly everyone's attention is riveted on the man standing in front of us. One of the cameramen who had hastened to help an ailing Aries is hunched over, grabbing his chest. A second later, he collapses to the ground.

Aries jumps up, totally healthy and alert. "What's wrong?"

"I think he's having a heart attack," the other cameraman says, hurrying to attend to his friend. "Someone call an ambulance."

When Aries came stumbling out of the woods, people were cautious, unsure how to act, as though her stunt was a dress rehearsal for a crisis. Now everyone rushes to the cameraman's side. I realize I don't even remember his name, and a shadow of shame falls over me.

"Is he okay?" I ask the question aloud, to anyone, but it's Petra who answers.

"I don't know," she says. "Hank has a bad heart. He takes medicine for it."

Hank. That's his name. I watch him writhing in pain on the ground, hoping I'm not about to witness a man take his final breath.

"A bad heart?" Aries says, looking at her.

"Yeah." Petra has a sharp edge to her voice. "As in he shouldn't have any sudden scares."

Aries's pallid countenance is genuine now. She covers her mouth with a hand. "I didn't know. I was just playing around."

"Give the guy some space," Cole says, rushing to Hank's side.

Most people seem frozen in place, but I'm overcome with the urge to escape. My body won't keep still. I look down at my hands, stained with Aries's fake blood, and recall the storm of emotions that reeled through me. Shock, sadness, relief. And now fear. Because no one is faking this emergency.

I tear away from Petra and Aries, marching in the direction of the main house. I don't recognize any of the faces I pass, don't register anything until I've stomped up the stairs and entered my bedroom. I reach for my purse, digging until I find the medicine bottle. Hurriedly, I unscrew the cap and pop one of the pills into my mouth. I need this panic to go away. I close my eyes and take a deep breath, waiting.

"What are those?"

Leo is standing in the doorway, staring at me, but not at my face. His gaze is fixed on the pill bottle in my hands.

"Pills," I say, stating the obvious. "For when I get stressed out."

Leo enters the room, and before I can move, he yanks the bottle out of my hands. He turns it around, inspecting it.

"It doesn't even say what they are." He looks at me now. "Where did you get them?"

"My agent gave them to me."

"I don't remember Hollywood agents being licensed to write prescriptions. Did he tell you what these are?"

"No. I mean, he said they'll help me stay calm. I only take

them when I'm feeling overwhelmed. He gave them to me after we shot our first scene together."

My cheeks flush at the memory of our embarrassing first encounter, which now seems a lifetime ago.

Leo sits on the bed, holding the bottle of pills loosely in his hands. "Shooting our first scene stressed you out so much you had to start taking pills?"

"It's not like that," I say, sitting beside him. I run my fingers along his wrist. Is it me, or does his body tense at my touch? "I don't take them every day. Only when I need them."

"You know who else says that?" He waits. "Every addict before they become an addict."

"It's not like that." I exhale. "I've struggled with handling the pressure. You know, I'm the Final Girl. It's up to me to carry this thing, and that's a lot of stress."

"I get it. I do." He gives the bottle a shake, the pills rattling against the plastic. "But this is dangerous, Ella. Do you know how many people start leaning on drugs and alcohol to cope with the stress? They think it's helping. They don't realize it's destroying them until it's too late. Until their careers and their lives are ruined."

I put my hand over his again, this time squeezing tighter. "That's not what's happening here. I promise. I've only taken two or three pills the whole time I've been here."

He twists around to look out the window, even though we can't see what's happening from here. Leo shakes his head. "I don't know what Aries was fucking thinking."

"She didn't think she'd give the poor guy a heart attack," I say quietly.

Why do I feel the need to defend her? Aries is always pulling stunts for attention. She thrives on it. I'm afraid of what would happen to me if I stepped out of Aries's corner.

Leo looks down at the pills one last time before handing them over. "I'm not trying to tell you what you should and shouldn't do. It worries me. I don't want the industry to change you."

"It won't."

I discreetly slide the pills back into my purse, dropping the bag on the floor. I wrap my hands around Leo's neck, pulling him onto the bed with me. We don't kiss or fondle each other. We simply remain quiet, enjoying each other's presence.

"Do you think Hank is going to be okay?"

"I hope so." He sighs. "Up until today, I'd thought this had been the perfect job. I guess something bad was bound to happen."

"Let's not think about the bad," I tell him. "Let's focus on the good."

At that, Leo raises himself up, locking eyes with me, those light blue pools seeming to stare into my soul. He kisses me, and the uncertainty and panic and fear all melt away.

20

Now

My head turns from left to right, waiting for another shriek to echo around me. Before the interruption, I'd felt wholly safe in Leo's arms. Just like last time, when a different scream tore through the night, signaling the beginning of a bad dream I haven't been able to escape.

"What was that?" I lean in, finding refuge in the hardness of Leo's chest.

"I don't know," he says, pulling me closer. He appears as alarmed, and I wonder what's going through his head, too. If our minds are connected, recalling the same memory, the very same moment.

Footsteps approach, trampling through fallen leaves. Aries darts out onto the trail, breathless, a hand resting on her chest.

"Aries?"

Before she can respond, Cole staggers behind her, uproariously laughing. "No worries, guys. Everything's fine."

"What happened?" Leo asks. "We heard a scream." He drops his arms to his sides as I take a step away from him. Aries and Cole are too involved with each other to recognize what they've interrupted.

"I snuck up behind Aries," Cole says. "She's as jumpy now as she was two decades ago."

"And you're as immature. No one has the patience for your stupid pranks," she says, rubbing her chest like she's still trying to catch her breath. "I'm trying to find Austin."

"You still haven't found him?" I ask.

"No one was at the house when I went back. At this point, I think he's avoiding me," she says, annoyed. "He promised to give me a glimpse of the interviews we shot earlier. I want to make sure I look okay."

"Why do you care so much?" Cole asks. "It's not like he's going to scrap the entire interview on account of your crow's-feet."

Aries shoots him a dangerous look as Leo steps between them. "When's the last time you saw Austin?" he asks Cole.

"No idea where he is," Cole says. "Or the rest of his staff."

"The crew left for town over an hour ago," I say.

"Most of them did," he says. "Austin was supposed to ask a couple to stay. Clearly, he didn't. I can't even get into the crew cabins. He has the damn keys."

"Shouldn't you have a set?" Leo asks.

"Not my project," Cole says, bowing his head. "Although I'm starting to think that was a mistake."

"There you are!" Petra calls out. She and Riley are walking toward us from the direction of the lakeshore. I wonder if Cole and Aries's dramatics interrupted a romantic reunion between them, too.

"I was starting to think everyone had left," Riley says. The hems of his jeans are damp. I can almost imagine him and Petra sitting on the dock, dipping their feet into the water below.

"Everyone's here," Aries says. "Except Austin."

A phone pings. Instinctively, all our hands go to our pockets, but Cole is the only one to hold up his phone.

"It's a miracle," he says, tapping at the screen.

"What is it?" Petra asks.

"Is it Austin?" I ask.

"We have a brief moment of service," Cole says. The screen turns black as he slides the phone back into his front pocket. "Austin says he's in the main house, waiting on us."

"It's about time," Aries says, marching in that direction. The others follow, but Leo and I remain standing a beat longer, still tethered to the moment we shared.

He squeezes my shoulder in a disappointingly avuncular way. "One more night."

"One more night," I repeat like a mantra before following the others toward the main house. The moment between us is gone. Maybe it's for the best. My only goal is to complete this job and move on to the next; I don't need any other distractions.

Exterior lights illuminate Blackstone Cottage's silhouette as we approach, reminding me of the opening scene in *Grad Night*, when viewers are introduced to the setting for the first time. We mount the back porch steps, and Riley is the first to enter. The house appears quiet, empty. The honey-colored walls exude a warm glow in the dim light, shadows from the antlers on the deer head above the fireplace branching out like claws.

"Austin?" Aries calls up the stairs, but there's no reply. "Where the hell is he?"

Cole plods past, stopping at the fireplace. "I swear, if he doesn't—" His words end midsentence, and his voice changes into something strange and uncertain. "What the hell?"

"What is it?" Petra asks, moving farther into the room. When she makes it past the kitchen island, she gasps.

Aries and I trail behind her, wondering what's left the other two speechless. As I turn the corner, I see Dani, Austin's assistant director. She's hunched over on the floor, stuffed in the narrow space between the island and the kitchen sink.

Riley rushes over to her, placing his hands on her shoulders. Leo kneels on the other side, placing his palm to her forehead.

"What's wrong with her?" Aries asks, nibbling the skin around her ruby-red nails.

Petra, watching intently, says, "She might have passed out."

Dani's body slumps to the side, her torso resting against Leo's raised knee. As though the scene wasn't bizarre enough, another detail captures my attention. An envelope is in her lap, coming closer to sliding onto the floor each time Riley jostles her body. Suddenly, he steps back.

"What?" Petra asks.

"She doesn't feel right," Riley says, a nervous catch in his voice.

"What do you mean 'she doesn't feel right'?" Cole asks, agitation spewing. He doesn't dare step closer to the kitchen.

"She's cool to the touch."

"Come on, time to wake up," Leo says, trying in vain to reposition her body as Riley reaches for her hands. Dani remains motionless, her expression still as stone. We stare at her, the rest of us too stunned to speak or move.

"Dear God," Riley says at last, pulling his fingers away from her wrist. "I think she might be dead."

21

Now

My eyes examine Dani's body—young, healthy, yet totally lifeless. Nothing about this makes sense. I keep waiting for her to sit upright, admit she's been roped into one of Cole's pranks, but in all the time I've been watching, she still hasn't blinked.

"She can't be dead," Cole says, his body nearly flat against the cabinets. "What even happened?"

"I don't know," Riley says, looking at me with an expression of fear and confusion I've seen from him only once before.

"Look at her eyes," Petra says, pointing.

They're open, but only now do I notice their bloodshot color.

"She's been strangled," I say.

"How do you know?" asks Aries, flinching as she takes another look at Dani's body.

"You see how red her eyes are?" I dare another look, my lips curling in disgust. "That's caused by strangulation."

"Have you taken up detective work during your hiatus?" Cole asks, moving quickly across the room, putting as much distance as possible between himself and the body.

"No," I say dryly. "I was in an episode of *Law & Order: SVU* once. I remember." Disassociation from reality is the only way I can process what's happening in front of me. I pull on past experiences to center my focus, like acting.

"Maybe she had a heart attack," Aries says. She's in denial, reaching for any plausible explanation besides murder. "Or she fell."

"Dani wasn't here thirty minutes ago," Leo says. "We were all looking for Austin, and you didn't see her then, remember?"

"That doesn't mean she couldn't have shown up after we left," Aries says. "It could still be an accident."

Riley bends down, taking a closer look at Dani's body. He pulls back the collar of her shirt. "Look."

There's a dark purple ring around Dani's neck. The way her body was positioned against the cabinets made it hard to see before.

"You're right," Petra says.

"This wasn't an accident," I say. "Someone killed her."

Cole paces back and forth, fidgeting as though his body is covered with invisible insects. When he speaks, his voice is high-pitched, unsteady. "Why would someone do that?"

Leo shrugs and stares up at Cole. "Who else is here?"

"Only us," Cole says. "The rest of the crew went back to the hotel in town. The only people staying on the grounds are us."

"You said Austin asked some people to stay behind," Aries says.

"He was supposed to." Cole raises his hands, drops them quickly at his sides. "I don't know if he did. We still don't even know where he is!"

"Someone must be on the grounds," Riley says. "We've all been together."

Yet, as he implied earlier, it looks as though Dani has been dead for a while. She could have been killed hours ago, when the crew was still present, her body recently moved to the main house. And the six of us have been together for only a short time. I was alone by the lakeshore for almost an hour before I met Leo in the woods. There's no telling where Cole, Austin, Aries, Petra, and Riley were during that time. And it's unclear if any other crew members stayed behind.

Anyone could have had the opportunity to kill Dani, then move her body when we were distracted. Her killer could still be on the grounds. Might even be in this very room.

"We need to call the police," Aries says, her eyes locking with mine. There's an unspoken understanding between us: this is our chance to do the right thing, an opportunity we squandered last time we were in a similar situation.

"And what are we going to say?" Cole asks. "We don't know what happened."

"It doesn't matter," Riley says. "Even if it was an accident, we need help."

"There aren't any cars," Petra points out, her gaze falling on the front door.

"When will the buses be back?" I ask Cole.

"Not until morning," he says, holding his phone in the air. "And the reception here is shit. We're not getting through to the cops."

Leo leans Dani's body to the left, gently resting her on the kitchen floor. He stands slowly. "Austin texted you, remember? The message said to meet him at the main house."

"I don't have any bars now," Cole says. "He could have sent it hours ago, and I just now received it. What's your point?"

"Maybe Austin knows what happened."

"Or he could be involved," Aries says under her breath, rubbing a palm against her chest.

"What about the envelope?" Petra asks.

I'd momentarily forgotten about the strange placement of the paper on Dani's body. Now it lies beside her, sliding beneath her like it's trying to hide. I bend down to retrieve it, careful not to touch Dani in the process.

"This could tell us something," I say, peeling back the unsealed flap.

My fingers slide out a small rectangle of paper. The words, in hurriedly scrawled handwriting, read, *You know where to find me.*

The message startles me, but when I flip it over to see the other side, my heart stalls in my chest.

"What is it?" Petra asks, leaning over my shoulder to try to see.

The answer seems stuck in my throat, my eyes still fixed on what's in front of me. It's a photograph. I've never seen the picture before, can barely remember taking it, and yet small details in the image speak to me. The heavy makeup painted on my face. Leo's arm, warm and protective, slung over my shoulders. The person behind the lens.

Five smiling faces stare back at me. Leo, Aries, Riley, Petra, and me. We're scrunched together, trying to fit into the frame, all wispy hair and glassy eyes and bright smiles, completely unaware of what would happen next.

The picture was taken before the *Grad Night* wrap party.

My stomach lurches, sharp and quick. I think I might be sick.

You know where to find me.

"Let me see that." Aries swipes the photograph from my hands, studying it. "Why would Dani have this?"

"Maybe she didn't," Leo says. "Someone could have left it after she died."

"Why leave a random picture of us from the original set?" Riley asks.

It's not the picture itself that bothers me. It's the precise night when it was taken, the five of us at the wrap party.

"I knew Austin had something to do with this," Aries says. "He's trying to stir up drama for his reunion."

"By murdering someone?" Leo asks. He sounds equal parts disturbed and skeptical.

"Austin wouldn't do something like this." Cole's eyes are fixed on Dani. It's sinking in that someone has died on set, that his passion project's societal reintroduction is forever tarnished.

"Austin kept going on about how real he wanted the reunion to be. Said he wanted the audience to feel like they were in the movie with us," Aries says. "Would he really go this far?"

"What about the cameras?" Petra asks.

Her words inject me with the adrenaline I need to snap out of my fearful trance. I kneel before the living room console, looking for the lens from yesterday. Sure enough, it's still there, though the light is no longer flashing.

"The cameras would have caught what happened to Dani," I say, looking over my shoulder at Cole. "Are they still working?"

"They should be," he says, but his face is blank, like he's not sure of anything anymore.

"How can we see what's on the cameras?"

"The control room is in one of the crew cabins. We could go there and play it back," he says sheepishly before his expression changes to one of purpose. "There's a CB radio in there, too. The crew used it to communicate with truckers when they were bringing in equipment."

"You're saying we could use it to call for help?" Riley asks.

"Sure," Cole says, nodding, "but I don't have the keys."

"Let's go now," Leo says, already pulling open the back door. "We'll break in if we have to."

The six of us rush outside, hurrying in the direction of the crew cabins, leaving Dani's lifeless body on the kitchen floor.

SCENE 7

EXT. BACKYARD/BLACKSTONE COTTAGE

Ella cautiously moves toward the body on the ground. With each step, she's hoping it's the masked killer, praying it isn't Leo.

Finally, she reaches him. We get a close look at Leo's face. Handsome, young, naive, and utterly lifeless.

Ella crouches beside his body. She touches his hand, his chest, his face, and begins to sob.

Ella's cries are interrupted by the CRUNCH of twigs nearby. She is not alone. She stands and turns around.

When she sees the MAN in the lion mask, she screams, but she remains frozen. Her body is rigid, still, filled with fear.

                    MAN
        Hello, Ella.

The calm introduction catches her off guard. She stops screaming.

                    ELLA
        Who are you?

He takes a step closer, but not in a threatening way. With one hand, he lifts the lion mask, revealing his face. Benjamin RHODES (50s, muscular, tired).

                    ELLA (CONT'D)
          Mr. Rhodes?

                    RHODES
          I always liked you, Ella. I thought you
          were different.

Ella looks back at the ground, sees Leo's
still body, and gasps. It's finally hitting
her that this is all real.

                    ELLA
          Why did you hurt him? Why did you hurt
          any of them?

                    RHODES
          They deserved it.

Ella isn't understanding. She can't fathom
how any action warrants the carnage that's
happened here tonight.

                    RHODES (CONT'D)
          I lost everything because of them. They
          ruined me.

A look of knowing crosses Ella's face. She
understands now. The video. The firing. Riley
and Leo.

                    ELLA
          What they did was wrong. But that
          doesn't give you the right to kill them.

                    RHODES
Doesn't it? You know I lost my job because of them. You were there when it happened. I lost everything because of that video.

                    ELLA
They didn't know that was going to happen—

                    RHODES
They didn't know *this* would happen either. (Pause.) Every action has a reaction. They took a video of me. Posted it online. I lost my job. My wife lost her insurance. I was forced to watch her wither away in pain, and there was nothing . . . nothing I could do about it.

                    ELLA
Mr. Rhodes, I'm sorry about your wife—

                    RHODES
I put up with it for years. Class after class of wiseass students, their excuse-making parents, the weak administration. I didn't do it because I liked it. I did it because that's what I had to do. It's what we all have to do. Buy time. Wait.
   You know what types of students I've taught over the years? Most of them drop out of college. Some of them end up in jail. I've taught addicts, abusers, rapists. Even murderers. I've watched all of them flounder during their formative

years, knowing exactly where they'd end
up. Never accomplish half of the things
I did in my life.
 And then it's all taken away by two
punks?

Ella senses this is all too far gone. All
she can do is stretch out this moment.

              ELLA
Mr. Rhodes, please.

              RHODES
Were you in on it, Ella? Did you help
them?

              ELLA
No, I swear. I didn't know.

              RHODES
I've always liked you, Ella. (Slowly, he
puts the mask back on.) I'm going to
feel guilty about this.

He lunges at her, but she's too fast. He
trips over Leo's body still on the ground,
while Ella runs for the tree line. We see
her disappear into the dark, gloomy forest.

EXT. DEEP FOREST/BLACKSTONE COTTAGE

Every footstep results in a CRUNCH or a
SNAP. Ella's breathing is heavy. She has a
head start, but she's not sure how long it
will take her to outrun him.

That's when she sees it: a sliver of moonlight falling over the rippled water of the lake. She runs toward it.

A hand reaches out, grabs a chunk of Ella's hair. She yelps in pain.

                    RHODES
   I can't let you leave.

She's holding on to a narrow tree trunk, the weight anchoring her in place as he pulls her in his direction. She knows if he wins this fight, she's dead.

On the ground to her left is a fallen branch. She stares at it for a beat. Then she reaches down, palms it.

He pulls her back right as she lifts the branch, striking him hard over the head. She hits him two, three, four times.

Rhodes slumps to the ground and falls back against the trunk of the closest tree.

Ella looks at the branch, sees the blood staining the bark, her hands.

She drops the weapon and faces the moonlight. She runs in the direction of the lake.

22

Then

We gather around the monitor, watching.

Leo's death scene was shot earlier in the week, but it's also the first scene that's been fully edited, and Cole offered to share it with the group.

We're in the living room of Blackstone Cottage, the same room where the fictional friend group convenes at the beginning of *Grad Night*. And yet now, as I look around the room, Petra and Riley sitting on the stone hearth of the fireplace, Aries leaning against the wall beside them, Leo standing close to the monitor, taking it all in, I can't help thinking how lucky we are. That life has imitated art, minus the death, and now we're all friends.

We aren't the only ones in the room. Ben sits beside Leo, a wide smile across his face, so at odds with the revenge-obsessed killer he plays on the screen. Cole, Jenny, and a handful of editors have joined us, eager to show off their own handiwork after weeks of our talent being on display. They've taken the raw material we've given them and turned it into something real. A story. A movie. There's something beautiful about watching it all come together.

On-screen, Leo lets out a loud scream. We cut to my character running away from the house and catch a glimpse of something falling behind her. A deafening thud. The angle changes, giving us a close-up of Leo's bloodied body on the hard ground. The screen cuts to black.

"And that, everyone, is the first completed scene in *Grad Night*," Cole shouts, turning to take in our reactions. "What does everyone think?"

The room breaks into applause. Riley and Petra are the loudest revelers. Even Aries joins in, reluctant to admit that Cole was able to pull it off. Ever since Jenny's outburst, there's been a noticeable shift in the way Aries approaches Cole. I wonder what's going on between the two of them—between the three of them—behind the scenes and whether there will be another blowup before shooting wraps.

"It's excellent," Monica says. She's standing close to Cole. I'd omitted her in my previous scan of the room. I've been doing my best to ignore her ever since our altercation. Somehow, watching the scene together erases all the drama on set. None of it matters in the presence of witnessing what we made.

"It is," Cole says. "The tension and the buildup. That raw emotion when you think Leo might get away, only to realize all hope is lost. It's fucking brilliant."

His reaction would typically come off as braggadocio, but in this instance, I believe he has earned it. We came together with limited experience, and an even smaller budget, and we've managed to create something that rivals *Cabin Fever* or *Friday the 13th*, big contenders in the genre.

"It's one scene," an editor adds hesitantly. "There's still a lot of work to be done. We haven't even finished shooting."

"That's right," Cole says, his eyes bouncing between me and Ben. "Tomorrow night, we'll shoot our last scene. The moment when the Final Girl bests the killer. It's going to be epic."

At the beginning of filming, I felt insecure, unconvinced of my worth as an actress. Now, after watching how Cole and the rest of the team were able to put everything together, I feel capable. Excited. Maybe that's why the crew decided to break protocol and give us a small glimpse into what we created, to inspire us to keep going.

"Okay, we have a lot to get ready for tomorrow. And it's going to take even longer to pack everything up and leave the lot in time. I'm heading in for the night," Cole says. "Don't stay up too late."

One by one, the crew members leave. Cole and Jenny and Monica. Riley pulls Petra in for a kiss on the lips before she takes off after them, leaving only the cast behind.

"What do you say?" Leo says. "Should we turn in early tonight? Get ready for tomorrow?"

"Ben and Ella are the only ones still filming," Aries reminds him. "As far as I'm concerned, my job here is done. I have a few days left to enjoy the mountains, or whatever. I don't care what Cole says, I'm not joining the cleaning crew."

"She has a point," Riley says. "We could start celebrating the end of our first feature film."

"I'll leave you guys to it," Ben says, standing. "But while I have you all together, I wanted to give you each something."

He pulls a black backpack from behind the chair where he was sitting and begins rummaging through it. He takes out a small gift bag with blue tissue paper springing from the top.

"I've enjoyed working on this project," he begins. "I may only have a handful of lines the whole movie, but in between chasing you around and ramming props into your sides, I've been lucky enough to work with each of you individually, and I see a lot of young talent in this room. I wanted to give you all something."

He pulls the tissue paper out of the gift bag, revealing four rectangular picture frames. Inside is a crisp one-dollar bill with his signature on it. He hands a picture frame to each of us.

"Each of you is so different, your individual strengths so pronounced." He pauses, looking down at his hands, which are now empty. "I started in this industry when I was young, like all of you. I've worked with some of the greats, even if I never headlined a movie on my own. This is my forty-second film, and I go into each one of them like I do the rest. Make enough money to pay the mortgage, put down another reference that will lead to the next job. As much as there is disappointment in this industry, there is also hope. This dollar represents that. The first role in the string of many. The first buck in what I hope will one day be millions."

I stare at the frame in my hands, thinking of everything Ben has said. His career is admirable, even if he's never been a leading man. It's an honor to work in this field, to be considered even for the smallest of roles. I think of all the sacrifices I made to get to this point. The sacrifices my mother made. Without realizing it, my eyes start to fill with tears.

"This is so nice, Ben," Aries says. Is there a hitch in her voice? "Thank you."

"Yes, thank you," Riley adds. "When I heard they'd scored you to play the killer, I was beside myself. It's been an honor."

"I know we've cracked a bunch of jokes along the way. Another horror flick at a cabin. All the tropey stuff," Ben says. "After watching that scene, I'm starting to think we might have something here."

"Thank you," I tell Ben, although I want to say more. I can't find the right words to adequately express how grateful I am for this experience, for every person in this room.

"That was sweet, Ben," Leo says. "I thought the wrap present was saved for the last day of filming."

"That's another thing," Ben says, sitting back down in the chair. "Ella and I will shoot our final scene tomorrow night, but as soon as we wrap, I'm leaving." He shoots a glance at Aries. "I won't be able to stick around for the cleanup."

"Well, aren't you lucky," Aries says. "Why are you getting out of here? Have another job lined up?"

"I wish." He smiles weakly. "A week after I accepted this role, I got a phone call from my doctor. Looks like I've taken on the role none of us ever wants to play. The Big C."

"You have cancer?" Leo asks.

"My doctor is optimistic," Ben says. "They have a treatment plan ready, and I'm going to do everything I can to fight this. It was important to me to finish this first. To have one last movie at the end of my career."

"Don't say that," Riley says, resting a hand on Ben's shoulder.

My throat aches. I look down at the gift Ben gave each of us. This dollar bill takes on a new meaning. It represents not only our first movie together but potentially Ben's last.

"Cole has been understanding about the whole thing. We've made sure to get everything they need from me on film, and then some. If they need to shoot any extra scenes, there will be a stand-in wearing a mask. No one will know the difference."

"We will," Aries says, a rare offering of kindness. "There's no replacing you, Ben."

"I appreciate that."

We move closer to him, each of us wrapping our arms around him, offering more thanks and well-wishes. When we pull away from him, I see tears falling from Ben's eyes.

"And with that, I'm going to turn in," he says. "Tomorrow will be a big scene. I'm looking forward to it."

"I am, too," I say.

Suddenly, shooting this scene with Ben seems more important than it did before because of its significance to him. He stands and walks outside, heading in the direction of his cabin. We remain silent, each of us watching him and thinking.

"Poor guy," Riley says, finally breaking the silence.

"I can't believe he's been dealing with this the whole time and none of us knew," Aries says.

"Cole knew," I say. I suddenly have more respect for our director, that he knew about Ben's challenges and continued to work with him, even kept it a secret from the rest of us.

"Who knew that bastard has a heart after all," Aries says.

"Come on, Aries. Can't you give the guy a break?" Leo says.

"The guy with cancer. Sure, he can catch a break. Cole? He's an asshole."

"An asshole who's giving all of us a chance," he counters.

"And that means we should overlook everything? Because we need something from him?"

Silence fills the room. It doesn't sit well with any of us, the idea that we'd be willing to put up with anything for this opportunity. Maybe that's because it makes us sound desperate, or maybe it's because it's true. Everyone is chasing their big break. No one said that wouldn't cause fractures along the way.

"You saw the scene," Riley says finally. "It was good. Cole is doing better than any of us expected."

"Yeah, I saw it," says Aries, her eyes landing on Leo. "It was great." She kicks off the wall, arms crossed, and walks to the front door. "I'm sure it will make all of us household names. Including Cole."

I watch the doorway, where she disappears into the night. The frequency of the room feels altered, different with Aries gone.

"What is that girl's problem?" Leo asks.

I follow Aries outside. Instead of pondering her dilemma, like I did when Cole and Jenny had their public scuffle, I'm going straight to the source.

She's off the porch, almost at the tree line when I catch up.

"Aries!" I shout after her. "I want to talk."

She's wearing a white pullover, appearing like a ghost against the forest backdrop. She turns slowly.

"Are you upset I got into it with your boyfriend?" she asks.

"It's nothing like that. I'm wondering what's going on with you," I say. "The rest of us are thrilled with the way the scene turned out. You seem disappointed."

She exhales, pulling her sweatshirt tighter around her.

"I'm not disappointed. I'm happy for you and Leo and Riley. I am. After seeing that scene, I think this movie might be more than a straight to DVD flop." She pauses. "I'm not the biggest Cole fan, and I like him even less after this experience."

I don't understand. Cole always praises her talents. The two often banter, but there's invariably an element of flirtation involved, like when I overheard their conversation in the woods or caught them in the lake together.

"Do you have history with him? Is that why you're upset?"

"History?"

"I heard you two talking one day in the woods." I pause. "I thought you two were together."

"In his fucking dreams." She laughs harshly. "There's nothing romantic between us."

"Maybe there was before?" I push. "I know he's with Jenny now—"

"You don't know anything. Cole is a ruthless bastard who will do whatever it takes to get what he wants." She takes a step closer, her words beginning to sound more like a threat. "It doesn't matter, okay? We've almost finished this job. We'll be on to the next one soon enough. That's how it works."

"If *Grad Night* is a big hit, we won't go our separate ways. There will be a press tour. Interviews. All that. If you have issues with Cole, or any of us, I think we should hash them out now."

The look on her face is hard to describe. I sense Aries has already considered all of this. That the real reason she's upset is because she knows how successful *Grad Night* will be. She knows our time together isn't over, and that angers her.

Sure, Aries has the most star power out of all of us, but this is still her first major film. She doesn't want to be known as a child actor forever. I can't understand why she isn't as thrilled about the film's success as the rest of us.

A sound echoes from the tree line. A falling branch, a snapped twig. I can't be sure. I'm suddenly filled with the sensation that Aries and I aren't alone out here. We're being watched by someone. She studies the woods, then turns to me, a look of understanding on her face.

"Are you meeting someone out here?"

She places herself between me and the woods at her back.

"Look, I appreciate you checking in on me," she says. "It's nice. But I'm a big girl and can take care of myself."

I simply nod. Whatever Aries has going on with Cole, I'm no longer convinced it's some type of love triangle. I think it's something else. Something worse. Something in which I don't want to get involved.

"Go get some rest for tomorrow." She squeezes my shoulder, dismissing me. "You're going to be great."

With that, she turns, disappearing into the shadowy forest. All the fear and paranoia that surrounds me whenever I enter these woods doesn't affect her. She welcomes it. And I can't decide if that fearlessness makes Aries brave or dangerous.

23

Now

Along our trek to the crew cabins, each step away from Blackstone Cottage brings relief, carries us further away from the moment we found Dani dead on the floor.

None of us want to believe she died due to foul play, but those bloodshot eyes, the dark ring around her neck, the picture of us left beside her body—*You know where to find me*—it seems like a morbid strategy, not an unfortunate coincidence.

Still, I try to convince myself that the worst possible situation—that another person has died on the original *Grad Night* set—isn't real. That's what the brain does during trauma, isn't it? Convinces itself that everything will be okay, even when that's far from the truth.

"I don't fucking get it," Cole shouts, pounding his thumbs into his phone. "There was service an hour ago, now nothing."

"I'm not getting any, either," Aries says, her own device in her hands.

"Do you think Austin's behind this?" Petra asks. She's on one side of me, Riley the other. The three of us hang back, lacking the fervor for confrontation the others have.

"Austin's vision for the reunion has always pushed boundaries, but killing Dani would tank the whole project, not to mention ruin his career," I say. "I can't figure out why he'd do that."

I look at the picture in my hand, which has grown slimy with sweat. The smiling faces staring back at me are like strangers, naive of what fates lie ahead of them. We're equally clueless as to what's unfolding in the present.

"I can't get over seeing Dani like that," Riley says.

The placement of Dani's body is eerily reminiscent of the *Grad Night* screenplay, except in the fictional version, Riley's character died from an axe, not strangulation. There's enough difference to make me question whether I'm being paranoid.

"Don't you think it's weird this was left behind?" I say, holding out the picture for them to see.

"It's from the original shoot," Riley says. "There's tons of memorabilia scattered around the cabin."

"It's not just any picture," Petra says.

"It was taken at the wrap party. That night." I lower my voice. "We couldn't bring it up in front of Cole because he wasn't there. He still doesn't know what we did."

"And you think someone does?" Riley asks.

"I don't think it's a coincidence someone would leave a picture of the five of us beside a dead body."

"Who could know?" Petra says. "We were the only ones there."

I shake my head and say, "I don't know. Maybe I'm crazy."

"You're not crazy. We're all trying to process what happened," Riley says. "If we can just get our hands on that radio, we'll call for help, and everything will be okay."

"It's this one," Cole says. Up ahead, three narrow cabins sit in a line. He goes to the middle one and yanks on the door, but it doesn't budge. "Told you. Austin is the only one with a key."

Leo inspects the cabin, moving around the area, searching for another way inside. He disappears behind the building, and when he returns, he's holding an axe in his hands. Again, my mind flashes to scenes from the film. Instead of a fictional Rhodes wielding the blade, it's Leo in the present.

"Good thing this was nearby," he says. "We can use it to break down a door."

"That's not a prop," Aries says. "Do you know how to use that thing?"

"It's made to chop through wood," he says, seemingly annoyed.

He rears back, holding the axe high above his head. He heaves it down, the blade making a dull clank as it hits the wooden door.

"I thought you'd be in better shape after those superhero movies," Cole says.

"You want to give it a try?"

Cole and his spaghetti arms move to the side.

Leo aims at the door a second time, a third, a fourth. Finally, a vertical chunk of wood breaks free, falling through to the other side. The hole is large enough for him to insert his hand and unlock the doorknob.

"I'm impressed," Aries says, storming past him to enter the cabin.

Leo drops the axe by the front door and walks inside. Riley, Petra, and I follow, then Cole.

The small room is fitted with two desks. Large monitors hover over each one, a mess of cords dangling below. Normally, I'd wait for Cole to signal which one we need, but there's no use. The screen to each monitor has been shattered, intentionally destroyed with angry force.

"What the hell?" Riley says.

"Someone's gone completely mental in here," Petra says, her confused expression moving from one screen to the next.

Cole hurriedly flips open one of the laptops on the desk, typing in codes and clicking the mouse. "No, no, no. Everything is gone."

"If someone did kill Dani," I say, "they made sure there was no evidence of their crime."

"They made sure we couldn't call for help, too," Riley says. He stands at the end of the other desk, holding another damaged device in his hands. The CB radio.

"And ruined the reunion in the process," Cole spits.

"Are you serious?" Riley is seething with anger. "Someone is dead, and all you care about is some stupid movie."

The irony of the statement alarms me. Twenty years ago, when we were confronted with another death, we were all more concerned with saving the project and our reputations than doing what was right, a decision that haunts us to this day.

"What the actual fuck?"

Aries jumps back like she's trying to avoid stepping in a mess.

"What is it?" I ask, moving around the others to get a better look.

"Is that fucking blood?!" Aries is practically straddling a swivel chair, trying to get as far away from the direction in which she's staring as she can. A smear of dark crimson originating from beneath one of the desks snakes through the rest of the cabin, stopping in front of a closed door.

"What's in there?" Riley asks, his eyes fixed on the door.

"The bathroom," Cole says.

"It's fucking everywhere!" Aries squeals. She's right. Now that she's brought it to our attention, I see droplets of blood splattered around the room as though one of the containers of prop blood exploded.

"Calm down," Leo says, approaching the door with caution. "Let us think."

"We have to go in there," Petra says, her lips almost touching my ear.

Riley steps forward. He twists the knob. It gives easily, but another beat passes before he has the courage to push the door in.

The door swings open, bouncing against the wall on the other side. Sitting directly in front of us is Austin. He's slumped atop the closed toilet seat. Sprays of blood cover the walls, the ceiling, the floor. Countless vertical gashes decorate his chest and torso. He looks like one of the decoys used on the original *Grad Night* set, but he isn't. All of this is real. The smell of rot and iron invading my nose makes me want to puke.

I try to turn away, but Petra and Leo have already beat me to the door. Cole stares ahead wide-eyed, like he can't believe what he's seeing.

"Austin?"

No response, other than the panicked cries of those around us. Whatever life was inside him left long ago. I peel my eyes away from the blood and gore, my vision focusing on one bizarre element before I leave: a VHS tape on the floor beside him in the pool of blood. Its presence is so unexpected, I wonder if I imagine it, if my mind is somehow trying to connect this discovery to whatever fiction I've witnessed before.

Next thing I know, Leo's hands are on my shoulders, pulling me away.

24

Now

I'm going to be sick. Each gulp of humid air does little to settle the disgust roiling around inside me. When I close my eyes, visions of Austin's mangled body haunt me.

"That was . . ." Aries is hunched over beside me. "Why would someone . . ."

For once, words fail her. It's impossible to make sense of what we've seen. The others—Leo, Petra, Riley, and Cole—stagger around, avoiding one another and afraid to veer too far away at the same time.

"They mutilated him," I say, when I'm able to catch my breath.

Petra, panting, says, "Like in the movie."

Earlier, I'd made a connection between Riley's on-screen death and the discovery of Dani's body. Still, there was a hint of plausible deniability, a chance her death might have been an accident we didn't understand.

Austin's death leaves no room for ambiguity. He was murdered, butchered like one of the characters from *Grad Night*.

"What do we do?" Leo asks. "Who would have done this?"

Riley runs back into the crew cabin, a confusing decision, but all of us are too traumatized to make sense of it or follow him. When he returns, he holds a VHS tape in his hand.

"Maybe this will tell us. It was in the same room where we found Austin," he says. "When is the last time you've seen one of these? It can't be a coincidence."

I was so shocked by the discovery of Austin's body, I'd wondered if I'd imagined the tape. I hold up the photograph still clenched between my fingers.

"There was something left behind when Dani died, too," I say.

"She's right," Petra says, standing beside me.

"Someone snuck on set to kill Austin and leave an old VHS tape?" Cole says. "That doesn't make any sense."

"Let's see what's on it," Riley says to him. "Is there a VHS player inside the control room?"

"I'm not going back in there." Aries points at the crew cabin, still hunched over like she might be sick.

"There's one at the main house," Petra says.

I nod vigorously. "I remember seeing a VHS player in the living room when I first spotted the camera."

"I saw it, too," Leo says. "We'll have to go back to the main house to watch the tape."

"This is ridiculous. There isn't time to watch some stupid tape," Aries says. "We need to call the police before we do anything."

"We don't have service," Riley reminds her. "And the radio is destroyed."

"Then let's walk back to the lake. Or toward town," she says. "We'll get a signal eventually."

"We should see what's on the tape before we do that," Cole says hesitantly.

Before anyone else can offer a suggestion, Leo plucks the tape from Riley's hand and starts walking back to Blackstone Cottage. Cole and Riley follow.

"Hey, you can't leave us here," Aries says, waving her hands at Petra and me.

"Come with us," Cole calls over his shoulder.

Petra whispers to me, "Two bodies and two messages. They must be connected, right?"

Petra and Aries chase after the guys. I glance back at the crew cabin, the front door still ajar. I shudder at the memory of Austin's mangled body inside.

And again, when I realize that the axe Leo used to break down the door is now gone.

Forcing myself to look ahead, I jog faster, trying to keep up with the others. Moments later, we're back in the dimly lit living room, the deer's beady eyes bearing down on us as Leo fiddles with the VCR beneath the giant flat-screen.

"I can't remember how to work this stupid thing," he says.

"Let me see it," Riley says, walking over.

"Wait, I think I've got it."

The six of us stand back, our eyes fearfully fixed on the screen. Dani's dead body, which lies only yards away from us, is disturbing, but I'm grateful to be away from Austin's corpse and a scene grislier and more grotesque.

The television screen turns black. We all stare ahead, waiting to see what will appear next. An image comes into focus. A video. Hard to see, and taken at an awkward angle, as though it was being recorded in secret.

"What is that?" Petra whispers to me.

I shake my head, unsure. "Did someone make a video at the wrap party?"

"No," Leo answers. "The video is newer than that."

"It's me," Riley says, moving closer to the television.

Now I see it. Riley is sitting on a black sofa, his body drooping to the side. He looks like he's inebriated, on the verge of passing out. There are other people in the room, but his is the only face visible from that angle. Whoever else is there, all we see are glimpses of elbows and shoulders.

"Do you know what this is?" Aries asks Riley.

"No." He's mesmerized by what's on the screen.

"You're in it," Leo says.

"I look wasted. I don't remember when this was. I don't know—"

Before Riley in the present can answer, Riley on-screen begins to mumble. We each take a step closer to the TV, trying to hear what he's saying.

"We didn't mean to do it," Riley says on the video.

His eyes are closed, his head leaned back. In the background, music blares, making it hard to hear. Then:

"We killed a girl," Riley says. "We didn't mean to . . ."

His words drift away, but someone else, a male voice, slurring, speaks. "What the fuck are you talking about?"

In the video, Riley lifts his head off the sofa, only for a moment, then he settles back down.

"It was an accident."

"This guy is wasted," the second voice says, laughing. It's clear whoever is speaking is the person recording the video, likely on a cell phone.

Riley mutters again, "We killed her." His body slumps to the side, the drugs in his system slipping him into unconsciousness.

SCENE 8

EXT. FOREST/BLACKSTONE COTTAGE

Ella is running. We can hear her heartbeat thumping in her chest, her feet pounding against the ground. She's breathing hard. She darts through the trees, getting closer.

EXT. LAKESHORE

Ella makes it to the shoreline. She stops momentarily to look behind her. She sees and hears nothing.

By the edge of the water is an overturned canoe. It appears worn and out of use, but it's her only chance at survival.

She overturns the boat, hitting it repeatedly to dislodge dirt and cobwebs. Then she crouches to push the canoe at full speed onto the lake. Once it begins to glide on the water, she jumps over the side. The boat wobbles for a minute—she's afraid she might capsize it—then it steadies.

She can hardly see anything, but the full moon illuminates the lake. In the distance, we see lights from other homes on the far shore. That is her destination.

A strange sound cuts through the night. She looks back in time to see Rhodes emerge from the trees. He's still wearing the lion mask.

Ella is scared, but only for a moment. She has a good enough start in the water. She grabs the paddle, starts moving it from side to side ferociously.

That's when she hears another sound, closer. The THUD-THUD-THUDding of Rhodes's footsteps. He's sprinting down the dock. He jumps off the edge, into the water.

Ella is afraid now. Still paddling, she waits for the sound of Rhodes breaking the water's surface for air. There is nothing. She pauses for a moment. Waits, listens.

A beat passes; all she can hear are crickets chirping and the gentle lapping of the water.

Rhodes, no longer wearing the lion mask, breaks the surface. His hands grasp the side of the boat. Ella screams.

Rhodes is trying to climb in, his weight coming dangerously close to overturning the boat.

                 RHODES
  I can't let you leave, Ella. No one will
  understand what I've done.

Ella looks around the boat, frantic. She picks up the paddle, raises it above her head, and slams the wood down on one of Rhodes's hands.

He yelps in pain.

Ella hits him again, this time on the head, close to the spot where she hit him earlier. This blow disorients him. His head lolls, but he maintains his grip on the gunwale.

                    RHODES (CONT'D)
          What I did to her was a kindness. You
          need to tell people that.

Ella doesn't understand his confession. She
continues to scream.

                    RHODES (CONT'D)
          . . . but they needed to pay. They had
          it coming.

                         ELLA
          And you deserve this, you sick fuck.

She strikes him over the head again, this
time hard enough to break the skull.
   Rhodes's eyes go blank. His hands slide
away from the boat, and he sinks beneath the
water.
   Ella looks over the edge, the paddle
gripped tightly in her hands, prepared to
take another swing.
   When Rhodes emerges, he's face down in the
water, his arms and legs outstretched, empty
of life.
   Ella stares a few seconds longer, unsure
whether to let her guard down. She looks
back at the cabin, which she can barely see
in the distance. She looks as though she is
about to cry.
   Then she turns and gazes across the lake
at the shoreline, the house lights twin-
kling. She takes the paddle and starts pushing it through the water.
   As we pull away, we get a glimpse of Ella
in the boat. We can still see Rhodes's body

floating in the water, can see Blackstone Cottage in the distance, and ahead, the re-assuring shoreline.
  Safety.

                                          FADE OUT

                    END

25

Then

It rarely works out this way. The last scene of the movie being the last one filmed. They aren't putting the cameras away yet. There are still some exterior shots they'll need to take, but as far as a full scene—with hair and makeup and dialogue and props—this is it.

I'm standing in the boat, having mastered the precise foot placement needed to keep my balance. Ben is in the water, his hands holding on to the side of the boat, waiting for Cole to decide whether we need another take of the death blow.

"One more time," Cole says.

After weeks of filming, I've learned that *one more time* can mean countless shots ahead, but everything we've done today has felt right, organic, like we've finally worked out the groove of what *Grad Night* is supposed to be, how it's supposed to end.

"Places," Jenny yells, although it's more a warning to the cast and crew gathered around the lakeshore than it is to me or Ben, who has been in the water for almost an hour.

Following Cole's cues, I raise the paddle over my head, bringing it down close to Ben's body. He feigns being hit, his hands shaking as he lets go of the boat's gunwale and sinks into the water. He'll quickly swim away, out of the camera's view, but I must stand still, remain in character. I know Cole is trying to get extra footage of my face, my expression.

I think of Ella, not me per se, but the one in *Grad Night*. She watched her friends get slaughtered. She witnessed her boyfriend take his last breath. What was supposed to be a night of new beginnings, a promise of the future, turned into something she didn't deserve, and she had to dig deep inside herself to find enough strength to keep fighting. As she looks down into the water, the paddle gripped tight in her hands, streaks of blood across her shirt, it's not the horror of her experiences she sees. It's her own reflection, strong and fearless, for the first time in her entire life. She's a survivor.

Those are the feelings I'm trying to convey.

I don't change my expression until Cole's voice calls, "Cut!" from across the lake. Seconds pass, all of us turned in his direction, waiting.

"That's a wrap," he announces at last. "Bloody fucking hell, that was good!"

His words are followed by a loud round of applause from the lakeshore, hoots and hollers echoing through the night forest. A smile spreads across my face, so wide it's almost painful.

I did it. We did it. My first project as a leading lady is a wrap.

The water breaks beneath me, and I look down. Ben is clapping his hands. "Bravo, Ella," he says.

"I couldn't have done it without you." I dip my head at him, do a small curtsy in the wobbly boat. "Let's get back to shore and into something dry."

The praises and applause continue once we're back on land, people squeezing my shoulders and slapping Ben on the back. The excitement in the air has reached new heights, different than it was when we captured any of the other important scenes, bigger than last night when Cole gave us a glimpse of the first completed scene.

The crowd parts, and I see Aries, Riley, and Leo standing together. They begin clapping. Once Ben and I are nearer, Riley reaches out an arm and pulls us into an embrace. The five of us, our limbs wrapped around one another.

"Let's hear it for our cast," Cole shouts, and the applause grows louder.

All of us have a rosy flush to our cheeks, goofy smiles on our faces. Even Aries, who always comes across as effortlessly cool, seems a little awestruck at the reaction we're getting, at what we've been able to achieve.

"Now what?" Leo asks.

"We have two days until our rental agreement expires," Cole says. "We'll use that time to make sure we have all the backup shots we need and clean up."

"So, what do we do?" Riley adds.

"Whatever you want," Cole says. "Get some rest. It'll be all-hands-on-deck tomorrow."

The crew, knowing already that they'll be doing the brunt of the work, trudge back toward the house. Petra remains at the water's edge, giving the cast a few minutes with Ben. He waits until we're alone to speak.

"Well, that does it for me," he says. "I hope you guys have fun the next couple of days."

"Really?" Aries asks. "You're leaving just like that?"

"I told you I needed to head out after the last scene."

"It's, like, two in the morning."

"I have a car waiting. Honestly, we finished up faster than I expected." He looks at me. "You were really something out there."

"Thanks, Ben. You're a great scene partner."

"I appreciate that." He smiles and looks down. I don't want to imagine what he's thinking right now. That the joy we all have for completing our first film is small in comparison to the despair he must feel about this potentially being his last.

Leo holds out his palm for a handshake. "We wish you luck, Ben. You're a great guy."

"Seriously, if you need anything, give us a shout," Riley says, his voice scratchy with emotion. "We'll see you in a few months. Once the promotional schedule is set."

"I hope so," he says. He doesn't sound confident but optimistic. I think that's all a person can be when facing a dire diagnosis.

Ben gives us each a hug before walking in the direction of the house. I see Cole standing alone on the back porch, no doubt waiting for him. They must have their own goodbyes they need to share.

"That's the saddest thing," Leo says.

"Ben'll be all right," Riley says with confidence. "He's a tough guy."

"So, what's next?" Petra wanders back over, fiddling with the crescent-shaped pendants on her necklace.

"You heard Cole," Leo answers. "Last-minute shots and cleanup."

"I think you're forgetting an important part of that plan, my friend," Riley says.

"What?"

He smiles wickedly. "The wrap party."

"I didn't know there was one," I say.

"Hell, we're planning it. One last hurrah before we all head our separate ways." He squeezes Petra a little tighter. "What do you say?"

"Let's do it," Aries says. "I'll get Carlos to score us some booze."

"Do you think Cole will mind?"

"Doesn't matter if he does," Aries says. "Besides, he's Hollywood royalty. If anyone knows about partying, it's him."

"I'd feel better if we talked to him about it," Leo says.

"Then let's go," Riley says.

The others start walking toward the main house, leaving me alone by the lake. It's a beautiful night, the bright moon painting ripples on the clear-glass water. Hard to imagine that in two days everything will come to an end.

"You coming?" Petra asks.

"I'll hang back a bit longer," I say, looking out over the water.

"I'll stay with you," she says, signaling for Riley and the others to go ahead. "I'm not ready to sleep anyway."

For several seconds, we stand in silence, listening as the rippling water laps against the shore. Another sound disrupts the moment.

"Do you hear that?" I say, turning to Petra.

Her chin is raised, signaling she hears it, too. "What is that?"

I stand still, trying to listen. It sounds like muffled sobs. Someone is crying. I walk forward, stopping when I see a dark figure hunched in the sand.

Petra, only a few steps behind me, says, "Jenny?"

Sure enough, Jenny sits in the sand, knees pulled to her chest. She turns in our direction, wiping her face.

"I thought I was alone," she says.

"We're about to head back," Petra says, kneeling beside her. "What's going on?"

"Nothing." She forces an unconvincing smile. "I get like this sometimes when a project ends."

I have the same fears and anxieties about what comes next, but my career is just starting. I would have thought Jenny, with her experience, wouldn't feel so lost.

"Is this about Cole?" I ask her. I feel Petra's eyes on me. The relationship between Jenny and Cole is something we've all whispered about from time to time, but we've never addressed it head-on.

"Everything comes back to Cole, doesn't it?" Jenny scoffs. "This is his big project, after all."

"You've been beside him every step of the way," Petra says. "He wouldn't have gotten this off the ground without your help."

"That's for sure." Another pitiful laugh escapes Jenny's mouth. "Did you know I wrote the original screenplay? Cole read over it to give me some notes. Next thing I know, it's being pitched as his feature project."

My head shakes in disbelief. I've read the script more than a dozen times by now. Jenny's name isn't attached to it at all. "Why didn't you say anything?"

"That's bullshit," Petra says. "You should confront him."

"I'm a nobody, remember? Cole's connections are what got this project off the ground. It just stings knowing he'll take all the credit for my work."

Whatever the relationship is between them, it's obvious Cole doesn't value Jenny. He doesn't respect her. Fooling around with Aries is bad enough. But this? Taking ownership of her hard work?

"You deserve better than him," I say, squeezing her hand.

"I know." She wipes her face again. "Look, don't say anything about it? Please. The shoot is almost over. We don't need any more drama."

"We won't say a word," Petra says. As outraged as we are on her behalf, we know all our voices are small when stacked against the likes of Cole and his Hollywood pedigree.

"Thank you." She sounds relieved. "At the end of the day, I'm just happy to be involved. This whole industry is magical to me. I'll miss it one day."

"The guys are putting together a wrap party tomorrow," I tell her, trying to lighten the mood. "You should come. We can end all this on a high note."

"Cole be damned," Petra adds.

We stare ahead, watching as the moon sinks closer to the water in the distance.

26

Now

I'm still trying to make sense of the video we watched, understand how it connects to Dani's and Austin's deaths.

"What the hell was that?" Aries is the first to speak.

"Oh, Riley," Petra says. "What did you do?"

"I . . . I don't know." Riley's back is to the television now, ashamed to watch further.

"I think it's pretty fucking clear," Leo says, his voice strong and aggravated. "It's Riley on camera, confessing to what we've done."

"That's not . . . I—I don't remember," Riley stammers.

"No shit you don't remember," Leo fires back. "You were so wasted, you don't know who you told!"

"I know I've never told anyone about what we did in the woods."

"Then how is there a video of you confessing?" Leo is standing in front of Riley, their faces only inches apart. There's an intensity in Leo's eyes I've never seen before. A combination of fury and panic. If Riley says the wrong thing, I'm afraid Leo might hit him. Aries, Petra, and I are huddled together near the back wall, watching. Cole stands apart from our group, his expression wearing the same shock as the rest of us.

"I know I've never told anyone when I was sober," Riley says. "You saw me on the video. I was out of it. No one took it seriously."

"Then how did that clip make it onto a tape?" Leo asks. "And why was that video left here, with Austin's body?"

"I don't know."

"Well, you need to start thinking," Leo says. "You fucked up and started running your mouth *on camera*. We don't need your drunken confession being traced back to us."

"Enough." Cole stands between the two men, pushing them apart. "There's no use fighting about who fucked up in the past. We need to worry about what's happening now."

I look behind me at Dani's body. For a minute, I think he's talking about her. Then Cole adds, "Whoever has this video could leak it to the press or sell it. Then we're all fucked."

Pricking waves radiate through my body. "Wait, do you know?"

"Know what?" Cole asks.

"About what happened after the wrap party?!"

"Of course I know."

"Shit," Petra says.

"How?" Aries roars. "We were the only ones out there."

Cole's lips flatten into a thin line as he exhales. His eyes dance around the room, landing on Leo.

"I told him," Leo says.

"You did what?" I gasp, my chest aching like it's been punched.

"I had to," he says. "It was too big a secret for us to keep all those years."

"But we kept it!" Aries says, rage building. "I told no one. Ella, did you?"

I shake my head, too dazed to speak.

"We were supposed to be the only ones who knew," Petra says.

"You're giving me hell for opening my mouth when I was wasted off my ass, all while you spilled the tea years ago?" Riley shouts at Leo.

"You were rambling about murdering a girl in a room full of strangers!" Leo says. "Anyone could have gone to the police. I told Cole to protect us."

"Yeah, right. How is Cole going to protect us?" says Aries. "He'd rat out his own mother if it meant getting ahead."

"I bought the land," Cole says defiantly. "Canceled that stupid Grad Fest they had here. If there had ever been a whisper about someone being murdered, I could have done something about it. More than any of you could have."

"I didn't have a choice," Leo says. "Year after year, I'd see pictures online of all these kids getting fucked up and wandering around the woods. We couldn't risk them finding a body. And then Jenny's aunt started running her mouth all over television. What if the police had decided to take her claims seriously? Search the land?"

"I made sure none of that would happen," Cole says. "After Leo told me."

"You knew this the whole time," Petra says to him.

"You knew this morning in the interview, when Austin was toying with you about Jenny's disappearance," I say. "How could you?"

"I was doing what I always do. Spinning a story. I was only playing into the haunted narrative that's followed the franchise all these years," he says. "I would never say anything that could jeopardize any of us."

"This is no longer some publicity stunt to pad your next box office. We're talking about another dead body." I motion back toward Dani. "Now two! Someone knows what we did after the wrap party, and they didn't run to the police. Or the press. They came here. Why?"

"And why kill Dani?" Aries mutters. "And Austin?"

"Maybe they saw something they shouldn't have," Leo says.

Riley, arms crossed over his body, shrunken in shame, says,

"Or maybe the person who left the video only cares about making us pay for that night."

There's a somber tenor in his voice, like part of him has been expecting this all along, waiting for the day when the universe might settle its score.

27

Then

The makeup trailer is different tonight. Instead of following reference cards for continuity and rushing to meet our call time, all the women are scrunched inside, styling one another's hair and raiding clothing racks in hopes of finding something to wear to the party.

Eventually the conversation turns to the film, which leads us to discussing our favorite scary movies.

"I'd have to go with *Halloween*," I say. "It's a classic. There would be no *Grad Night* without it."

"That's the traditional choice." Aries puts her finger to her lips, thinking. "It's corny, but my favorite is *I Know What You Did Last Summer*. That movie scared the shit out of me when I was a kid."

"What about the second one?" Petra asks.

"I love it! A revived serial killer, a hurricane, Brandi. Total entertainment." Aries looks around, stopping at Jenny. "Which movie is your favorite?"

Jenny raises her head, thinking. "I'd have to say *Scream*. The whole movie within a movie thing intrigues me. I like how it pokes fun at all the tropes in the genre."

"It makes sense you'd like *Scream*, seeing as you work behind the scenes," I say, my mind going back to last night's conversation at the lakeshore. I can't imagine how helpless Jenny must feel, knowing that Cole is taking credit for all her hard work.

"I don't even have a favorite franchise," Petra says. "Scary movies were never my thing, but a job is a job, right?"

Petra finishes her own makeup and instructs me to sit in the chair. As I'm taking my seat, Leo and Riley squeeze through the front door of the cabin.

"We have good news and bad news," Leo says.

"That's never a good way to enter a room," Aries says.

Riley sets a brown paper bag on the table in front of me. I can see the streaks of condensation weakening the fiber.

"Turns out most of the crew didn't get the memo about the wrap party. That, or they didn't care. A lot of them are heading out tonight before it gets started."

"Bummer," Petra says. "Any idea who is staying?"

"All of us. And Cole," Riley says. "I think some of the camera guys. And Monica."

I try to mask my disappointment. Monica is the one person I was hoping would ditch tonight's event.

"What's the good news?" I ask.

"More booze for us," Riley says, putting another bag on the table. "And we lucked out with our driver, too. He gave us a contact for some good bud. Prepare yourselves to get high on some homegrown mountain weed."

"Total score," Aries says, sashaying over to inspect the bag.

"Sounds fun." Petra looks at me in the mirror. "Do you smoke?"

"Not really."

"I don't, either," Jenny adds, sitting at the back of the room. Aries walks over to her and starts sifting through one of the wardrobe trunks, still on the hunt for some gaudy accessories to go with her ensemble.

"Come on," Riley says. "It's a party."

"Don't pressure them," Petra says.

"We all need to have fun tonight," he says. "We deserve it, right?"

"Yeah, we do." Leo bends down, putting my duffel bag and purse on the floor. "I hope you don't mind. Cole wanted everything out of the main house. I grabbed your bags for you."

"You didn't have to do that," I say.

"I guess he doesn't care if we trash the small cabins, since we brought those in, but he wants the main house to be spotless before the owners show up tomorrow afternoon," Leo says. "Riley and I are going to set up for the party in Cabin Six. I think it's the only one that's vacant."

"Check this out," Aries says. She reaches into the trunk and pulls out a Polaroid camera. "I haven't seen one of these in ages."

"There's no telling what you might find in there," Jenny says. "It's one of those relics that gets moved around from set to set."

Aries aims the camera at the wall and presses the button. The device flashes, spitting out a square photo. She begins flapping it in the air. "Holy shit, it works."

She stands, walking over to us and holding out her hand. "Everyone, get together."

We fold into one another, everyone trying to get in position around me in the makeup chair as Aries strains to hold out her arm. After a few seconds of maneuvering, Jenny steps away from the group.

"Here," she says, holding out her hands. "I'll take it for you."

"No, we want you in it," Aries says.

"It's fine. You're all good friends. You'll want to remember this."

The five of us—Leo, Petra, Riley, Aries, and me—huddle together, the camera's flash blinding us. We remain together, watching as the sepia foil changes into a photograph.

"Okay, you guys head out so we can finish getting ready," Petra says, shooing them away. "See you in about an hour?"

Leo steps forward, kisses me on the lips. "By the way, you look . . ."

He swings his eyes to the side and whistles, as though he can't find the right words. I smack his chest playfully.

Riley walks over to Petra and gives her a kiss on the cheek. "See you soon."

"I'm heading out, too," Aries says. "I need to make sure my stuff is packed because I have a feeling that I'll be nursing one helluva hangover tomorrow."

"I'll join you," Jenny says. She looks back at us before following the others out. "It's been fun getting to know you guys. I wish I'd done it earlier in the shoot."

The others leave us, and I'm grateful to have a few moments alone with Petra. She's the first person who made me feel comfortable on set, the first person to put me at ease when Cole was being ridiculous. It's hard to believe our month together has already come to an end.

"What are you doing after we wrap?" I ask. "You could join me on the press tour, if there is one."

"I would love that. You could ask Gus to hire me as your personal makeup artist," she says. "I've got a job lined up, though. It's a period piece. Should give me some good experience."

"I'm serious about working together again, too. You've been the highlight of this job for me."

"You too, babe." She stands back. "Now, get a look at yourself."

Petra moves so I can see my reflection in the mirror. The heavy makeup is different from what I'm used to wearing, but it looks good. I can't help thinking of female characters in nineties romcoms who get a haircut and swipe on some lipstick, suddenly converting into a "hot" girl. The longer I stare at my reflection, the more transformed I feel.

"Have you and Riley talked about what's going to happen after tomorrow?"

"Riley doesn't have another job until next month. He said he might fly out to visit me on set."

"That's great."

"Yeah. I didn't think he'd want to keep it going. You were right about giving him a little more credit." She pauses, playing with the shell necklace around her neck, the one Riley made for her. "What about you and Leo?"

"We still haven't talked about it. I guess I thought I'd see how tonight goes. I'm a little nervous."

"It's a party. You make it sound like you're going to marry the guy." She must catch the look on my face. "What is it?"

"I was thinking tonight might be the night we, you know, go all the way."

"Sex? You two haven't done it already?"

"No. I haven't done it with him. Or anyone."

She raises her eyebrows. "Wow. I had assumed . . ." She smiles, uncertainly, then genuinely. "Well, that is a big deal."

"Don't make me more nervous about it."

"I'm not trying to make you nervous." She puts her hands on my shoulders. "I mean, it's a big step, but you should feel good about it. If it's what you want to do."

"I think it is. I've never felt this way about someone before. And I think if I don't do it tonight, I'll regret it."

"I think you have your answer, then." She looks at the alcohol left by the boys. "We need drinks to celebrate."

"I don't think I'm going to drink very much. I don't want to be so wasted I forget my first time." I bend down and start rummaging through the bags Leo brought in until I find my purse. I take out the pill bottle. "I might take one of these instead."

"What is it?"

"Something to help with my anxiety. Gus gave them to me."

"Agent of the year." She takes the bottle from my hand and gives it a shake before handing it back. "We could split one? Looks like both of us have nerves to settle."

She pops open the lid and thumbs out one pill. She breaks it in half with ease, offering part to me.

"To what comes next," she says, placing half of the pill on her tongue.

I do the same, struggling to swallow it dry. "Let's go have a night to remember!"

28

Now

We're all stunned by the discovery of Austin's body, and the shock of Riley's confession video, but we need to figure out who has uncovered our secret, and exactly what the person plans on doing with the information.

"Someone knows what we did," I begin. "And they didn't go to the police. They waited until we were all here to let us know the secret is out."

"Who would do that?" Petra asks.

"Someone must have talked," Leo says, looking at each of us. "I already admitted to telling Cole. And Riley blabbed about it on video."

"I didn't necessarily use with the most upstanding members of society," he says. "Still, if anyone had taken what I said seriously, they would have gone to the cops."

We all look at Cole.

"What? You think I'm involved—"

"Answer the question," Leo says.

"I haven't told anyone."

"How do we know you're not behind this?" Aries saunters

over to him. "You could have found this video and planned on using it against us."

"And why would I do that?"

"To take the focus away from your MeToo drama," she says coldly. "We've all heard about it. Women coming forward, saying you coerced them into having sex. That you drugged them—"

"Those are only allegations."

"I know how PR works. Plant a bigger story than the one that's already out there," she says, her voice firm. "Instead of Cole the Rapist, it's Cole the Crime Stopper, solving a decades-old murder."

Petra locks eyes with me and whispers, "She has a point."

I agree. Aries's argument is compelling, but I'm not sure whom in this room I can trust. Twenty years is a long time, and we've all changed.

"If you know so much about Hollywood, you know there's plenty of B-list actresses willing to lie to get their name in the papers," Cole says, continuing his argument with Aries. "How do you explain Austin? You think I'd set this whole thing up to take pressure off me, then murder my protégé?!"

"I wouldn't put anything past you."

"Me either," Petra adds.

"Austin is a big name. People will notice if he goes missing. Let alone if he turns up dead," he says, his face turning red. "He's not some no-name crew member no one cares about."

"She was a person," Riley says. He clenches his jaw as he charges at Cole. "People cared about her."

"I'm sorry, okay?" Cole raises his hands, defending himself against an angry Riley. "I can't imagine what that night was like. For all of you. You've been carrying this secret for years, but someone knows now. We need to find out who."

"If none of us told anyone," I say, "then whoever this is must have been part of the original shoot."

"And they waited until we were all together again," Riley says. "Austin made a big deal about bringing the old cast and crew together. If someone was wanting to confront us with what they know, this would have been the perfect time to do it."

"So, what we need to do is figure out who on the reunion crew was also associated with the original film."

Again, we all look at Cole.

"Okay, there's a list of names somewhere—"

"We don't have time for that," Leo says.

"Just think," Petra says. "There aren't that many people."

"Okay, okay." He clenches his jaw and closes his eyes. "Austin brought in his own people, but from the original crew, we have some of the camera guys . . . hair and makeup."

"This could go on forever," Aries says.

"Will you shut up and let me think?" He pauses.

"None of them are here," Leo points out. "The crew and handlers left hours ago."

"Oh, shit," Cole says.

"What is it?" I ask.

"There's one person still here. She was supposed to get a ride back to set."

"Who?" Aries asks.

Cole hesitates. "Monica."

The head of hair and makeup. The person who had a vendetta against me for taking the role she believed should be hers. She was a dark presence on set twenty years ago, and she's here again now.

"Why would she come back?" Riley asks.

"We had, um, plans," Cole says. "She was going to stay the night with me, but we didn't want to make a big deal about it."

Aries exhales in frustration. "You are such a sad stereotype, Cole. Thanks to you and your dick, we're all in danger."

"We don't know it's her," he says.

"When was she supposed to get back?" Riley asks.

"She was going to meet me outside the cabin after dark."

"It's been dark for hours," Leo says. "She could be anywhere."

It's difficult to focus on anything outside the fact that Monica seems like the ideal culprit. She has resentment toward all of us, especially me. Once she uncovered our biggest secret, she snatched the opportunity to dangle what she knows over our heads.

"We need to find her," Riley says. "Before she finds us."

"And what are we going to do then?" Cole says. "Jump her?"

"If we stick together, she'll be outnumbered." Then Riley adds, "Or we'll end up like Austin and Dani."

"The picture," Petra says under her breath, grabbing my attention.

It's like an explosion going off inside my head. I lift the photo that's still pressed between my fingers. "The note on the back says, 'You know where to find me.' She's telling us where to go."

"What's that even mean?" Aries asks. "We don't know where to find the killer."

"No." I close my eyes. "We know where to find the body."

29

Then

The rustic look of Cabin Six is at odds with the vibrant buzz in the air. The loud music is almost disrespectful in this serene setting that we've called home for the past month. My chest vibrates with each thump of the bass.

The furniture has been moved against the walls, giving us more room to walk around, but it still feels cramped. Leo and I sit in a chair meant for one person, my legs over his. Riley and Petra are sharing the same-sized seat across from us. Jenny and Monica have staked out a spot on the floor. The others are standing around, leaning against the narrow breakfast bar in the corner, pouring drinks and snorting powder off the countertop.

Aries is in the center of the room, presently hopping.

"A kangaroo," Riley shouts.

She shakes her head.

"A flamingo," says Petra.

She shakes her head again, more vehemently.

"A rocker from the eighties hopped up on quaaludes," Cole shouts from the direction of whatever is going on at the counter.

"Time," Leo calls.

"I was a fucking rabbit," Aries says, bending down to retrieve her drink, which she'd left on the floor. "And since when do flamingos hop?"

"I couldn't figure out what you were doing," Petra says.

"Who'd have thought a group of actors would suck this much at charades?" Cole says, wandering over to us. The people he'd been standing with in the makeshift kitchen, Carlos and a few of the other crew members, stay back.

"I don't think any of us are in our right minds," Riley says, taking another sip of his drink.

Rather, they're all royally drunk. The guys started passing out drinks the moment people arrived and haven't stopped. Even I feel woozy, despite having only had a couple of drinks. My head lolls to the side, resting on Leo. He squeezes me protectively.

"Having fun?" he asks.

"A blast," I say, and I can't decide whether it's true or not. It's entertaining to watch the others, but I feel as though there's a glass pane between me and them, something keeping me from the revelry they so eagerly welcome.

"We can take a walk, if you want," he says. "Chill out for a bit."

"I don't want to be the first ones to leave," I say.

I'd rather the others head out first, spare me the jokes and hoots and hollers as Leo and I make our exit. Our attempt to keep our relationship under wraps at the beginning of filming ended a long time ago, but I still don't want the extra attention. Especially tonight, when I'm so close to taking the next step with Leo.

"Who is next?" asks Cole.

"I'm done with this game," Aries says, taking another swig straight from the wine bottle. "And I'm getting bored."

"I don't know what to tell you," Cole says. "We're in the middle of nowhere. We can't very well head out to the next place."

"That's not true," Carlos calls out. "There is a bar in town. We've visited a couple of times."

Cole scoffs. "I can't even imagine how lame it is."

"It's a sight to be seen. It's like a real-life *Road House*," Carlos says. "Jukebox in the back. Middle-aged guy behind the bar."

"How are the girls?" Cole asks.

"Drunk and willing," Carlos says.

"Why are guys such dogs?" Aries asks. The question is rhetorical, but Cole can't stop himself from taking the bait.

"Right, Aries," he says. "Like you've never gotten all dressed up and decided to go looking for some ass."

"It's what your whole world revolves around," she says. "I mean, you have more opportunity than everyone in this room put together, and all you can think about is getting your dick wet."

I'm still cringing at the term *dick wet*, but it's clear Cole is bothered by the suggestion that his life is easier because of his last name. What upsets him most is that it's true. We somehow shot an entire movie without anyone confronting Cole's privilege, but it's not in Aries to pass up the opportunity.

Cole stares at her for a beat, a wicked energy coursing between them.

"Fuck it," he says, looking back to Carlos. "Let's check it out. Maybe it would do me some good to be around girls with a little less culture."

"I'm down," says Carlos.

"Me too," adds another crewmate.

"You're more than welcome to join us, guys," he says to the rest of the room. "Y'all could be my wingmen." He looks at Aries. "Or wingwoman."

The awkwardness in the room is palpable. If there's one thing I won't miss, it's the never-ending love-hate drama between Cole and Aries.

The song changes to Britney Spears's "Toxic." Riley, the eternal peacemaker, seizes the moment to break the tension.

"This is my song!" He hops up, holding out his hand for Petra to join him. Half-drunk herself, she's happy to oblige, and they begin to prance goofily around the living room.

"There you go," Cole says. "Some good, wholesome fun."

I whisper to Leo, "I'm going to use the restroom."

He nods, his eyes turning back to the dancing couple in the center of the room.

The bathroom is as narrow as the rest of the house. I can't sit on the commode without my knees touching the sink cabinet. As I'm washing my hands, I stare at myself in the mirror. Whatever Riley put in those drinks is strong. My cheeks are blushing, and my vision is a little hazy.

Thunder rumbles. Seconds later, I hear the rattle of raindrops hitting the metal roof. Some cool night air might calm my nerves, even if I get drenched in the process. I'm about to exit the bathroom when someone starts banging against the door.

"Let me in," says Petra, continuing to knock.

I barely make room for the two of us as I open the door and push it shut behind her. There's a feverish look in her eyes, and I don't think it's from the dancing.

"Can I have another pill? Aries is right. This party is getting lame, and I need a little boost."

My purse is still wrapped over one shoulder. I unzip it, feeling around for the bottle. "It looks like you're having a good time without it."

"Yeah, but I'm ready to let loose. And I don't feel like sharing with the douchebags over in the kitchenette."

"What do you think they're doing over there?"

"Probably cocaine. Not my thing. I try to stay away from the hard stuff." She holds out her hand, and I drop the pill into her palm. "You must have transferred your nerves to me. For some reason, I can't stop thinking of this being my last night with Riley."

"Don't go there."

"I'm trying not to, but . . . I don't know." Sadness falls over her face. "I have a feeling things will never be this good again."

Now my thoughts are on Leo. What we're about to do. Worrying that what it means to me is so far beyond what it will mean to him.

"I want to get out of here," I say. "I wish some of the others would head out first."

"I don't think it will be much longer. Cole is all about taking a road trip into town."

The music cuts out, and voices get louder. Petra and I share confused looks before reentering the main room.

"Last call for whoever wants to go into town," Cole says. Carlos and the other crew members are already standing at the door. "Any takers?"

"What the hell," Monica says, standing. "I'll check out the place. Gotta be better than this dump."

He looks at Jenny. "You coming?"

"I'm too tired."

"Tired? You didn't work today. What do you have to be tired for? And you've barely had anything to drink." He walks into the kitchen, grabbing the martini shaker and pouring it into a nearby glass. He walks back to Jenny. "Come on, loosen up a bit."

"My car will be here early in the morning." Jenny doesn't raise her eyes to meet his. I wonder if, in addition to not wanting to go to the bar herself, she resents him for going.

"Yeah, so will ours," Cole says with a slack jaw.

"She said she doesn't want a drink, Cole," Aries says.

"I'm talking to her." He holds up a hand. "Not you."

Aries stands directly in front of him, piercing him with an intense stare. "Well, it sounds like you aren't getting the message."

Cole pauses. That same charged energy passes between them. He holds out the drink, offering it to Aries.

"Then you take it," he says. "It's the least you could do, considering I'm giving you your big break and all."

Aries remains still only for a moment. She takes the drink, and a second later she raises it, pouring the contents over Cole's head.

"You fucking bitch," he says, his shoulders rising as the cold liquid slides down his back. It's hard to tell if he's genuinely angry or amused, but the action attracts laughs from the rest of the room.

Everyone but Jenny and me, that is. It's like we're the only ones to recognize the pulsating anger behind her action. Jenny moves toward them; I'm not sure if she's reaching for Aries or Cole when she slips on the wet floor. She falls forward, clocking the side of her head on the countertop.

"Jenny!" I call, rushing forward. Everyone inside the cabin moves immediately, scrambling to help her up.

Cole gets to her first, grabbing her shoulders. "Are you okay?"

"Fine," Jenny says, touching her forehead. When she pulls back her hand, her fingers are stained with blood.

Leo hurries to the small sink in the kitchenette, running water over a rag. He hands it to Jenny.

"Give her some space, Cole," Riley says, standing behind her.

"I'm not the one throwing drinks," he says, pointing at Aries.

"I'm sorry, Jenny," Aries says, her cheeks red with embarrassment. "I didn't mean—"

"I'm fine," Jenny snaps, leaning against the counter as she stands. "Really."

As people move away from the mess on the floor, Leo walks to the front door. He locks eyes with me, motioning for me to follow.

"Are you sure you're okay?" I ask Jenny.

She nods, escaping the crowd of people at the counter. The others drift around the cabin, the lively spirit of the party officially ruined by Aries and Cole.

"Looks like we're making a run for it," I whisper to Petra.

"Get out while you can." She squeezes my hand. "Have fun."

I give her a knowing look, making a beeline for the exit before the rest of the partygoers notice. I steal one more glance at Jenny and the wet rag still pressed against her bleeding forehead, but then I turn to leave.

Outside, the cool night breeze is in contrast with the stifling atmosphere inside Cabin Six. Rain falls softly around us, dampening our shirts and hair. Leo squeezes my hand.

"What do you think is going on with them?" I say, looking back at the cabin. "Aries and Jenny and Cole."

"Some kind of weird love triangle, if you ask me."

"Aries says that's not it."

"And you believe her? Look, I'm not trying to bad-mouth Aries, but she's not really a girl's girl," he says. "It wouldn't surprise me if she's befriending Jenny so she can sink her claws deeper into Cole."

Leo's assessment of Aries is harsh, but not completely inaccurate. I hear more raised voices coming from the cabin, and I turn back to look.

"I hope Jenny is okay."

"Quit thinking about them," Leo says. "This is our last night here. I want to enjoy it."

I shake my head, trying to forget everyone else's drama. Other things should be on my mind. I squeeze Leo's hand tighter. "Let's get inside before the storm picks up."

Even though Cabin Four is the same size as the one we left, this one appears homier. There are appliances in the small kitchenette, a double bed in the center of the room, and a small door at the back, which I assume leads to the bathroom. An air conditioner hums in the corner, and a shiver rattles through me, my damp shirt now sticking to my torso.

"I don't think I ever entered this cabin."

"It was Ben's place," Leo says. "I guess he wanted his own space, you know."

I'm saddened to think about Ben. We've all taken this experience for granted compared to what he's facing.

"You want another drink?" he asks, walking into the kitchen.

"Let's just talk."

I sit on the bed, and Leo joins me. We smile at each other, that tingle of desire growing every second. My head is swimming, and when he reaches for my hand, it's like hot sparks explode throughout my body. I'm afraid my own nerves will ruin this moment between us.

We kiss. I lie back on the bed, pulling Leo on top of me. He's hesitant at first, chivalrous even, but his instincts soon take over, and he's on top of me. Layers of clothing are removed, and as each garment makes its way to the floor, I feel another reeling sensation of excitement and . . . fear. I've decided what I want tonight to be, what I want it to mean, but I'm still anxious.

Leo puts his hand between my legs, and I writhe with lust. He gets on his knees, kissing me in the same spot, until it feels like fireworks are going off inside my head. When I reach the peak of ecstasy, I pull him closer, guiding him into me.

He pulls away. "Are you sure about this?"

"Yes." My voice is quiet but confident. "This is what I want."

Leo bends down to grab his clothes from the floor, pulling a condom from one of the pockets of his jeans. He waits another moment, then he's on top of me again, pushing his way inside. I brace myself for the pain, but it quickly morphs into pleasure. Soon, I'm not thinking about anything, only feeling. Craving Leo and everything he represents.

When we finish, Leo strides to the bathroom. I lie still on the bed, looking at the steepled ceiling. I smile. I don't think my first time could have been more perfect.

Then I hear it, slicing through the quiet night, ringing through the trees, ripping apart my contentment and happiness.

A scream.

Leo hurries into the room, staring at me with wide eyes. "Did you hear that?"

I barely have time to nod before another wail rings out. A woman's cries, echoing through the forest.

30

Now

Twenty years have passed since I've entered these woods at night. Twenty years of trying to forget what we did. Twenty years of trying to forget what we left behind.

"This is useless," Aries says. She's only a couple of steps behind me, using the light on her phone to guide her. "No one is going to come out here and dig up a body."

"What else could that sentence have meant?" I ask.

"It's someone trying to scare us."

"Austin and Dani are dead," Leo says coldly. He's at the front of the line, leading our group deeper into the forest. "This has gone beyond scaring us."

"Leo is right," Riley adds. "The video proves it. Someone knows what we did. They're holding it over our heads."

"What's the point after all these years?" Petra asks, walking beside me.

"It could be payback," I say.

When I raise my head, I see someone standing among the trees. I halt, my heart feeling as though it will leap into my throat. It's a person, their face covered by a lion mask. A long graduation gown dangles to their feet, and a glinting axe is in their hands. Paralytic fear squeezes my lungs, making it difficult to breathe. And yet, when I blink, the image disappears. I step forward, chasing the vision.

"What are you doing?" Aries asks, pulling me back toward the group.

"Did you see that?" I ask, blinking rapidly, as though the person might appear again.

"I didn't see anything," she says, pushing me forward. "Let's keep going."

Petra marches ahead. "We're almost there."

I follow her, trying to decide whether what I saw was real or imagined. The horror of finding Austin's body has reawakened past traumas. Maybe there isn't a person stalking us in the woods, but my own conscience is haunting me wherever I go.

"If Monica knows there is a body buried in the woods, why wouldn't she go to the police?" Cole asks. He's several steps behind us, the most reluctant voyager.

"I don't know," Leo answers. "She could be after something. Money, most likely."

"What if it's Jenny's aunt?" I say. "Maybe she finally put everything together."

Aries gives me a bizarre look. "She wouldn't have killed Austin and Dani."

Someone is trying to make us pay for what we did in the past, and the chaos in the present—Dani's and Austin's murders, that bizarre video—is connected to that horrible mistake we made.

"How do you guys even know where to look?" Cole asks. "It's been years."

Leo stops and turns. He shines the light he's carrying on me. "Did anything look strange to you when you were out here earlier?"

"No," I say. "Nothing looked out of place."

"You came out here by yourself?" Aries asks, a peculiar tone in her voice.

"I couldn't stop thinking about her," I say, trudging ahead. "It didn't feel right being back here without paying my respects."

"You should have known better," Petra says. "It's dangerous."

"That night haunts all of us," Riley says, his voice filled with understanding. "Probably why I was talking like that on the stupid tape. The guilt."

"Yeah, let's hope your *guilt* doesn't make us all guilty in a court of law," Leo says. He stops again, raising his arm. "We're here."

Hours have passed since I was last here, taking with them any sense of protection. Now the woods are dangerous, dark and deep, the wilderness primed to pull us back into the hell we escaped twenty years ago.

"This is it," Aries says aloud. There's a disbelief in her voice, as though she thought we might trek all the way out here and never find the spot, like what we did never happened.

Cole is the only one who isn't staring at the tree illuminated by our phones' flashlights. His shoulders are pulled tight to his head. He looks around nervously. "You just left her here?"

"We didn't have much choice," Leo says. He takes a step forward, staring at the tree. "Oh shit."

I raise my phone, as do the others, to train its light on the same spot: the small carved heart in the center of the tree's trunk. Except now the heart is covered by a message. The word *DIG* has been carved into the tree, the indentation of each letter manic and hurried. Was this message carved with the same axe that mutilated Austin's body? The memory flashes through my mind, and I shudder.

"Ella was right," Leo says. "Someone has messed with the body."

I point my light at the ground, and the others follow. The soil is dark and moist, recently disturbed.

"Oh my gosh," Aries says, taking a step back. "You don't think someone dug her up?"

Leo is already on his knees, clawing at the soil with his bare hands. "The ground didn't look like this earlier. Someone has been here."

"Why would they dig up the body?" Riley asks. He is now on

his knees, helping. They pull at the soil like it's an endless string they're trying to untangle. "They have the video. If they knew where the body was, they'd go to the police."

"Whoever is doing this doesn't care about that," Petra says. She's standing beside me, her gaze feverish as she watches the men. "They care about the truth."

"This isn't about going to the police," I say, agreeing with her. "They want us to know our secret is out."

"But why?" Riley pauses, his arms resting at his sides. "It's been twenty years. Why now?"

"Because we're all here together," Aries whispers.

"I'm not finding anything," Leo says, his hands still digging frenziedly through the dirt. "I think she might be gone."

I fall to my knees, helping them dig. The others stand behind me, watching, but they appear too startled to move. The soil is grimy between my fingers, the same consistency it was twenty years ago, when I was dazed, attempting to get rid of the body as fast as possible.

Then my hand hits something hard. Leo must have felt it at the exact same moment.

"Thank God," he says, sitting back against the trunk of a nearby tree. He lets out a huge exhale. "She's still here."

I keep feeling, making sure it's not some rock put here to deceive us. I take out my phone again, turning on the light.

Most of the body is covered by the ground. I'm thankful for that. After twenty years, I don't want to see what time and decay have done to the corpse. Light catches on something in the grave. I brush away dirt with my hands, trying to get a better look.

Terror races through me, and I jump back, dropping the phone.

"What is it?" Aries asks, daring to look closer.

"This isn't right." I'm feeling on the ground. My fingers find my phone, and I shine the light over the exposed grave.

It's a necklace. The light bounces off the chain, stinging my eyes. In the center of the necklace are two small shells, equal in size, shaped like crescent moons.

"Oh my God," I cry out, sobs rising from somewhere deep inside my body. "It's Petra."

For a moment, there's silence. The whooshing of wind through tree branches is the only proof that the world around us continues.

"Of course it is," Riley says at last. "She's in the same place we left her twenty years ago."

31

Then

A scream.

It's coming from Cabin Six, where we left everyone else.

Leo and I run as though our lives depend on finding the source of that terrifying sound. Rain beats on our backs as we try to maintain our balance on the slippery mud and gravel.

Leo opens the door first. I stand behind him, afraid of what I might see.

We've heard Aries scream enough during the past month, you'd think we would have been able to tell it was her. But this scream is different. Real. All her convincing screams on set are nothing compared to the sounds leaving her lips at this moment.

She's staring ahead, pointing at the ground.

That's when I see Riley. He's shirtless. His unbuttoned pants are pulled around his waist as though he hurried to get dressed. Kneeling on the ground, he pushes his arms up and down doing chest compressions on someone.

I must walk all the way inside the cabin before I can see.

It's Petra. She's flat on the floor, inert, pale. Her lips are parted, her eyes open.

"What the hell is going on?" I ask, trying to make sense of the scene.

"We were in the bedroom. She started flopping around," Riley says. "I think she was having a seizure."

"Did you see what happened?" Leo looks at Aries.

"Riley was screaming when he carried her out here. She was seizing, like he said." Aries's voice breaks. "Then she just stopped."

I stare at Petra, motionless on the floor.

"She's not breathing," Riley says, continuing to press on her chest. "Petra! Petra!"

"Let me help." Leo gets on his knees, crawling closer to the couple. He bends down, his ear hovering over Petra's lips, waiting for a breath. Dissatisfied, he sits up, presses two fingers on the side of her throat. "How long has she been like this?"

"It's been two minutes. Maybe three," Riley says, his voice breaking more and more with each new word. "I don't know what happened."

Two or three minutes. How could something so awful happen in such a short amount of time? It already feels like I've been standing here, frozen in fear and confusion, for an eternity. It's like the world never existed before I heard Aries's scream.

"I don't feel a pulse," Leo says, exhaling in defeat.

"Do something!" I cry. "Call an ambulance. Get help!"

"An ambulance won't get here in time," he says. "Where is everyone else?"

"Cole and the others said they wanted to go downtown. They left right after you two did," Aries says. "We're the only ones here."

"Where are the fucking phones?" Riley screams. "We need to call for help."

"No one can help her if she's already—"

"Don't even fucking say it. She's a perfectly healthy girl in her twenties," Riley says. "She wouldn't just drop dead."

"We were partying. Drinking. Smoking," Leo says. "Did she take something else?"

I feel it then, a realization as hard and brutal as a punch to the gut.

"I gave her something," I say.

"What?" Leo says, his eyes wide, afraid.

"She said she wanted something to take the edge off," I say. "So, I . . . I gave her one of my anxiety pills. She must have had a reaction."

Riley lifts Petra's head, searching frantically for a breath. He spins around to face me. "What the fuck did you give her? Xanax?"

"I—I don't know."

"What do you mean you don't know?!" Riley sounds unhinged. I've never heard him like this before.

"There isn't a label on the bottle," I say. "My agent gave it to me."

"It could be anything." Riley throws his hands in the air. "Why the fuck would you give her something without knowing what it is?"

"She didn't give her anything to hurt her," Leo says, moving his hands away from Petra.

"Oh my God. I think she's dead." Riley stares at Petra in horror. "She's really fucking dead."

Aries is on the ground now, crawling to Riley. She puts her hands on his shoulders.

"Get away from me." He pushes her, scooting his body until his back is flat against the far wall. He pulls his knees up and leans forward. He begins to sob. An empty, helpless sound I'll never be able to forget.

I stand motionless. It doesn't feel like I am even breathing, and yet I must be because I am alive, feeling every aching emotion of the moment, while Petra lies dead on the floor.

"I didn't mean to hurt her," I say. "I didn't know any of this would happen."

"We don't know that what you gave her had anything to do with this," Aries says. "She could have taken something else."

She didn't. Petra admitted as much when we were in the bathroom. If I was a better friend, I would say something, but I don't. I let that window of possibility remain open because it lightens the weight of my guilt. Anything is more acceptable than the reality that I have caused my friend's death.

"We need to call someone," I say. "Tell them what happened."

"There's no one to call," Riley says from across the room. "She doesn't have any family."

That's why there was such a deep connection between them. They were both islands that had somehow floated through the abyss and found each other. And just like that, Riley is back to being alone.

"Everyone went to town?" Leo asks.

"Yes," Aries answers.

"What about Jenny? I thought she was staying back."

"She changed her mind." Aries's eyes fall to Petra, a nauseous look on her face. "We'll have to tell them all what happened."

Leo doesn't say anything. He storms outside, the door slamming behind him.

Aries, Riley, and I are alone in the room with Petra's body. She looks like she is sleeping, but there is a stillness to her, a loss of vibrancy that is apparent, even in these early moments of death.

I begin to cry. "I'm sorry, Riley. She was my friend. I wouldn't have done anything to hurt her."

He is quiet for a long time before he lifts his head and speaks. "It's not your fault. Aries is right. We don't know what caused it."

But inside I know. It was me who killed her.

"An hour ago, we were dancing around the living room," Riley says in disbelief. "It doesn't make sense. How could this happen?"

Leo comes back into the cabin, carrying my purse with him.

"What are you doing?" I ask him.

"I'm grabbing our things. We need to figure out what to do."

Riley lifts his head and looks in our direction. "Is that your bag?"

"Yes," I say.

"Give it to me." He stands, tramping toward us. "I want to see what you gave her."

"I already told you," I say. "There isn't a label on the bottle."

"I might be able to tell by looking at it. They have those websites where you can type in what a pill looks like, and it'll tell you."

Leo jerks the bag away from him. "The pills are gone."

"What?" I ask.

"I got rid of them. Flushed them down the toilet in the other cabin before I came back."

"What?" Riley asks. "Why would you do that?"

"Because Ella didn't mean to hurt her," Leo says, a vein in his throat throbbing. "I'm not going to let her take the fall for this."

I feel a twisted mix of pride and shame. Leo is willing to defend me, even though I don't deserve his protection.

"We'll have to tell the police something," Aries says. "They'll want to know how a perfectly healthy girl dropped dead."

"We can't call the police," Leo says firmly.

"What do you mean?" Aries asks.

"We're all emotional right now. Understandably." Leo exhales. "Hear me out. What good does it do to admit what happened here tonight?"

"It's the right thing to do," Aries says. "A woman died. People deserve to know."

"She doesn't have any family. Her parents died when she was young. That's why she grew up the way she did." Leo looks at me. "Did anyone know she was working this set?"

"I'm sure people knew," Aries answers before I can.

"Anyone who would check up on her? Find it suspicious if they didn't hear from her?"

"She was taking another job soon," I say. "It wasn't with the people from here."

"Crew members bail on jobs all the time," Leo says. "It's how we got stuck with Monica."

"What's your point?" Aries says.

"I'm saying Petra has no family. No one would notice that she didn't come back from set. If we don't tell people she died, no one will even know."

"*We* will know," I say. "We can't act like this never happened."

"The woods are thick here. We've heard the locals talk about it. People get lost and never find their way out," he says. "It couldn't be that difficult to hide a body."

Riley charges at Leo, and it takes Aries and me to hold him back. "You cannot be fucking serious."

"Listen to me, please," Leo begs. "If we call the police, there will be an entire investigation. We've all been drinking. Some of us are underage. We all know there were drugs here tonight, too. She might have even taken some. All of us could wind up in trouble for a careless mistake.

"And not just with the law. If word gets out that a member of the crew died on set, there's no way this movie gets off the ground. Not even Cole's father could stop the press, and it would tank all of our careers."

"Don't tell me you're thinking about your fucking career right now?" Aries says.

"I'm thinking of my future. All our futures. I don't know about you, but I'm not good at anything else. This is all I know how to do." He focuses on Riley. "Do you want to head back to Kentucky? Work in a factory for the rest of your life?"

Riley shakes his head. "No."

"This is going to follow us. Wherever we go. We're always going to be those kids who let their friend die while they were shooting a horror movie in the woods. And it's not just us. Everyone on set, too. They'll question all of us. Tear all our lives apart, and there still won't be any justice for Petra because it was an accident."

"He's right," Aries says reluctantly. "Nothing good will ever come from this."

"Petra died, Leo. She is dead," I say. "We can't worry about our futures when hers was cut short."

"Whatever we decide to do, it won't bring her back," he says. "She wouldn't want her death to ruin our lives."

A beat of silence as we all consider this. In my mind, I'm still picturing Petra alive, cracking jokes and bestowing wisdom. It doesn't seem possible that those days are gone forever.

"What is your plan?" Aries asks at last.

Leo sighs. "We take her into the woods. Bury her somewhere deep. This place is rural and rugged. There's a slim chance of anyone finding her, especially if they don't know where to look."

"What about tomorrow morning?" I ask. "People will wonder where she is."

"We'll tell people she left tonight. If they even ask. Think about it, everyone is going to be hungover, their cars showing up at different times," Leo says. "They may not even notice she's gone."

I wince at the thought that Petra could be so easily overlooked, yet that's the premise we're banking on to help us conceal her death.

"And then none of us ever talk about it again," Leo says, ending his pitch. "I don't like this, either. Any of it. But it's better than all our lives being ruined over an accident."

I survey each face. Leo is already decided. Aries has been pulled into his corner. Riley's expression is painful to see, torn between grief over Petra and fear of ending up with the future he worked so hard to avoid.

I don't know what to feel. Can barely think a clear thought.

"It's getting late," Riley says at last. "If we're going to do this, we need to hurry."

32

Now

My ears thrum with the sound of my own heartbeat. I stare at the body in the ground, stare at the necklace in the soil, trying to make sense of it.

"This isn't right," I say. "It can't be."

"We should be celebrating," Cole says, his voice distant. "If Monica hasn't dug up the body, then there's still time. We might be able to find her before she goes to the police."

Celebrating. Police. Time.

It's like Cole is speaking an entirely different language. I'm struggling to understand why Petra's necklace is buried with the bones, fighting to make sense of what happened twenty years ago.

"Ella." Aries is bent down beside me now, her hand on my back. "Are you okay?"

I stand quickly. Riley and Aries are still kneeling at my feet. Leo is resting beside the tree, taking ragged breaths from his frenzied digging. Cole is several steps away, his arms crossed in front of his body. But there's no sign of Petra. Where has she gone?

"It's supposed to be Jenny who died," I say, staring at all of them, angry that they aren't as confused as I am.

"What are you talking about?" Leo asks.

"Jenny died that night."

"No, she didn't," Aries says. "She—"

"That isn't her," I shout, pointing at the uncovered grave. "Who is it?"

Riley stands now, coming close. He puts his hands on my shoulders.

"That's Petra, Ella. She died twenty years ago, and we buried her here." He stares at me, waiting for a reaction. "Don't you remember?"

I remember Jenny hit her head at the wrap party, a place to which I'd invited her. She was never seen again after that night. Her aunt even reported her missing. Gave interviews in the press. There was all that tension between Jenny and Aries and Cole. According to the *Grad Night* mythos, Jenny Cruise was the girl who disappeared from set. Not Petra. Over the years, it became easier to think Jenny died that night, that we'd left her in the woods.

Long-buried memories rise to the surface, tremoring through my mind and body. Sharing my pills with Petra. Riley's desperate attempts to revive her. Another sob catches in my throat as I look down. Without the light, it's impossible to see, but I know what's there. I know *who* is there. Part of me has known all along.

I take off running through the woods. Tree branches reach for me, clawing at my bare arms and legs.

"Ella, where are you going?" Aries shouts. It sounds like she might be following me.

I ignore her, running as fast as I can through the forest, away from Petra's body in the grave, away from the group of people who helped me put her there. It's so dark, I can't see anything in front of me. All that flashes through my mind are memories, glimpses of Petra and me.

My footsteps tread across the hard earth. I keep running until my chest feels so tight, I must stop. If I go any farther, I'll collapse. When I pause, I realize I'm in a clearing, close to Cloud Tops Rock. I let out a strange sound, part yell, part cry, filled with anguish and regret.

"Ella?"

I turn quickly to the sound of the familiar voice. Petra is standing behind me. I can see her as clearly as I have every day since I returned to set.

"Petra?"

"You know it's not me," she says weakly.

"But I've seen you," I say. "I've talked to you."

"You needed me to get through this weekend."

"I didn't know it was you," I cry. Then, more truthfully, "I didn't want it to be."

"You've been trying to survive," she says, her voice soothing. "You've leaned on me to do that."

"I thought it was Jenny. She's the one who went missing."

"Jenny has nothing to do with what happened," she says. "It was only easier for you to imagine her being dead."

The word hits like a rock at my flesh. Brutal and real.

"You can't be dead."

"I am. And you're alive. You've constructed a whole other story in your mind to help you cope, but you must let that go now. You have to see the truth."

I think of everything Petra has said to me since I returned to Blackstone Cottage. It was only my mind using her voice to fill in information I already knew, wishing so badly she was here, imagining what she would say if she was. If she hadn't died twenty years ago.

"I'm so sorry," I tell her. "I didn't mean for any of it to happen."

"I know you didn't," she says.

There's a warmth in her voice. She sounds so real, so loving. I wish to reach out and touch her, but I don't dare. The feeling of my hand sliding through empty air would be too painful.

"Why is this happening?" I ask her. "Why now?"

"I don't know."

"There must be a reason. You're here. We're all here. What am I supposed to do?"

"You need to stop living in your head," Petra says. "Your life depends on it."

I close my eyes, tight. All these years, I've grappled with our choices that night. I tried to pretend it didn't happen, and when that wasn't enough, I constructed a different story, one where the person rotting away in the earth was someone I barely knew, and not my closest friend. I pretended she was still living, still thriving, having the life she truly deserved to have. When I returned to Blackstone Cottage, I imagined she was still with me. It was her presence—whether real or invented—that made it possible for me to carry on.

"Ella?"

When I open my eyes again, Petra is gone.

Standing in her place is Aries, bent over and out of breath.

33

Then

You don't think about what you're doing, you just do it.

You don't think about burying your friend, only about what will happen if the truth comes out.

The entire trek out to the woods, my mind tries to trick itself into doing something different. I cling to any hole in the plan, hoping to tear the entire thing apart, but then there is another layer in my mind, talking me out of an idea as soon as it appears.

What if her family files a missing person's report?

She has no family. Petra has been on her own since she was a teenager.

What about her friends or co-workers who knew she was taking the job?

Petra's jobs were always last-minute. Sure, she might have told someone her plans, but they wouldn't know an exact location, not even the name of the film. How many indie movies are being shot around the country at any given time?

"Ella." Leo's voice pulls me from my foggy thoughts, brings me back to the cold and dark. "You need to keep digging. This is almost over."

Using a dolly from the equipment cabin, we wheeled her body

into the forest, rain beating down on our backs. We took shovels from the crew cabin. Thankfully, they hadn't all been packed. We each have one now, each take turns driving the metal into the soil.

"It's not deep enough," Riley says. "We need to go at least four feet or deeper."

"That could take until sunrise," Aries says.

Should we turn back now?

We can't. It would be clear we had tried to cover it up, which would only beg more questions. We'd look guilty, like we'd intentionally done something to hurt Petra. We need to finish what we started.

"There are four of us," Leo says, the unwilling leader of our group. "It won't take long."

Our time in the woods passes in a blink and lasts an eternity all at once. Filling in the hole didn't take nearly as long as digging it. By the time we finish, the rain has stopped; the ground is smooth again, freshly turned soil outlining a dark rectangle in the earth.

"If someone finds this, they'll know something is buried here," I say.

"Storms are coming," Riley says, his eyes fixed on the grave. "It will be nothing but dirt and brush within a week."

Surely, it can't be that simple, to cover up a death, an entire life, in a matter of hours, and yet that's what we are banking on, that and the idea that no one will come searching for Petra, that no one will care about her death.

Riley walks over to the tree closest to her grave. He pulls a knife from his pocket and begins carving into the bark.

"What are you doing?" Aries asks.

"Don't worry. No one is going to come looking for her, remember?" he says solemnly. "At least we'll know where she is."

When he finishes, there's a small heart carved into the bark.

"We need to clean up," Leo says, already marching back toward the crew cabins. "Hopefully, they're not back from the bar yet. We don't need anyone seeing us in the woods."

The main house and grounds are empty when we return. We take turns showering in the small bathroom of Cabin Four, washing away our crime and the remaining memories of Petra. I am the last to shower. I turn on the overhead faucet, when there's a knock on the door.

Two knuckles against the wood, casual and quick.

"Cole and the others just got back," Leo says without opening the door. "I left your clean clothes right here."

I don't respond and lean my head against the tile. It feels like I am closing in around myself, the walls inching nearer, trapping me inside.

Below, I watch as the grime on my body rinses away, the dirty water circling the drain, all while knowing I'll always be unclean.

The morning is exactly as we'd predicted it would be the night before—rushed and inconsequential. Cole and Carlos and Monica and the others stumble around the grounds, hungover and agitated, trying to load the last of the equipment into trucks before the property owners arrive. They are so distracted, they don't notice Aries's dark circles, Riley's red-rimmed eyes, Leo's shifty glances, or my own melancholy.

They don't notice one of us is missing.

They don't ask where she has gone.

In a snap of the fingers, it seems, we are loaded in the car, driving away from Blackstone Cottage, the setting of my first major film and final resting place of my dear friend.

34

Now

The pale moonlight hits Aries at exactly the right angle, making her look like a phantom emerging from the trees.

"You can't take off like that," she says between sharp inhales. "There's enough going on. We can't worry about you, too."

"I know, I just . . ." The words trail away. "I needed a minute alone."

Aries takes a cautious step closer. "Did you really not know Petra had died?"

My eyes dart from left to right, waiting for Petra to appear as she has during every other time of uncertainty since I returned. Now I know she was never with me; it was all in my head.

"I guess, after a while, it was easier to think Jenny was the one who died. And not . . ." I search the area again. No one. "And not Petra."

"The two of you were close," she says. "It can't be easy, especially seeing her again. Like that."

"Jenny was the one who went missing. It made more sense that it was her."

Aries exhales slowly. "Jenny was never missing. She is alive and well."

My eyes are wide, staring at Aries. "What do you mean?"

"That's the story that's out there," she says. "The story I helped put out there."

"Why?"

"I guess you're not the only one avoiding the truth." She sits down on the ground, and I sit beside her. "Jenny stopped being *Jenny* twenty years ago. She moved away and changed her name, took on a new identity. I helped her do it."

"I don't understand. Why?"

"Because of Cole. Well, not only because of Cole, but he was the biggest reason." She sighs. This isn't a story she's shared often. Maybe never. "Jenny and Cole had a toxic relationship. She needed to get away from him. Break free. But he wasn't going to let her go. He's dangerous, Ella."

"What do you mean 'dangerous'?"

"All those rumors about him drugging women and assaulting them. It's true."

My mind conjures images of Cole and these faceless women, imagines the unspeakable pain he's caused behind closed doors.

"How do you know?"

"Because he did it to Jenny," she says. Her expression is one of despair. "That's how their relationship started. He took advantage of her, and she didn't know what to do about it. We were living in a different time. An anonymous set girl couldn't make an accusation against Hollywood royalty and be believed. Even if someone did believe her, they wouldn't care. Cole was too big a monster to take down."

"That's why you've never liked him," I say.

"I *hate* him."

"Then why did you sign up for *Grad Night* in the first place?"

She winces, and I can see her shame. "I needed this role. Just like Jenny needed a job. Countless women are victimized because the sad reality is, we don't have better options. Cole knows that and exploits it."

I approach the next topic carefully. "Did he assault you?"

"No. Thank God. I came to set fully aware of the rumors about Cole."

"The night of the wrap party you poured a drink over his head."

"Because I knew what was in it. Or what was probably in it. He was trying to get Jenny to drink, and when she wouldn't, he handed it to me." She shakes her head, repulsed. "He only cared about Jenny when it suited him. If he thought he had a chance with me or Monica or someone else on set, he'd act like he didn't even know her." She smiles now. "So, I used that to my advantage. I knew if I humored Cole, even a little bit, he'd leave Jenny and the others alone."

"I saw you together in the lake. All those times you were flirting with him—"

"I was never flirting with that asshole. I was acting. Even better after he yelled 'Cut.'"

I think back to the interactions I saw between them on set. I always assumed it was some sexual tension at play, but according to Aries, it was all an act, orchestrated by her.

"He was trying to get into my pants. I was trying to get into his head," she says. "I had to create a distraction to keep him away from Jenny."

"Even if she didn't go to the police or tell anyone the truth about what Cole did to her, why stick around on set and work for him?"

"She needed the money. Like most of the crew, she'd signed on to work *Grad Night* as part of a contract deal. She wouldn't get paid for the projects she completed before unless she finished this one. And she needed the money to start over."

"But why take on a new identity? Change her name and everything."

Aries exhales, refusing to meet my eyes. "She was pregnant. She found out right before we started filming."

"Pregnant," I repeat. "Was Cole the father?"

"Yes, but he couldn't know about the baby." She looks at me, tears in her eyes. "Do you understand now?"

Their behavior from twenty years ago is starting to make sense, that weird relationship between the three of them I spent countless moments trying to decipher.

"She didn't want him to know about the baby."

"Cole would have forced her to get an abortion. Jenny didn't want that. If she'd refused, he would have found a way to take custody. Throw Jenny to the curb and keep the baby for himself, to be raised by nannies and guardians, like he was," she says. "Jenny knew if she wanted to keep her child, she had to get as far away from him as possible. Even though she hated Cole, she was excited about being a mother. She was ready to step away from the industry and leave it all behind, but she needed my help."

"That's why she was never seen again, after filming wrapped."

"This was her chance to make a clean break. She could get her paycheck from completing the movie and move. If Cole figured out her plan before she left, he would have found a way to make her stay. When I think back to making this stupid movie, all I think about are the hoops Jenny and I had to jump through to keep her and the baby safe."

"But her aunt? She's the one who went to the press talking about how Jenny went missing. Why would she do that if she knew Jenny was safe and living under a new name?"

"Cole wasn't the only person Jenny was running from. Her aunt wasn't any good to her, either. She'd started working in the industry to get away from her family. Hard life and all that. Jenny's aunt only wanted to track her down to take money from her, and I couldn't let that happen."

I think about Petra. She had a hard life, too. No one to turn to, no one to search for her. All she had was us. And we repaid her friendship by burying her in the ground, acting as though she never existed.

"Are you the only one who knows the truth?"

"Yes. Cole spent the first few weeks trying to find Jenny, but he eventually gave up. If he'd tried any harder, it would have been clear that she left him, which would only cause more embarrassment for him." She pauses and smiles. "Jenny has been living in Kansas ever since filming wrapped. She has a new name, a new job. Most important, she has a beautiful nineteen-year-old son. He's in college by now. She took good care of him, which is all she ever wanted. We stay in touch, but I've had to be careful. No one else needs to know what happened to 'the girl who disappeared on set.'"

"And you've kept this to yourself all these years?"

"I guess it's like you, pretending Jenny was the one who died." She pauses, raises her eyes to stare at the stars above. "I try to focus on the fact that I was able to help save Jenny, not that Petra ended up dying."

Dying. The word is so final, brutal. I look ahead, and for a moment I think I see someone standing in the trees. Petra? Has she returned? Is she watching me?

I think of those words I imagined her saying, knowing they're true: *You need to stop living in your head.*

I can almost hear her voice saying it.

Then a very real voice breaks through the trees.

"Aries? Ella?" It's Riley yelling for us. "Where are you?"

"We're here," Aries shouts.

Riley emerges from the trees. He bends over, hands on knees, trying to catch his breath. "There's someone out here."

"What do you mean?" Aries asks.

Cole and Leo join us in the clearing beside Cloud Tops Rock, the latter using a hand to cover his right shoulder. A smear of blood stains his shirt.

"What happened?" I say, running to him. When I touch him, he flinches.

"Someone attacked us," Cole spits. "We were busy looking for you two."

"Who was it?" I ask.

"We don't know," Leo says. "They were wearing a lion mask."

"And a graduation robe," Riley adds.

I'd seen the same person during our trek to the grave site. At least, I thought I did. I can't trust myself right now. I try to move Leo's hand to inspect his wound, but he shrugs me away.

"It's nothing," he says. "I fell and scraped my shoulder against a rock. I'm fine."

"Now we know someone is after us," Riley cuts in. "Monica lured us out to the woods for an attack."

"We need to stick together from now on," Cole says, slinging his vitriol at Aries and me.

"Let's go back to the cabin," Leo says. "We're safer there than we are in the woods. Once we're safe, we can figure out what to do."

There isn't enough time to sort out other options. We race toward Blackstone Cottage, hoping Monica, or whoever is behind all this, doesn't get there first.

35

Now

It feels like all five of us are pinned onto a target, the arrow closing in.

The jog back feels endless. When we finally reach the wooden steps of the cabin's back porch, I'm paralyzed with dread over what else we might find.

"There's a light on," Riley says as we approach.

"Maybe it was on before we left," Leo adds.

"I don't think so."

"What should we do?" I ask. "Just walk inside? How do we even know she's in there?"

"There are five of us," Aries says. "Only one of her. And she has nowhere else to go."

"Should we split up?" Cole adds.

"No!"

"Hear me out," he says, shushing Aries. "Leo and I can walk around the front of the house. The three of you go in the back. That way, no matter where Monica is, she's cornered."

"And what if she decides to attack us?"

"She's still outnumbered," Cole says. "I don't want her running out of the house. I'm not up for another chase in the woods."

Aries exhales, but it's clear she can't agree on what the best option is. This situation comes without a script.

"Fine," Riley says. "Walk around after I enter the back door."

"What do we do once we're inside?" I ask the others.

"If she's there, we can try reasoning with her. Explain what happened," Riley says. "But we have to remember that Austin and Dani are already dead. Monica is dangerous."

"It was all an accident," Aries says, almost to herself. "We never meant for anyone to get hurt."

Riley nods, acknowledging her statement, then turns back to the house, all business. Leo and Cole watch closely, waiting for their cue to run to the other side of the house. When Riley pulls on the handle, it doesn't slide open. He tries again, this time using his entire body weight, but nothing works.

"It's locked," Riley hisses, the plan we'd hurriedly thrown together already foiled.

"It wasn't when we left," Leo whispers. "If we all go around to the front—"

"We know it's you, Monica," Cole begins shouting, pounding his fists on the door.

"What are you doing?" Riley pushes him back.

"I'm sick of playing games. We know who's behind this." He cups his hands around his mouth, amplifying his voice. "It's time to talk, Monica. This is—"

Behind us, a heavy thud interrupts Cole's pleas. We all jump at the sound, which mimics that of a falling tree limb in the woods. When we turn around, there is someone lying on the ground beneath the second-floor balcony.

They've been thrown over the railing.

Just like Leo's death scene in *Grad Night*.

We approach hesitantly. The body is draped in a dark robe, the face covered by a lion mask. We exchange worried glances, unsure of what to do.

Leo and Cole inch forward. Riley does the same, approaching from the opposite direction. Aries and I move back, farther away from the house, our backs to the woods.

Leo is the one who bends down, lifting the mask to see the face underneath.

It's Monica, a deep gash across her throat. Her eyes are open, dull and lifeless.

"Monica isn't the killer," Cole says, raking a hand through sweaty strands of hair. "What does this mean?"

"Dear God," Leo exclaims, panic-stricken, and I soon realize why. He's not looking at Monica; rather, his gaze is upward, staring at the balcony above.

I step back, expanding my view of Blackstone Cottage's infamous balcony. A tall figure stands at the railing, also dressed in a graduation gown and with a blood-spattered lion mask covering the person's face, an axe with a bloody blade in their hands.

36

Now

Our plans for confrontation evaporate.

Not only are we faced with another dead body, but the killer stands before us now, welcoming a reaction.

Everyone responds differently. Cole and Leo dart off into the woods. Riley scrambles around the house, searching for a weapon. When he finds nothing, he retreats, too. I don't even see where Aries goes.

My reaction is neither flight nor fight. I'm frozen in place, staring at the startling presence before me. The killer commands the balcony, staring down at me, so like the scene Ben and I filmed years ago. Long dark gown. Lion mask. An axe, tinged with the blood of Austin and Monica, gripped in the person's hands.

That's when it hits me: this is all real. No props, no stand-ins, no script. It's a horrifying realization, but even that isn't enough to make me move. I'm cemented in place, unable to do more than blink, my eyes fixed on the horror above.

The killer turns, the gown drifting in the wind, and vanishes inside the house.

A hand grabs my shoulder.

"Ella, we need to run!" It's Aries. She hadn't left after all.

When I stare into her eyes, her fear and panic are hypnotizing; my body still refuses to move, as though inaction will prevent this situation from being real.

Aries begins to shake me. "Now, Ella!"

The urgency in her voice controls me. Petra's words seep back to me, too:

You need to stop living in your head. Your life depends on it.

Aries's fingers wrap around mine and pull. I run alongside her, trying to match her strides, my mind finally starting to connect with the rest of my body.

We dash into the forest. The landscape blurs together, everything shadowy and gray. Aries jerks my arm downward. She's hunched behind the stout trunk of a tree.

"Shouldn't we keep going?"

"Let's wait," she says, eyes wild like an animal's. "See what the killer does."

Sure enough, the killer appears in the backyard clearing. The back door never opens, so the person must have left through the front. The killer runs toward the forest, toward us, then stops. Their posture is confident and proud. Using two hands, the person grips the axe, swinging it up and down. Their head turns slowly from left to right, and I fear it's only a matter of time until we're seen.

"Where did the others go?" I whisper to Aries.

"Into the forest." Her eyes never move from the person in the lion mask. "We have to make sure we go in the opposite direction."

A crackling resounds from our left. The killer turns in that direction, watches for a beat, then takes off running.

Aries and I remain still, listening to the killer's footsteps plow through the forest. The crunching stomps eventually cease, and all I can hear is the pulsing of my own heartbeat in my ears.

"If Monica isn't the killer, who could it be?" I ask Aries.

"I don't know." She watches the place where the killer just stood, making sure they don't reappear. "All that matters is getting out of here."

"We don't even know where the others went."

"They got a head start. If the killer is after them, that gives us a chance to find help."

"How?"

"We can try running into town."

"We don't know where the killer went. What if they hear us. Or—"

"The killer is in the woods," she says, stealing a look behind us. "We'll sneak around the side of the house and start running from there."

Fear threatens to paralyze me into inaction, but Aries is determined. She seems convinced that we'll be able to do something to salvage the situation.

"You ready?"

We abandon our cover, escaping the trees and arriving in the clearing. The seconds that pass while we're exposed are excruciating. I'm afraid someone will see us. I'm afraid of the killer. When we make it to the house, our backs against the wood siding, I exhale in relief.

"Now what do we do?" I ask Aries, relying on her instruction to make it through.

"Let's take a second to catch our breath. From there—"

Aries's words are interrupted by the sickening sound of a blade connecting with flesh. I stare in horror as the killer comes from the other side of the house, their hands still gripped around the handle of the axe. They must have left the woods and crept to the other side to confront us.

The blade is stuck in Aries's shoulder. The laceration isn't deep, but the blood gushing from the wound is startling. Panic takes over. Aries's screams ring out, her eyes unable to look away from the cut.

The killer pulls back on the weapon, raising it again to bring it down on Aries.

"Run!" she calls out.

I turn away from her as she lets out another soul-crushing scream and run for the woods. I glance over my shoulder, daring for a look. Aries's body slumps against the side of the house. The killer has already retracted the weapon, is turning to chase me.

I stare ahead, determined to outrun the fiend behind me. If I don't, I know that I'll be next.

37

Now

The forest, once so mysterious and dangerous, is now my sanctuary. Where the others went barely registers. There is no one else on this earth, it seems.

Only me and the person hunting me with an axe.

A feverish sensation scales my back, like I'm being followed. Watched. I keep sprinting, looking for a place to hide. Tree branches bite and claw at my arms as I race through the forest. When I have a second of relief, a sound from behind reignites the tension.

Is someone following me? Is the killer close enough to attack? Will I be next?

I think of Aries. One second, she was standing next to me, our backs against the house. Then she was attacked, left for dead beside Blackstone Cottage. It could easily have been me. I wish I were brave enough to have stayed by her side, but I'm not. If I want to survive, running is my only option.

Running from what, exactly? From whom? Monica isn't the one behind this. Like Austin and Dani—and Aries—she's dead. Someone else is after us, and I don't know who it could be.

My chest wheezes with every inhale. Even though my life depends on putting distance between myself and the killer, I'm afraid my body will give out if I don't take a break. Squinting, I see the wide trunk of a tree in the distance. A brambly bush grows behind it, wide enough to conceal me for a little while. Waiting in the darkness is my best option, allowing the psycho in the lion mask to chase down Cole and the others. That's a selfish, weak thought, but bravery won't save me; my only concern is surviving the night.

I crouch down, leaning back against the tree. My hand covers my mouth, trying to silence my gasping. With every inhale and exhale, my entire body trembles.

Alone in the darkness, I try to think. Who could be behind this? Who could have uncovered our secret? It must be someone who cared for Petra, someone so outraged by her death that instead of doing the logical thing and going to the police, they decided to exact revenge. And yet, the initial victims—Dani, Austin, and Monica—were never involved in her death. They were only a means to whet our fear, so the killer could hunt down the rest of us, one by one.

It seems clear that the picture and video were left behind for the four of us. Five of us, if you include Cole—

A sound in the distance captures my attention. Pounding, like footsteps. Someone is coming. My heart begins beating faster, terror spiking.

"Still no fucking service!" It's Cole, and he isn't alone.

"We need to call for help," Leo says. The two of them must have taken off in a different direction and managed to stick together.

"I'm not getting the police involved."

"I didn't say the police," Leo says. "Just help. Someone. This is getting out of hand."

Part of me wants to draw their attention—strength in numbers, and all—but something, whether it's fear or plain exhaustion, keeps me still. Keeps me quiet.

"How are we going to get out of this?" Leo asks Cole, his whispers amplified by the night forest.

"We need to find out who is doing this," Cole says. "Three people dead. My God!"

"I'm talking about all of it," Leo says. "If we make it out of here alive, this clearly links back to what happened twenty years ago."

"I know that—"

"We're going to have to come up with a story. We'll never be able to keep the others quiet."

I want to join in their conversation, help create a plan for moving forward, but I'm afraid—the blade so easily took Aries's life. I remain motionless, my body concealed by the thorny bramble, and listen.

Cole says, "I'm not going to start worrying about some girl who has been dead for twenty years."

"Well, I think we need to be worried," Leo says. "We're the ones who killed her."

I gasp, but no one hears me. My hand covers my mouth again, attempting to smother my breaths, as I lean harder against the tree. Listening.

"*We* killed her?" Cole says. "I wasn't even there."

"It was your pills she took," Leo says.

That can't be true. Petra took *my* pills, the ones I'd given her out of my bag. I was the reason she died that night, not them.

"If you hadn't been busy trying to get in Little Miss Final Girl's pants," Cole says, "she never would have taken them."

Final Girl? Me? Cole gave Leo pills to give to me.

I recall the night of the party, the night Leo took my virginity. I'd been planning to sleep with him, but he didn't know that. Had he wanted to move things along by giving me one of Cole's pills? Leo had brought my bags when Petra and I were getting ready inside the crew cabin. My purse. Could he have swapped my pills for Cole's? The bottle wasn't marked. The tablets looked the same, so I wouldn't know the difference.

"How was I supposed to know she was sharing pills with her friends?" Leo asks, irritated.

"Have you met young girls? That's how they are with everything," Cole says. "Can't keep anything to themselves."

"I need you to stop blowing me off about this. We've managed to keep this secret for twenty years, but we can't do that anymore. We have to get our story together," Leo says. "We need to figure out what to tell the others. What to tell the police. What to tell whoever is running around killing people!"

"I'm not coming clean about anything," Cole says. "I didn't do anything to that girl."

"She took your drugs and died," Leo says angrily. "If it hadn't been her, it could have been Ella. Regardless, there's still blood on your hands."

"Do you know how many girls I've given those pills to over the years? She had a freak reaction. An accident. As far as the others know, they were Ella's pills, and she's the one who gave them to her," Cole says. "That's been the story for twenty years, and I'm sticking to it."

My mind is racing between the conversation I'm overhearing in the present and my memories of that night. For twenty years, I've been blaming myself. Now I know I'm not the one at fault.

Cole is.

And . . . and Leo.

My anger is so fierce, it overtakes my reason. I leap to my feet, whipping around the other side of the tree, and scream, "Petra took your pills that night?!"

Both men jump. They'd assumed they were alone in the woods, only looking over their shoulders for the masked killer. They didn't think I was so close, listening to their every word.

"Ella?" Leo says. "What are you doing here?"

Nothing matters anymore. What brought us here. Who is chasing us. All I care about is finding out the truth.

"They were your pills," I say, staring at Cole. My eyes drift to Leo. "And you gave them to her."

"Not exactly—"

"You *meant* to give them to me. You switched them out of my bottle. Were you that desperate for me to sleep with you?"

Despite the darkness, I can read Leo's face. His expression. His eyes bounce nervously between me and Cole. "It was a long time ago, Ella. I was a kid."

"Were you trying to drug me? And that's why you switched the pills?"

Leo stares at me, his jaw fixed. He refuses to answer.

I look back at Cole. "Those rumors about you drugging women. They're all true. You've been doing it since back then."

"Not every rumor is true—"

I cut Cole off before he can insult me with more excuses. "That's why Petra overdosed. She wasn't taking one of my anti-anxiety pills. She was taking something stronger. She'd been drinking, and she had a reaction. That's what killed her."

"We don't know that," Leo says, even though minutes ago, when he'd thought he was alone with Cole, he'd said something different. "It was still an accident."

"An accident caused by your own cruel intentions. You drugged her. No, you were *trying* to drug me. And for years, ever since that night, you allowed me to believe that what I'd given her led to her death. You let me think it was my fault."

"It was no one's fault!" Leo yells. "That's what I'm trying to tell you."

"You killed her!" I shout. "Both of you!"

"You're being ridiculous," Cole says. "I wasn't even there!"

"Someone is hunting us down because of what happened that night," I say. "Dani and Austin and Monica are dead." I almost choke on the next part. "Aries is dead!"

"And we will be next if you don't stop yelling!" Leo lunges forward until he's only inches in front of my face. He reaches out his hand and, for a terrifying moment, I think he is about to strangle me. The anger in his eyes is emotion I've never seen before. The secret we've all been holding for the past twenty years doesn't compare to the one he's been keeping.

And I'm the only person who knows the truth.

To the left, the sound of a falling branch grabs our attention. We look in that direction, and that's when we see. The killer, still dressed in the *Grad Night* robe and lion mask, is standing mere feet away from us.

"Run," Leo says, taking off deeper into the forest.

The sting of betrayal numbs temporarily, and I take off after him. My eyes haven't fully adjusted to the darkness, but I rush forward. As upsetting as hearing the truth is, I know that if I don't keep moving, the killer will catch me.

I hear a scream behind me. Cole's scream. I look back to see that he is on the ground. The killer looms over him, the axe held high. I watch the blade come down, landing in Cole's leg. My body recoils in agony at the sight. He lets out a pained howl.

I've lost sight of Leo, but I start sprinting with all my might. I must keep moving. Keep running. Maybe I can find a way out—

My foot tangles with an exposed root. I lose my balance and fall forward, the hard earth slamming against my chest. My ankle shoots out bursts of pain, but that aching no longer matters.

The killer has caught up.

The face of a lion hovers over me, the eyes behind the mask watching me squirm.

38

Now

Arms raise. A glint of moonlight strikes the blade.

I close my eyes, bracing for the brutality my body is about to endure. Instead of hearing the whoosh of the axe before it strikes me, I hear a dull thud.

When I open my eyes, the axe is on the ground, a large rock beside it. Something comes flying through the night sky. Another rock. This time, it smacks the person wearing the lion mask in the chest. The person doubles over in pain.

"Ella!" Riley's voice rings out. I look in that direction. He emerges from behind a tree, holding a rock with each fist. He aims them at my attacker, trying to give me time to escape. "Run! Now!"

I get to my feet right before the person in the lion mask lunges at me, but another rock strikes, this time hitting the side of the person's head. It's only a momentary distraction, but that's all I need.

I'm moving again, wincing with every step because of my injured ankle. It's painful, but I don't have a choice. Approaching footsteps startle me, and I turn to see Riley, close on my tail.

"What do we do?" I ask him frantically.

"Keep running."

I turn, ignoring whatever is behind me, focusing only on what's ahead. Safety. Help. Survival. To focus on anything else is failure, and to fail is to die. I'm not even sure where I'm headed, the trees like mirrors in a maze, looking the same and distorted in confusing intervals. Then I see the clearing in front of Cloud Tops Rock. I run toward it, not because it will provide cover—it does the opposite of that—but because it is familiar.

When I break out of the trees, a large branch swings down, hitting the side of my head. I crash to the ground. Looking up, I expect to see a low-hanging limb, but instead it's Leo standing over me.

"Ella, I'm sorry." He reaches out his hand to help me up. "I thought you were the killer."

"Don't touch me," I say, kicking away from him.

"What are you doing?" Riley gasps, catching up to me. "We have to keep running—"

Before he can finish his sentence, something slams into the back of his head, and he falls forward. I scream, afraid he's been hit with a bullet, even though I don't remember hearing a gunshot. That's when I see the rock beside his head. He's on the ground, whimpering, but still alive.

"Guess it's time I start taking plays from your book," says a voice.

The killer emerges from the forest, striding into the clearing. The graduation gown tugs at the ground with each step, the lion mask still on, loosely covering the person's face. In one hand, the person holds another rock, which they toss playfully into the air. In the other hand is the axe, spattered with blood.

Leo takes the same tree branch he used to injure me and holds it high over his head. The masked killer lowers the axe, bringing the blade dangerously close to the top of Riley's skull.

"No!" I shout, lurching forward but too afraid to move beyond that.

Leo lowers his weapon. He gives Riley a pitiful look, then turns his attention and anger toward our attacker.

"Who the fuck are you?!" he screams. "And what do you want?"

The masked killer takes a step back but is close enough to attack any of us on a whim. "I want justice."

"For what?" Leo argues. "For a mistake from twenty years ago?"

"There's no statute of limitations on grief," the person says. "Wouldn't you crave revenge for the death of someone you loved?"

I listen to the person behind the mask. The voice is familiar, but I'm confused by what's being said. Petra didn't have anyone who loved her besides me, and maybe Riley. Who would go to these lengths for her?

"We didn't mean to hurt her," Leo says. "It was a mistake."

"Someone has to pay, and I've decided it will be all of you."

The person drops the rock and uses that same hand to peel off the lion mask. And now I know why I recognize the voice.

"Fiona?" I say.

She shakes her tangled black hair off her neck, like a lion ruffling its mane, and takes a deep breath. "It sucks to breathe in that thing."

"Who the fuck are you?" Leo says.

Fiona looks at me. "Should I say it, or do you want to do the honors?"

"She's my agent," I say.

"I don't understand," Riley says. He's regained his bearings but is still on the ground, scooting as far back from Fiona as he can without going over the edge of Cloud Tops Rock. "Why are you doing this?"

After hours of confusion and chaos, the answer appears so clear. I recall our conversation back at Pendulum's, when Fiona first told me about the reunion. At the time, I'd thought she was trying to sympathize with me over the death of my mother. In reality, she was letting me into her own trauma.

"Your parents died when you were young," I say to Fiona.

A pained smile spreads across her face. "I was a resident of Miss Claude's Group Home."

"Just like Petra," Riley says, piecing it all together.

"I was only twelve when my parents died," Fiona says. "I didn't have any family who could take care of me, so I was shipped off to that forsaken orphanage with all the other outcasts. I was never the same after their deaths and being at that place only made it worse. For years, I was lonely and scared and miserable." Her smile morphs into something sweet and genuine. "And then Petra arrived. Sometimes it was easy to forget she'd endured just as much heartache as the rest of us. There was this vibrancy about her. We became best friends, and she saved me from whatever fucked-up path I was on."

Petra had provided that same sense of comfort for me. I remember my first day on set, the way her friendliness brushed away my nerves and insecurities. An open book, flipping her pages to make me feel a little less alone.

"I don't understand," Riley says. "Petra said she wasn't in contact with anyone from the group home."

"Once I aged out, I took off for Los Angeles to start interning at PR firms. Petra started working odd jobs on the East Coast. I was the one who got her involved with the industry, something I'll never forgive myself for," she says, her expression turning remorseful. "The last time we spoke, she was headed off to work on some indie film, but I wasn't sure which one. It took years to find out that she was on the payroll for *Grad Night,* and then the trail went cold. I always wondered where she ended up. I'd started building my own reputation by then. I wasn't a hard person to find. If she wasn't reaching out to me, I knew it was because she couldn't."

"Petra worked on the set, but none of us stayed in touch after filming wrapped," Leo says. It's the worst performance I've ever seen him give. He can't possibly think Fiona would be willing to write everything off as a misunderstanding, not when she already has the blood of five people on her hands.

"I would have believed that line a few years ago." She looks down at Riley. "But then I saw your little video, remember? 'We killed a girl.' An original cast member from *Grad Night* wasted off his ass talking about a girl who had died. I knew it couldn't be a coincidence."

"How did you even get that video?" he asks.

"How do you think I got it? I'm an agent. Some dipshit druggie at the party was shopping it around the tabloids, and my agency put in the bigger offer to kill it. Everyone else who saw the video thought it was Riley being a dumbass. But me? I knew there was truth in what you were saying.

"Everyone had heard the rumors about that film. I figured a lot of it was pure gossip to help promote the movie, but I knew the rumors about Cole were true. And now someone was claiming they'd killed a girl on set."

"That video doesn't prove anything," Leo says.

"It put everything in motion. All I could think about was Petra and what might have happened to her. How her death had been covered up. It's not like I haven't done my own share of dirty work over the years. Spinning stories and hiding the truth just because someone has a big bank account and loyal fan base. It never bothered me before," she says with a shameful shake of the head, "until I realized it was girls like Petra paying the price. I had to know what happened to her. The *Grad Night* reunion had been in talks for years, and I made it my mission to make it a reality. I knew that if I got enough people from the original set back together again, I could figure out what Riley was talking about in that video."

"You blackmailed my agent with the bar fight video," Riley says.

"Really, Riley, you've got to get your shit together," Fiona says. "Everyone has a cell phone these days."

"You pressured Aries, too," I say, remembering what she told me about the contract ensuring we were all involved. "You've been planning this since the beginning. Since before you even took me on as a client."

"Didn't you ever stop and wonder why I'd agree to represent you? You've always been a loose cannon. It's how you lost your career in the first place. You were the hardest to influence, but if I could just get you to trust me, I knew I could convince you to do anything."

My insides reel with regret. Fiona had been playing me from the very beginning. She sniffed out my desperation and used it against me, even when my every instinct had warned me not to get involved, not to come back.

"Thankfully, Cole had enough reasons to want to participate," Fiona says. She looks at Leo. "And wherever he goes, you follow. You're his little lap dog. Always have been." She laughs. "I mean, sure, there was always the possibility that nothing would come of it, but I had to take my chances. The original cast together again in the same location. The last place Petra was ever seen. This was the closest I'd ever get to finding out the truth."

She hoists the axe in the direction of the woods, then aims the blade at me. "And then you led me right to her body. When you left with Leo, I started digging around the tree with the stupid heart on it. I didn't have to look very far. Finally, after all those years of searching, I had my answers."

"Fiona, you need to listen to us," Leo says. "No one meant for Petra to get hurt."

"Then why didn't you tell anyone something went wrong? Why weren't the police involved? I don't know what happened that night, but I know you were the last people with her."

"What about Dani and Austin and Monica?" I shout, fresh rage rising to the surface. "They were never involved. You didn't have to kill them. You didn't have to dress up in that ridiculous costume and chase us through the woods with an axe!"

"Dani was my point of contact when it came to the reunion," she explains. "She knew how determined I was to get this off the ground. I was afraid she'd be able to connect everything back to me. I killed her before I left the property and hid her body in the laundry room at Blackstone Cottage."

"How did you make it back here?" I ask. "I saw you get on the bus."

"Monica had arranged for a driver to bring her back to the cabin, so I tagged along. I killed her in the upstairs bedroom before anyone knew we were back."

"Why Austin?" Riley asks. "He wasn't even involved with the original production."

"Monica and Dani are nobodies, just like Petra was. But Austin McKinty? The press will eat up the murder of an up-and-coming director. That's what this was about." She tightens her grip around the axe. "Making this weekend as violent and splashy as possible. No one will be able to cover it up in the woods, like you did last time.

"I waited for Austin inside the crew cabins. While I was there, I trashed all the footage from the secret cameras stashed around this place. I sent Cole the message from Austin's phone to start you all on your chase through the woods. I figured it was fitting, after all the years I wasted trying to track down the truth."

Fiona puts the axe blade on the ground and leans on it. "So, now I need to know, what did happen?"

"It was an accident," Riley says. "She took a pill the night of the wrap party. She had a reaction and died."

"You said, 'We killed a girl.'"

"I felt like it was my fault. I was with her when it happened. After she died, Aries, Leo, Ella, and I buried her in the woods because we were afraid of getting in trouble," he says. "And you're right. We should have gone to the police. Done anything but discard her in the woods like trash. She was so much more than that."

His sincerity touches Fiona, but only for a moment. She glares at me like she already knows the answer to her next question.

"Who gave her the pills?"

"I did," I say.

"Figures. 'Ella needs pills to get out of bed in the morning.' That's what your old agent told me."

"It was an accident," I say. "I didn't know—"

"It doesn't matter. You all helped bury her in the woods. You all deserve to pay for what you did." She pauses, her tone changing. "But I'm going to let one of you live. I need someone who can corroborate my story. We'll say one of the cast members lost it and started killing people, and I can walk away unscathed."

The situation makes no sense, further highlighting Fiona's madness. She can't possibly think she'll get away with this, or that one of us would turn on the others—

"I'll do it," Leo shouts, interrupting my thoughts. "Whatever you want me to say, I'll say it."

"Are you serious, man?" Riley's voice is equal parts anger and hurt.

"We saw what she did to the others," Leo says. "I'm not going out like that."

"Works for me." Fiona raises the axe, prepared to bring it down on Riley's head.

"No!"

My body reacts before my mind can process what's happening. I charge forward, slamming into Fiona right as she lowers the blade. The collision knocks her off-balance, sending us both flying.

The forest floor rises to meet us, unforgiving as a slab of steel, knocking the air from my lungs. Still, I keep moving, trying to wrangle my body around Fiona. The axe is within reach, but her legs tangle beneath the gown, and she struggles to move. I seize the opportunity, beating at her hands and wrists as she reaches forward, and she shrieks in pain.

She raises her knee, striking my already aching chest. The pain forces me to shudder, and before I know it, I'm on my back, Fiona hovering over me. She stretches her arm, her hand grabbing the weapon.

"Stop! You said you want justice. Revenge. But that's not what you want," I say, desperate to strike a chord of reason. "You want the truth."

Fiona halts, still struggling to catch her breath. "The truth?"

I look at Leo, repeating Fiona's line from earlier:

"Should I say it, or do you want to do the honors?"

39

Now

Leo's skin flushes red, his eyes bouncing nervously between us. My comment might have saved me from being hacked to death, but even that doesn't quelch Leo's anger.

"What is she talking about?" Fiona asks. She points the blade toward Leo as she stands. "And why is she looking at you?"

"I have no idea," he says.

"None of us knew the truth about what happened that night," I tell Fiona. "I only just found out."

"Found out what?" Riley asks. Now that Fiona is distracted, he's moved away, is now leaning against a large rock. All Fiona's attention is focused on Leo and me.

"One of you better start talking," she says.

"She's spitting nonsense," Leo roars.

Fiona and Riley are staring at me, wide-eyed and ready for answers. Leo is not going to tell them what they want to hear, which leaves me the responsibility.

"You were right. I gave Petra a pill," I tell Fiona, standing. "But they weren't my pills. Gus had given me medicine for anxiety. I thought that's what I was giving her. But Leo switched them."

I cut my eyes over to him. His face is fully red now, almost purple, his jaw clenched tight.

"Why would he do that?" Riley asks me.

"Cole had given him something different. A drug of some kind. Leo knew I was relying on my anxiety meds to get through the shoot. He switched the pills on that last night because he was hoping they'd loosen me up enough for me to sleep with him."

"Your own boyfriend tried to drug you?" Fiona asks.

"Yes. And because I didn't know what he'd done, when I shared my pills with Petra, I unintentionally drugged her. She took more than I did and had been drinking more, too." I look at Riley. "That's how she overdosed. It wasn't because of anything we had done."

Riley is on his feet now, darting over to Leo. "You killed her."

"I didn't know what I was doing," he says. "I wasn't trying to kill anybody."

"You knew what you were doing was wrong," Fiona says. "You were trying to drug Ella and ended up killing Petra in the process."

"It was a horrible, horrible mistake," Leo says, his voice breaking with emotion. "I feel awful about what I did, and I've carried this secret with me for a long time."

"Please. Don't act as though you're suffering from guilt," Riley says. "You've been thriving ever since that night. Not like Ella, who walked away from her career. Not like me, who could only cope with drinking and drugs. Even Aries struggled. She was a recluse for years."

"You don't know me, Riley," Leo says. "You don't know what I've struggled with since that night."

"I know from the moment Petra died, all you cared about was covering it up. You're the one who convinced us not to call the cops. You're the one who insisted we should bury her body in the woods. You even told Cole, hoping he'd protect us. Protect you! Apparently, the two of you have been in cahoots since the very beginning."

"And you flushed the pills," I add, that tiny detail now returning into focus. "You claimed you got rid of the drugs to protect me, but you destroyed them so they wouldn't be traced back to yourself. You couldn't risk anyone finding out what you and Cole did."

"It was a mistake," Leo says, punctuating each word with a solemn pause. "I didn't mean for any of it to happen. I didn't mean for Petra to die or to ruin so many lives. I was a kid. All I did was move on the best way I knew how. I'm sorry that wasn't so easy for the rest of you."

"It wasn't easy for us because we cared!" I shout. "We loved Petra."

"All you cared about from the very beginning was your career," Riley adds. "Even now, all you want to do is save yourself."

"Damn right I do!" Leo yells, a frightening rattle in his voice. "I'm not going to let one mistake ruin the rest of my life. You are all fools for not doing the same. There's only one person I can depend on. Me. I've worked hard to get where I am. I've made my own sacrifices. Hell, maybe even my soul was one of them. But I'm not going to let some dumb girl from twenty years ago ruin what I have now."

Fiona charges at Leo with the axe raised, but Riley is faster. He tackles Leo to the ground, begins beating his fists into that beautiful face. Leo lets out a yelp, then starts fighting back, trying to wriggle Riley off him.

I stand back. Even Fiona seems shocked into stillness. There's something animalistic about the fight taking place before us. The brutality of it. Maybe it's because Leo and Riley used to be friends. Maybe it's because both of us share in Riley's rage, knowing Leo so carelessly and callously brought Petra's life to an end, and concealed the truth for so many years.

The two men continue to tussle, but eventually they both get on their feet. Leo is tired and out of breath, but Riley keeps charging. The scene is surreal, my eyes flitting from Fiona in her *Grad Night* garb to the two men beating each other to a pulp.

"You're going to pay for what you did to Petra!" Riley yells. "You're going to pay for what you did to all of us."

"You're a fucking loser, Riley. You know that?" Leo says. "You've always been a loser. All of you. Wasting your lives worrying about things you can't change. You've let it ruin you. That's what separates you from me. I'm great because I choose to be. I refuse to allow anything to get in my way."

His speech does little more than infuriate Fiona, her original mission clear. She rushes forward, using her elbow to push Riley out of the way. The axe blade slices Riley's forearm, and he cries out, but Fiona keeps charging until both her hands are on Leo's shoulders.

"You're a monster," she shouts. "You don't even care about what you did to her."

Leo opens his mouth to respond, but it's too late. After his fight with Riley, he's winded and struggles to find his balance. It makes Fiona's strength deadly as she continues pushing forward and forward, until Leo's feet are on the edge of Cloud Tops Rock.

For the first time tonight, I sense genuine emotion from Leo, regret over what he's done, shame over the person he's become. He grips Fiona's gown.

"Please," he whimpers. "Don't."

From this angle, I can't see Fiona's face. I can only imagine what she's thinking. All the useless blood that's been shed to bring her to this point, at last confronting the person responsible for Petra's death. For two decades, he's reaped the benefits of her confusion and pain and loss. Only now, at the edge of a cliff, does he ask for mercy.

Leo's last two words are quickly followed by a tight scream, the sound decreasing as Fiona pushes him over the edge, and his body falls to the ground below.

Silence.

I wait, thinking Leo might make a sound. Thinking one of us might run to his rescue, but we stand still, replaying everything that's happened. Even if we could save him, I don't think he deserves our compassion. He never extended that kindness to

Petra. I realize now that any affection he showed me was nothing more than a self-serving manipulation.

"Do you think he's dead?" Fiona asks, her back to us, the front of her body still searching the darkness beyond the drop-off.

"It's a forty-foot drop," Riley says, exhausted and out of breath. "He must be."

A crude thought enters my mind. I could run forward now, push Fiona over the cliff. Put an end to all of this and keep Riley and myself safe. When I take a step forward, Fiona turns around.

"Was all that true?" she asks me. "What you said about Leo switching the pills. Or were you saying that to confuse me?"

"It's true. I overheard Cole and Leo talking about it in the woods. Before you . . . before you found us." I pause, and she waits. "For years, I thought it was my fault. I blamed myself. I didn't know the truth about what they had done until tonight."

Fiona turns in the direction of Riley. He leans against the rock again, this time nursing his wounded forearm. "And what about you? Did you know Cole and Leo were to blame for Petra's death all along?"

"I found out when you did," he says. "If I'd known, I would have done something about it sooner."

"We shouldn't have buried her in the woods," I say. "We were young and unsure. Afraid. If I'd had the chance to do it over, I would have. That's what has bothered me for so many years. She was my friend, and I couldn't forgive myself."

"You said you loved her."

"I did. She was so good to me," I say. "I believe we'd be friends today, if she were still alive."

"I loved her, too," Riley adds.

"Sometimes, I even pretended she was here," I say. "I couldn't forgive myself for my part in ending her life."

I'm staring at Fiona, fully aware that at any moment she could charge at me, finish what she came here to do, and yet there's a peace falling over me. I'm finally speaking my truth. Behind her, I think I see movement beyond the wall of trees. Perhaps it's a trick of my mind. A creature of the forest. Or maybe it's Petra, coming to say goodbye.

"I'm sorry," I tell Fiona. "We shouldn't have taken her from you. I wish we never did."

"For years, all I thought about was getting revenge. I've been angry for so long." Fiona looks down at the axe in her hands. "Never knowing the truth."

"I've been angry, too," Riley says. "I understand."

"Petra was a trailblazer and edgy and cool," Fiona says. She lets out a pained laugh. "All the things I wanted to be growing up, but beneath that tough exterior was a kindness I never had."

"That's what was great about her," I say, smiling as I remember. "She wouldn't have wanted this. All this death and violence and heartache."

"You're right." She looks down at the axe again. "I wanted the world to know what happened to her. I don't regret what happened to Cole and Leo. But all the others? Dani and Monica, Austin and Aries."

"Aries?" Riley asks, fresh sadness washing over him.

"If Petra were here right now, she'd be so ashamed of the woman I've become," Fiona says. "Of the things I've done."

"For what it's worth," I say, "I think she'd be ashamed of all of us. We let that night ruin our lives, but it's only because we loved her so much. I don't think Leo or Cole ever knew what it was like to care about someone beyond themselves."

"And now I'm like them. Hurting everyone, trying to fill this hole inside," she says. "Even now that I know the truth, it's not going away."

For a second, I think she's about to grip the axe tighter, but her hand unclenches, and the blade falls to the ground. Fiona walks over to the edge of the Cloud Tops Rock, where she'd pushed Leo moments ago. She raises her head, looking out at the endless sky. It's beginning to turn orange, the sun rising from behind dark clouds.

"Well, I guess I came here to do what I had to do. I found out the truth," she says. "Now there's nothing left."

She jumps forward.

I scream after her.

It's too late.

Petra's avenger now rests alongside her killer, and only Riley and I are left in the dark.

40

Now

I don't dare look over the cliff's edge. I know it's impossible that either of them could have survived the fall. For a moment, I consider everything that was revealed tonight, everything that was lost, and my loneliness consumes me. Then Riley speaks.

"Are you okay?"

"Yes. No." I close my eyes, trying to stop my brain from going back in time. "So much pain and suffering stems from that one night."

"I know," he says, filled with sadness. "Now we know the truth about what happened to Petra. It was never our fault."

"Leo lied about it for all those years. Cole, I can understand. He always cared only for himself. But Leo?" I close my eyes, still struggling to accept his betrayal. "I thought I knew him."

"He was a better actor than we gave him credit for," Riley says. "He'd hurt any of us as long as it meant he could protect himself."

How could I have been so blind? I wonder. At eighteen, I wasn't reading the signs that were in front of me. I only saw the best in Leo and the world and the others around me. I never believed my own boyfriend would try to take advantage of me. Now I know that our relationship was never rooted in love or respect, but even that acknowledgment doesn't erase the devastation of his sudden death.

"Come on," Riley says, placing his hand on my shoulder. "It's over. Let's go back."

The sky is changing from navy to blue, sunrise on the horizon. We've spent the entire night in these woods fighting for our lives, and there are only two of us left standing. As we get closer to Blackstone Cottage, a voice rings out.

"Help! Help!"

Riley and I exchange shocked glances before breaking into a sprint, getting closer to the voice.

We find Cole on the ground where Fiona left him, unable to stand or walk because of his wounded legs. He's waving his phone like a weapon but stops when he recognizes us.

"Oh, thank God. It's you," he says, panting. "Where's the person in the lion mask?"

"Dead," Riley says dryly. "We're the only ones left."

"Leo?"

I shake my head.

"Oh God." Cole looks away, his mouth opening and closing like he can't decide what to say. "Who was it?"

"Petra's housemate."

He shakes his head, then asks, "They're dead now?"

"Yes," Riley says.

"Good. Okay." He pauses, thinks. "We need to call for help."

"I'm heading to the main house now," Riley says. "If I have to hike until I get service, I will."

"Wait, wait!" Cole is desperate. "We need to figure out what we're going to say."

"What do you mean?" I ask.

"People will want to know what happened here, and we can't tell them the truth," he says, his voice gaining strength.

"We need to get our story straight. If the police trace what happened tonight back to Petra, we'll need to explain that, too."

Riley bends down so that he's eye level with Cole. He glares at the wounded director.

"I know what you and Leo did." He leans forward, placing his weight on Cole's injured leg. Cole shrieks in pain. "I'm not covering up anything for you."

"Please, look. It's not just me," Cole says. "Think about yourselves. Your careers. Your freedom."

"Enough!" I scream. "I'm done spinning stories."

Riley and I walk in the direction of the main house, ignoring Cole's cries. It wouldn't be right to let him die. We'll call for help and leave this forest together, but it's time Cole pays for what he's done.

The door is still locked. Riley uses a fallen tree branch to break the glass and let us inside. The house is quiet, ghostly. I keep my eyes low, avoiding the sight of Dani in the kitchen. We search the living room for anything useful to call for help but come up empty.

"Nothing," I say. "We're going to have to hike down the mountain."

We unlock the sliding glass door and exit just as the sun rises over the trees. A loud slapping noise grabs our attention, and we both jump back. Blood-soaked handprints make a pattern along the back deck. A body, slithering like a worm, moves closer, and that's when I see her.

Aries.

"You're alive?" I ask, my voice cracking.

"Barely." She falls forward, allowing her body to rest.

I bend down, cradling her in my arms. "It's safe now. We're going to get help."

Riley hurries around to the front of the house, his cell phone in hand. Hopefully he'll contact someone, and an ambulance will be here within the hour.

"I can't believe you're okay," I say, swiping her blood-soaked hair away from her beautiful face.

"Jealous you're not the only Final Girl this time?" Aries is weak and losing blood, but her spitfire personality remains. In that moment, I know she is going to make it through this.

We all are.

41

Nine Months Later

Truth.

It's hard to accept, even harder to share with the rest of the world.

But we did.

Aries, Riley, and I—each of us wounded and weary—told the truth about what happened at Blackstone Cottage, both during the bloody reunion shoot and what took place twenty years earlier, when we buried Petra Adamos in the rocky soil beneath the pine trees.

We could have spared our own involvement, but as I told Cole on that last day, I'm done spinning stories.

A car zooms by me on the highway, splashing muddy rainwater over my orange vest with the reflective stickers. I look down, surveying the damage.

"Keep it moving, Hollywood," shouts the sheriff's deputy overseeing the trash pickup along the highway.

I keep my head down, tending to my work for the remaining twenty minutes of my court-mandated shift.

Riley, Aries, and I took plea deals, and miraculously, none of us received prison time. The harsher sentence will be reserved for Cole, whom we all agreed to testify against. Not only is he charged with manslaughter in the wake of Petra's death, he's now facing charges for the sexual assaults alleged against him. Since the *Grad Night* reunion, even more women have come forward. Accusations are stacking hard and high; I'm not sure when he'll have his day in court, but I'm confident he'll never hurt another woman.

I only wish Leo could have faced the same punishment.

And I wish Fiona could have been held responsible for the lives she took, although as time passes, I have more sympathy for her than I do the others. Something had been taken from her, and she was driven to the point of madness to try to get it back.

"Load up," the deputy calls.

Single file, we enter the bus and ride back to the sheriff's station. Eyes linger on me from the other women, but I'm rarely confronted. We've all made mistakes in getting here. When we arrive at the station, I sign the required paperwork and hurry across the street, where my Uber is waiting. I slide into the back, immediately pulling out my phone to avoid conversation.

The latest headline reads, "Riley Gives Back: What Tragedy Taught Him About Life and Death." I begin reading.

Amazingly, Riley has maintained his sobriety. He was even the first one to step back on set. To think I signed up for the reunion because I thought it was the only way to revive my career. Ever since we took our plea deals, my phone hasn't stopped ringing. There are endless interview requests, and I even have agents fighting to represent me. I wonder what it says about our society when someone can commit a crime and become an even bigger celebrity.

"You look familiar," my driver says.

"Oh, yeah?"

If there's one positive from this situation, it's that *Grad Night* is no longer what people think about when they see me. It's usually the true story about the reunion.

"I know it," he says. "You were in that television show. They have some of the old episodes on Netflix."

I sigh in relief. "That's me."

Thankfully, not everyone follows the news.

The car pulls up to the small apartment I've been renting for the past month. I'm back in New York City, thanks to the plea agreement that allowed me to leave Tennessee. Once I decide on the right agent, I'm still hoping to revive my career post-scandal.

My place is small, a blank slate, but that's what I need right now. A picture of Mom hangs by the front door, a constant reminder of my roots, regardless of where I've been or where I might go next. As shaken as she would have been to know what we did all those years ago, I believe she'd be proud of me for finally speaking the truth and continuing to pursue my dreams in the face of hardship.

The television remains on at all hours of the day because I don't like walking into quiet rooms; I'm paranoid that danger lurks around the corner. The channel is fixed on an entertainment network, a familiar face on the screen.

"I'm here with a person whose name has been splattered all over the news lately," the anchor begins. "Aries Roberts joins me to talk about her experiences in the past year."

Aries looks beautiful as ever, but more important, she looks happy. At peace.

The anchor continues, "And she's not alone."

The camera pans to the right, revealing a face I've not seen in more than twenty years. Jenny Cruise. Now that her son is an adult, and the truth about Cole's abuse has been revealed, she no longer lives in hiding. She brushed away the cobwebs of her former life and came forward to reclaim her identity.

"Ladies, are you ready to share your story?" the anchor asks.

Aries looks directly into the camera, reveals that dazzling smile.

"I am," she says.

"Me too," Jenny adds.

We've each found our truth.

We've found a way forward.

Together. A far better fate than being a Final Girl.
My mind flashes to a memory of Petra, our first day on set.
What's your story?
Except it's not my story anymore. It's all ours.
And we get to share it with the rest of the world.

ACKNOWLEDGMENTS

I'm forever grateful to the many talented people that contributed to the publication of this book.

Thank you to my literary agent, Jessica Errera, for believing in this story and my writing. Jess, your feedback and passion for this project were critical in finding it the perfect home. Thanks also to the supportive team at the Jane Rotrosen Agency, including Allison Hufford for overseeing my foreign rights.

Thank you to my editor, Jenny Chen. Your enthusiasm and support were instant, and I've had so much fun working on this nostalgic, spooky thriller with you.

Thank you to Annette Szlachta-McGinn and Cara DuBois for your attention to detail during the copyedit. Thank you to everyone else at Bantam and Penguin Random House for all your hard work on this book.

Thank you to my film agent, Angela Cheng Caplan. Your insights into the entertainment industry improved the story's authenticity, and I so enjoy discussing all things horror with you!

Thank you to Regina Flath for designing the dark, distorted cover of my dreams. I can't wait to see this stunner in bookstores!

When I was a child, my father owned a video rental store. The constant exposure to movies and diverse storytelling nurtured a love for cinema that I've never been able to shake. My mother inspired my writing career by pushing me to read books and express myself creatively. Mom and Dad, your influence on this story and my life is undeniable. Thank you for all the love and support you've given me over the years.

To my sisters, Whitney, Jennifer, and Allison, some of my favorite memories from childhood involve binge-watching movies and television together. Those experiences influenced this story as much as anything else. To Chris, thank you for going on this journey with me. Thank you to my extended family and friends for your endless support and for continuing to shout about my books.

Harrison, Lucy, and Christopher, I love you more than anything. Big dreams and hard work are a winning combination. It took more than fifteen years for this dream to come true, and now we get to celebrate together!

Thank you to the book bloggers, librarians, and booksellers for all of your support over the years. I love seeing your thoughtful reviews and beautiful pictures. My biggest thanks go to every reader who took a chance on this book. None of this would be possible without you. I hope you enjoyed this one!

ABOUT THE AUTHOR

MIRANDA SMITH writes psychological and domestic suspense novels. Her work often focuses on complicated women, dark impulses, and Southern settings. She is drawn to stories about ordinary people in extraordinary situations.

mirandasmithwriter.com
Facebook.com/MirandaSmithAuthor
Instagram: @mirandasmithwriter
TikTok: @mirandasmithwriter
X: @MSmithBooks

ABOUT THE TYPE

This book is set in Iowan Old Style. Designed by noted sign painter John Downer in 1991 and modeled after the types cut by Nicolas Jenson and Francesco Griffo in fifteenth-century Italy, it is a very readable typeface—sturdy-looking, open, and unfussy.